A PLUME ~~

JUNO'S DAUGHTERS

Kim Wade at SilverBox Photographers

LISE SAFFRAN is a graduate of the Iowa Writers' Workshop, where she was an Iowa Arts Fellow. Her short fiction has appeared in a variety of literary magazines and in the anthology *Family Wanted*. She lives in Columbia, Missouri, with her husband and two sons. This is her first novel.

Juno's Daughters

Lise Saffran

A PLUME BOOK

PLUME
Published by the Penguin Group
Penguin Group (USA) Inc., 375 Hudson Street, New York, New York 10014, U.S.A. • Penguin Group (Canada), 90 Eglinton Avenue East, Suite 700, Toronto, Ontario, Canada M4P 2Y3 (a division of Pearson Penguin Canada Inc.) • Penguin Books Ltd., 80 Strand, London WC2R 0RL, England • Penguin Ireland, 25 St. Stephen's Green, Dublin 2, Ireland (a division of Penguin Books Ltd.) • Penguin Group (Australia), 250 Camberwell Road, Camberwell, Victoria 3124, Australia (a division of Pearson Australia Group Pty. Ltd.) • Penguin Books India Pvt. Ltd., 11 Community Centre, Panchsheel Park, New Delhi – 110 017, India • Penguin Group (NZ), 67 Apollo Drive, Rosedale, North Shore 0632, New Zealand (a division of Pearson New Zealand Ltd.) • Penguin Books (South Africa) (Pty.) Ltd., 24 Sturdee Avenue, Rosebank, Johannesburg 2196, South Africa

Penguin Books Ltd., Registered Offices: 80 Strand, London WC2R 0RL, England

First published by Plume, a member of Penguin Group (USA) Inc.

First Printing, February 2011
10 9 8 7 6 5 4 3 2 1

 REGISTERED TRADEMARK—MARCA REGISTRADA

LIBRARY OF CONGRESS CATALOGING-IN-PUBLICATION DATA
Saffran, Lise.
  Juno's daughters / Lise Saffran.
    p. cm.
  ISBN 978-0-452-29673-2 (pbk. : alk. paper) 1. Mothers—Fiction. 2. Teenage girls—Fiction. 3. Mothers and daughters—Fiction. 4. San Juan Island (Wash.)—Fiction. 5. Domestic fiction. I. Title.
  PS3619.A355J86 2010
  813'.6—dc22   2010015044

Printed in the United States of America
Set in Adobe Garamond Pro
Designed by Eve L. Kirch

For Robert, Clay, and Jonah. Always.

ACKNOWLEDGMENTS

I would like to express my gratitude for the several writing communities to which I have been privileged to belong, including the Iowa Writers' Workshop, the MacDowell Colony, and Hedgebrook. My parents and brother comprise an unparalleled cheering section in all matters, and my husband, Robert, is as thoughtful, insightful, and enthusiastic a partner as anyone could wish for. The collection of guitar strummers, banjo pickers, and washtub bass players that I call my extended family is also deserving of appreciation.

Juno's Daughters owes a significant debt of inspiration to Island Stage Left, which graced us with a virtually private performance of *The Tempest* one magical summer. They bring excellent theater to the San Juan Islands for free, but any further similarities with the company in the novel are purely coincidental and unintended. I would like to thank Shannon Kelley for her generous and detailed e-mails about life on the islands.

Acknowledgments

The *San Juan Islander* served as a further resource and in particular Susan Vernon's *San Juan Nature Notebook*. Miko Lee and Andrea Maio provided crucial backstage details; Kevin Perry shared his knowledge of Seattle street kids; and Amy Stambaugh deserves credit for Rascal. Meg Klein-Trull and her girls helped me understand challenges specific to the lives of beautiful teenagers, and Jo Luloff, Melanie Fallon, Kate McIntyre, and Julie Christenson all read and commented on early portions of the novel.

Finally, thanks aplenty to my perfectly brilliant editor at Plume, Denise Roy, and to my agent, Nathaniel Jacks, for his good sense, dedication, and friendship.

Juno's Daughters

CHAPTER I

Here in This Island We Arriv'd

There was one day in early June of each year when theater-loving residents of San Juan Island, Washington, listened more eagerly than usual for the echoing horn of the ferry in Friday Harbor. It was the day the Equity actors, professionals from New York and Los Angeles and Ashland, Oregon, arrived on the island to take their roles in the annual Shakespeare production. They came in their city clothes, or in brand new fleece and Gore-Tex, and fanned out to the spare rooms and converted garages and guest cabins happily offered up by islanders.

To the tourists who poured in from Seattle and Portland and San Francisco, it was a day like any other, an opportunity for bike riding on Lopez or whale watching in Haro Strait or strolling through the Westcott Bay Sculpture Park & Nature Reserve. Islanders who, like Jenny, helped with the sets or took the smaller parts, looked forward to this day the way they watched for the blooming of the red columbine. It meant that summer had finally come.

Dale and Peg, the founders of Props to You, had come to San Juan Island from the Oregon Shakespeare Festival in Ashland fifteen years before. They had arrived like so many of their neighbors: burnt out from the city or unhappy in their jobs or marriages or looking for a safer, more uncomplicated place to raise children. Back then you didn't have to be a Microsoft millionaire to buy a plot of land on San Juan or Lopez or Shaw. The ratio of old hippies, glassblowers, and lavender farmers to heiresses and rock stars was still higher than visitors to the islands could believe when they looked out their hotel windows at the views of Mount Baker.

The pair of actors had arrived with all their worldly goods in a VW camper van and bought five acres of land on Egg Lake Road. At the time it was just a pasture and a barn. They lived in their van for two years until they could finish their cabin and then immediately thereafter had framed a stage out of two-by-fours covered in plywood. They had begun casting their first production before the plywood was even painted. *A Midsummer Night's Dream*. People who had been around a while still talked about how the guy that Dale had convinced to come up for the summer and play Puck went for a psilocybin-induced walkabout on Turtleback Mountain and had to be rescued by the Washington Wing Civil Air Patrol. They talked a little less about what went on between him and Peg that summer, though they all knew. Everyone liked Peg.

It was in February of each year that Dale and Peg revealed the play they'd chosen for the coming summer. In no time, copies would be passed around from bed-and-breakfast owners to groundskeepers to whale watching captains to real estate agents. By May it would not be at all surprising to hear the owner of an art gallery and a souvenir shop clerk on a bench overlooking Friday Harbor speculating on how mistaken identities complicated the plans of young lovers or laughing about the machinations of this or that clever servant.

This year it was *The Tempest*, and by arrival day everyone on the island knew that Miranda had played a girl with multiple personality disorder on *Law & Order SVU* and that Trinculo and Caliban were regulars at New York City's Roundabout Theatre. Ariel was coming from Seattle, where he had recently starred in a production of *Peter Pan*. Prospero? Well, of course Prospero would be played by Dale himself.

His waist had thickened over the years and his beard, once streaked with gray, was now entirely white. It was easy to picture Dale in a long robe promising *calm seas* and *auspicious gales*. Speculation had been rife for weeks about who from the island would be selected to fill the minor roles. There was the question of the O's (Alonso, Gonzalo, and Stephano). There were the three spirits, Ceres, Iris, and Juno. There was the Boatswain.

Jenny had read this year's selection with particular interest. Lord knew she was no scholar like the shipwrecked Prospero. She had dropped out of college in her second year to marry a rock musician and spent her days working in an antique store and weaving table runners and place mats from home-dyed alpaca wool. She was, however, the mother of two teenage daughters. She knew as well as anyone what it was like to raise girls on an island. She would have loved to see Prospero, even with the help of his two magical companions, Caliban and Ariel, try to keep her older daughter, Lilly, out of trouble.

Jenny's daughters were four years and several worlds apart. Thirteen-year-old Frankie had her sister's jet-black hair, wide-set eyes, the same ability to sing harmony, and a dislike of what she and her sister both called "hairy fruit." At times, that seemed to be all they shared. Her older sister, Lilly, could be foolish, but she was canny. She could tie a sailor's knot at seven and drive a car at fourteen. She was in kindergarten when Jenny finally got up the courage to leave Monroe, and Jenny couldn't help thinking that it had to explain at least some of the difference between her girls.

Frankie was just a nursing baby when she last laid eyes on her father. It was that, believed Jenny with a confidence bordering on the mystical, that accounted for her younger daughter's blessed innocence. No one had ever been unkind to her. Nerve endings, which in Lilly's case had very early been tuned to the moods of men (and she had proved remarkably adept at that), had been free in the person of Frankie to concentrate on salt breezes and birdsong and the scratching of insects moving over the island soil.

Jenny thought of both her children often as she read the play. She tried to decide which of them was most like Prospero's daughter Miranda. Frankie might have Miranda's innocence, she decided, but there would be no doubt in anyone's mind, least of all her own, that it would be Lilly snatching up any young prince who happened to wash ashore.

Jenny had worked for years alongside a handful of her friends and neighbors building sets and sewing costumes for the show. She had read the play twice through by that day in June and had been excited for weeks about the possibilities for incorporating yarn. Lately she had been hand-painting raw wool that she bought at a discount from the alpaca farm on the east side of the island. It was too soon to tell if there would be a market for the stuff, but she could already see it swinging from the trees on Prospero's island.

She was behind the desk at work, picturing a vest woven of silver and gold thread to look like armor for Ferdinand, when the bell rang at the front of the store. Her eyes traveled down the aisle packed with Native American baskets and totems, Victorian butter churns, sleds, musical instruments, paintings and prints, lamps, skeleton keys, silver tea sets, and an ever-changing collection of miscellaneous treasures, and she saw two skinny teenage girls in matching pageboy caps. She broke into a wide smile, but it melted when she realized it was only two o'clock. Friday Harbor middle school didn't let out until three-thirty on Tuesdays.

"Frankie?"

"Relax, Mom. It was a teacher workday, remember? We got out early."

"We turned in our last book-share of the year on Monday," said Frankie's best friend, Phoenix, with a reassuring smile.

Frankie and Phoenix. The girls had been friends since before they could walk. They wore their long hair tucked under their caps in a style they must have invented because neither of them owned TVs and so far they weren't much interested in computers. On their matchstick wrists they wore bracelets woven from strands of Jenny's leftover alpaca wool, dotted with clam shells that they turned into ornaments the Indian way, by rubbing the highest point of the curve against a stone until a small hole wore through.

Now that Jenny remembered the teacher workday she realized that the kids had been out of school for an hour or more. In three days they would be out for the summer.

Lilly had graduated barely a week before. Though ostensibly working at a landscaping job, she was perpetually short of cash and had called Jenny earlier asking to borrow ten dollars. At Frankie's age, Lilly would have taken advantage of a free afternoon to careen around the island with deckhands from one of the big yachts, a joint tucked into a hollowed-out tampon container in her purse. Once or twice Jenny had almost had the sense that Lilly did what she did in part to say to her mother *this is how it's done. This is living.*

From the back door of the store Jenny could look straight down the hill to Friday Harbor and see that the ferry was just pulling away. It was the inter-island ferry, running regularly between the major islands. The large boat, cutting slowly through the water past the fishing and pleasure craft, sent a quick jolt of excitement through her.

The show moved around during the short season, performing on San Juan and Lopez and Shaw. Major props had to be small enough to fit into a framed backpack. The set for *The Merry Wives of Windsor* had depended largely on the collection of oversize beer steins Jenny had found at the shop where she worked and whatever big tables could be located on the island they happened to be on for the play.

Before the play opened in one of the big venues, there was a smaller, private performance on Waldron, one of the tiny islands without ferry service. Only the cast traveled to Waldron for the show, and the audience consisted entirely of the people who lived there without city services of any kind. Rocky and wild, Waldron was farther off the grid than most. There were just a hundred or so residents, and they grew their own food, rode bicycles or drove unregistered vehicles, and read by the light of generators. There was a community school, but no telephones or ambulances or stores. Nor (it was rumored) were there any wild animals larger then mice. The rabbits, deer, and even possums supposedly had been eaten by the islanders.

As a builder of sets rather than an actor, Jenny had to rely on the firsthand reports of those who had gone. She'd heard that Waldron's entire population came to the beach for the show. She could picture it. Even islands like Orcas, which rose into evergreen-covered peaks and harbored mountain lakes and streams, and others like Lopez, which were flat and mild and rural, all had private coves that were dotted with bleached driftwood logs and hidden by ancient stands of pine. It was on one such spot on Waldron that the summer play was performed each year.

During the first half the children swarmed over the benches

and on top of the rough-hewn picnic tables near the beach, their eyes shining in the setting sun. They ran off to play in the woods during the intermission and then crept back again when the play started, like raccoons inching toward a campfire.

When Monroe first brought Jenny and Lilly, then two years old, to the San Juans, he had talked about wanting to build a cabin on one of the islands without ferry service, like Waldron, Obstruction, Crane, Cypress, or Doe. There was something about the wildness of the Sound, the rocky shores and ancient trees, that made even a chain-smoking guitar player feel like he could build a house out of logs. You still had to buy the land, though, and in the end all they could afford was a two-bedroom trailer on a hillside near Cattle Point Road on San Juan Island. In retrospect, it was a very good thing, too. She shuddered to think of what might have become of her and her children had they settled in someplace seriously remote.

Jenny looked at Frankie cooing over some china animal figurines and tried to imagine her changing so much in a few years that she would skip out of a job at Café Demeter to caravan to the Oregon Country Fair as her sister had done just the previous summer. She couldn't picture it.

In addition to the cap, Frankie wore cords with frayed hems and a Hello Kitty T-shirt that her sister had picked up for her at a secondhand store in Seattle. She had a spray of small pimples on her forehead and a bandage on her thumb where she had cut herself trying to saw a piece of driftwood in half.

And she couldn't remember her father at all. Thank God.

Jenny remembered for the both of them. The clap of Monroe's hand hitting the side of her face; strangely, she heard the sound before she felt the sting. The very last blow he'd landed had had such force behind it that it sent her reeling. She had been knocked to the floor and the baby had screamed in outrage at being clutched so tightly to her chest.

Jenny's best friend, Mary Ann, owned the store that she had worked in ever since she had arrived at her friend's door with an infant sleeping in a sling and a kindergartener crying at her side. It had been thirteen years now, but Jenny would never stop being grateful.

She could still remember the iron taste of her own blood in her mouth, from the times that Monroe had hit her in the face. It tasted like shame, her own blood. Though she knew now that it had been the start of a better life for them all, she could remember feeling so sorry for herself on that drizzly afternoon they fled to Mary Ann's, and for her daughters. Especially Lilly, who had arrived with mud-splattered tights and only a small portion of the things she owned stuffed in her mother's backpack. Frankie had conked out in the sling— walking always put her out—but Lilly wouldn't drop off that night until midnight, and even then Jenny could remember the shuddering breaths she took in her sleep. Jenny had felt sorry for herself, and for her girls, and even for Monroe, who had hurt her.

"Didn't we have good times?" he had asked on the phone, pleading with her to come back.

When she hadn't answered immediately, he had listed them

himself, describing each as if he held a happy snapshot of the event in his hands: camping on the Oregon coast, on tour with his band in Las Vegas, their wedding on the Russian River. He drew the pictures vividly in her mind, until she could almost taste the grapes they had swiped from a vineyard growing close to the road. The dusty burst of sunshine in your mouth. What he didn't understand, though, was that, if you were afraid, the good times never really burrowed in. Fear was like a screen that kept them just out of reach.

Jenny rubbed her biceps, which were suddenly covered with goose bumps, though the store was warm. She was slender enough to have been more than once mistaken for Lilly from the back, but she was stronger than she'd been before. Her legs could take her up Mount Constitution on a bike and she could use a chain saw to get rid of dead trees on her property, push a wheelbarrow loaded with cinderblocks for a garden wall, and if she ever needed to, run with four times the weight of baby Frankie in her arms.

Frankie and Phoenix jostled each other on their way to Jenny and, having arrived, dipped their slender fingers into the jar of peppermints that Mary Ann kept on the table with the cash register. Jenny smiled at the way Frankie held the candy in her cheek like a squirrel.

"Where's Lil?" Frankie rolled the mint in her mouth.

Jenny glanced at the clock on the wall. "She's coming by any minute. And then I think she said she was heading over to Snug Harbor to help wash Jack's boat." The ten dollars was allegedly for soda and snacks at the small camp store.

Lilly must have seen Jenny fall to the ground holding her baby sister. She was five years old—where else could she have been? She must have been watching, but Jenny couldn't remember noticing her. What she did remember was the way Lilly raged after Monroe left for work and Jenny began packing their things. She would *not*, she insisted in all her kindergarten fury, go to Mary Ann's without telling her father good-bye.

Frankie nodded. "In Elliot's truck?" She looked over at Phoenix. "Maybe they have room for us?"

Jenny raised her eyebrows. "Elliot Cooper? Is she involved with him?"

Frankie nodded. "Don't tell her we told you, okay?"

"I won't, honey."

Jenny tried to imagine Lilly hooking up with the lanky, brown-eyed boy she had known since junior high. He had a big Adam's apple and a talent for drawing comic book figures. Working at his very first outdoor summer job, he must have been caught off guard in the sudden tractor beam of Lilly's attention. Lean and dreadlocked and gorgeous, she burned through boys like kindling. All the more likely contenders on the island were probably exhausted.

She reached out to straighten the woven bag that her daughter wore over her shoulder like a small quiver for arrows. She heard coins clinking against whatever treasures she kept in there: polished stones, abalone shell buttons, loose beads. She lifted the cap off her head and pressed a kiss against the milk white part in her black hair.

The bell jingled and the door swung open. Bright sunlight

shot through the dark corners of the store and Lilly's laugh carried to the back, along with the words, *"Tell me later,"* no doubt shouted across the street to someone perched on the front porch of Café Demeter.

Frankie jerked herself out of her mother's embrace with a fraction of a second to spare before her sister appeared before them in ripped shorts, work boots, and a T-shirt that said *Peace, Love, Entomology.* No bra.

Jenny looked from Frankie to Lilly and sighed. The moment you became an embarrassment to your children always snuck up on you. You went from lawful spouse to backdoor lover in the blink of an eye.

Lilly grinned and reached for a peppermint. "Hi kiddos."

Frankie hopped from one foot to the other in delight. She was bursting from the news she had to tell her sister. "You would not believe what Mr. G wore today in Social Studies. I tried you on your cell, but all I got was voice mail. He had on those plastic sandals, you know, with the dark socks pulled all the way up to the knee." She glanced at Phoenix, and they both giggled. "But the thing was, instead of shorts I swear he was wearing swim trunks. And I think they must have been Steven's, too, because they were *too small.*"

Phoenix nodded. "Way too small."

"He probably got behind on the laundry," said Jenny sympathetically.

No one else appeared to have heard.

Lilly pressed her hand to her stomach and grimaced. "Don't, Frankie," she said. "I just ate something."

Jenny raised her eyebrows. "So you won't be borrowing ten bucks after all?"

"*Mom.*" Lilly glanced toward the door, outside of which Elliot Cooper was no doubt waiting, his leash tied to a tree.

Frankie began digging in her pockets for cash to hand over to her sister. "Can we come with you?" She glanced at Phoenix for confirmation. "Cleaning Jack's boat will go a lot faster if you have us helping."

Jenny saw a look pass over Lilly's face and she guessed that boat-cleaning was the last thing on her older daughter's mind. "Look, Franks," said Jenny. "We only have an hour or so until we have to get ready to go to Dale and Peg's. Why don't you and Phoenix go to our house until then?"

"Yeah," said Lilly, avoiding her mother's eyes. "I'll catch up with you guys at the party."

"I can't go," said Phoenix. Her pert features composed themselves into an expression of utter despair. "We're spending the night in Anacortes."

"Tonight?" asked Frankie and Lilly in unison.

Frankie reached for Jenny's bag. "Your mom must not know that Dale and Peg's potluck is tonight." She fished around for the cell phone, her hand emerging like a diver with a pearl, her fingers already punching in the familiar numbers.

Phoenix shook her head. "She won't care. She has a doctor's appointment."

"In the evening?" asked Jenny, and then wished she hadn't.

Phoenix's mom, Theresa, was in her early forties, like Jenny. She was also a single mother. As members of the year-round community, particularly those who didn't have much extra money, they had often relied on each other to pick the girls up from school and had traded tips on where to find kids' clothes cheap.

Many of the people who visited the islands or bought summer houses there were rich in a way that Jenny had rarely even imagined when growing up with her sister, Sue, in Sacramento. Sue lived in Marin County, California, now and would not be out of place among the people who rented slips in Roche Harbor for the yachts they named *Twenty One* or *Golden Girl* or *Megabite*. On visits to Marin, Jenny felt the distance between herself and her sister acutely.

It helped that on the island there were bald eagles but no high-end shopping malls. She walked over the hill to Roche Harbor and enjoyed standing on the pier and watching the boats chug in to their slips, even though she knew she'd never possess one herself. The tanned couples on board owned the boats, she thought at such times, but they didn't own the sight of them bobbing on the water or the light reflecting off the sails. And she would walk back over the hill content.

That peace of mind had seemed to elude Theresa, especially lately. She'd grown incrementally more tense these past months as Phoenix inched toward adulthood. Groceries had always been expensive, but now they were "highway robbery." Clients at the home day-care center she ran on the south side of the island were nosy and small-minded. The tourists were a pain in the neck. She never mentioned the eagles.

Jenny looked at Frankie and Phoenix, standing with their

slender bodies tilted toward each other like saplings, their arms pressed together in a jumble of faded fabric, pale skin, and alpaca bracelets, and she could see what the two of them with their four bright eyes couldn't: It was only a matter of time before Theresa left for the mainland. Phoenix would be going with her, whether she wanted to or not.

Standing behind Frankie and Phoenix, Lilly was also clearly planning her escape. She mouthed the words, "Just ten dollars?" over Frankie's head.

Jenny took her cell phone from Frankie and dropped it into her bag. She then extracted the money for her older daughter, who snapped it up and blew them all a kiss on her way out.

Jenny watched Lilly go. She had had a fully-formed woman's body for years now, and seeing her in shorts and a tank top, Jenny felt a mix of recognition and nostalgia for her younger self. She could remember the power of that youthful beauty, the way it got her backstage at concerts, invited to Florence by a sculptor who had received a summer fellowship there, and attracted, with mixed results, the attention of the kind of man Monroe had been when she met him: a brooding lead guitar player for a semisuccessful Seattle band. Lilly exasperated her and worried her in equal measure, but the worries were based in a deep sense of familiarity. She could easily see her making the same mistakes that Jenny herself had made.

Frankie, standing in a doorway with the light reflecting off her hair and her collarbones rising from her chest like a whalebone corset, was different. Frankie and Phoenix had taken to sketching little cottages where they imagined they would someday live. Together. Some of them were directly on the beach with French doors and English gardens. Others were suspended entirely in the trees by wires, with spiral staircases leading down to the forest floor.

"What do you girls want to do until Theresa comes to get Phoenix? Do you have any drawing paper?" she asked them.

"Let's go to my house," proposed Frankie. "We have hard-boiled eggs in the fridge."

She had recently mastered a recipe for deviled eggs and made them at every opportunity. Jenny figured they went through more paprika these days than all but the most dedicated Hungarian families.

"Bye, Mom."

"Wait," said Jenny, thinking to remind them that the lasagna that was in the fridge was for Dale and Peg's. By the time she spoke the bell on the door had already rung them out.

In a moment they had vanished, just like Lilly had. They were quick on their feet, those girls. They were gone in an instant.

CHAPTER 2

A Thousand Twangling Instruments Will Hum About Mine Ears

Jenny's truck sat mud-splattered in the lot behind the store. The sun was still high, shining all the way to Mount Baker in the distance and warming her through her alpaca wrap as she walked over the lot.

Tonight it would set on Ariel, Miranda, Caliban, and Trinculo. As in seasons past, she would mostly think of these new friends in terms of the characters they played. Sure, there were circles inside of circles. (No one but the cast and director attended what was jokingly called the Naked Rehearsal—a final rehearsal that took place in an undisclosed location off-island and featured the cast in their ordinary clothes one last time before the full dress rehearsal. At least that's what Jenny assumed went on. Nobody talked.)

Jenny fished in her alpaca bag for her keys. She cupped them in the palm of her hand, unwilling just yet to duck out of the sun or take her eyes off the water. In this light, even the trees seemed to glisten. In summer it was like God took the lid off their northern world; there was more light, more people, more everything. Winter was when the islands could seem crazy-making claustrophobic or just super-cozy, depending upon whether or not you liked hearing the results to your most recent Pap test when you bumped into your gynecologist on the ferry to Lopez. The party was at five, and it was only four-thirty. She was sure she had time to pop into the grocery store on Main Street for a few minutes before heading home.

In the grocery store there were definitely signs that the summer traffic was picking up. The ferry had disgorged the usual combination of families with impatient children reaching for saltwater taffy, killer whale refrigerator magnets, and pirate flags on pointed sticks; wealthy-looking older couples; and those who looked like they might be on a first or second anniversary or even their honeymoon. Jenny smiled at a pair of middle-age lesbians picking out pasta and she dodged a broad, silver-haired man in yachting clothes who took up a narrow aisle while he regarded the Scotch selection with a critical gaze.

She took a second look at a pair of men waiting for service at the deli section. One of them was young, in his mid-twenties, and stood lightly and sway-backed like a dancer. He was African American, which was noticeable up in Puget Sound. He had close-cropped hair and a diamond stud in his ear. The other was white and closer to her age, though still under forty, she guessed. He stood firmly planted, with his Nikes on the floor and his basket tucked under his arm like a football. He was handsome, startlingly so. There was something about a boyish thicket of hair (a mop that needed cutting or a woman's thin fingers to untangle it) combined with a man's broad shoulders and sunburned neck that always made her heart beat faster.

She saw them and caught her breath. They were actors, she was sure of it. And a couple? She pictured them cooking a meal together in some stylish urban kitchen. They would dart and weave in and out of each other's way in the domestic choreography that she had achieved occasionally with one post-Monroe man or another, but never for long. She imagined herself sitting at a tall stool at the counter with a glass of wine in her hand, gossiping about people in New York or Los Angeles or Milan.

A man in a Mariners cap steered a shopping cart of beer toward her and Jenny stepped out of the way. She wanted to stand there for as long as she could, relishing that her world was about to change. Suddenly, the man in the Nikes looked in her direction. He smiled and she saw (or was she imagining this?) her interest returned. It was more than just the friendly curiosity of a newcomer to the island. He gazed frankly back, taking in her high cheekbones and wide mouth, the hair falling over her dyed wool wrap, her narrow legs in faded jeans. Her eyes.

She glanced away quickly, blushing, and hurried to the cash register with her eggs and paprika. She forgot about the milk altogether. How long, she found herself wondering, had it been since she'd kissed a man? When the days ran together like they did, full of work at the store and pots of rice boiling over and homework that needed to be checked, it was easy to lose track of time. Months and even seasons could pass by during which the only hands you felt on your skin were your own. And then suddenly it was summer, and you felt the sun on your bare back in the morning when you went out to check the mail or a strange man's blue eyes resting on your face, and you remembered what it felt like to have a tongue brush the velvet underside of your lip.

Jenny paid for her groceries and walked to her truck without looking back. Her heart didn't stop pounding until she had pulled around the corner and was headed away from the harbor on Beaverton Valley Road. She followed the two-lane road past the isolated houses and pastures. The greens and yellows and browns of the landscape began to soothe her and she allowed her truck to slow. Time wasn't really passing more quickly now that her girls were growing up, it just felt that way sometimes.

The other day when she was looking for her checkbook in Lilly's room, she came across a cache of love letters in her desk drawer. They looked like random notes at first, scrawled in pencil and blotchy pen on the backs of coupons or ripped fragments of lined paper. Until she noticed there were more stuffed behind the one she held and that each was written in a different handwriting. Until she noticed the word *love*. Some were signed and her first thought (well, her second, after thinking that maybe she shouldn't be reading them at all) was to wonder that the very same boys who flooded Lilly's inbox with blunt texts asking, "wll u do me?" would use a pen and paper to compose sentences like, *You are the only one I will ever love.*

Please don't tell anyone I've written to you and *I have never felt this way about a girl in my life before.* She stuffed the notes back in the drawer and what she had thought then was: Will anyone write me a love letter ever again?

Jenny swerved as a pair of tourists on rented mopeds careened past her going the other direction. Glancing at them in her rearview mirror, she caught a glimpse of her own widow's peak and forehead. Her dark brows and blue eyes. A look passed between the two of them, Jenny and her reflected self, a look that held the somewhat exasperated question: *What has happened to you?*

Before Monroe she might have walked right up to those men in the store and asked their names. She would have joked with them easily and flirted. She would have turned on her heels, her hair swinging, and known that the eyes of at least one of them might be following her to the cash register and out the door. She might even have felt entitled to their attention.

The previous summer she and David had whiled away pleasant hours working on costumes together or speculating about visiting actors late at night. He was an easygoing carpenter, a guitar player, and, like most of the single men in her age group, someone she had known for years and years. Since she'd settled on the island, Jenny's relationships all occurred within the boundaries of her small community, which made them more like a series of arranged marriages rather than torrid affairs. After endless bonfires and picnics, potlucks and gallery openings, small dinner parties and large celebrations, she and some preapproved local guy might appear to drift together like leaves on the wind but, really, it would be more like two planets revolving into each other's orbits, anchored in the strong gravity of their mutual friends. Mary Ann had pushed hard for David in particular.

"What is wrong with him?" she had asked Jenny, exasperated, after the two of them had broken up.

"Nothing's *wrong* with him exactly."

"*Exactly?* What then?"

Jenny had sprayed vinegar onto a rag and used it to wipe down the window sills, the desk, and the cash register. Each of the old things they brought in to sell carried a lifetime of dust with it. "It's stupid. I don't want to say."

"Oh, come on. Spill it." Mary Ann ripped open a cardboard box that had come in the mail from an estate sale in Bellingham.

"He started fixing things around the cabin."

Mary Ann paused in her work and looked at the younger woman with incredulity. "You mean like leaky faucets?"

Jenny lifted a pile of out-of-print books from the older woman's arms. "Faucets, the catch on the front door, other stuff." Mary Ann was still staring at her in disbelief, so she set the books down and put her hands on her hips. "He put shelves up in the shed. Without asking!"

"Why didn't you tell him to stop?"

"I didn't want to hurt his feelings."

"So you started sleeping with Phinneas? Because you didn't want to hurt David's feelings?"

"That just proves that he's better off without me."

Mary Ann shook her head. "If I were a psychoanalyst, I might wonder if you didn't think you *deserved* a nice guy," she muttered.

"That's why you're an antique dealer, sweetie," Jenny had said, softening the words with a smile.

David would be at the party, of course, with his harmonica and green chile enchiladas. Phinneas would be there, and Mary Ann, and Lilly and Frankie's teachers (first through fourth grade), and the postmaster, and just about everyone else on the island who wasn't out of town or a recluse.

Dale and Peg's welcome for the professional actors had become a beloved tradition. Old friends played guitars and banjos and even a washtub bass (brought by Phinneas). Dale dragged logs and tree limbs into the pasture for a raging bonfire. In addition to the casseroles, muffins, and home-brewed beer, they would feast on potatoes in foil, marshmallows, chestnuts, and all manner of other things you could throw into and roast over a fire. One year they had arrived to find a small pig turning over a spit.

Chad, the chef at the Hotel de Haro, made a wild duck ragout that people traveled miles to try, but in certain circles what he was most famous for were his batches of "enhanced" brownies. During the long months of winter a hash brownie or two could often be a welcome addition, and everyone who'd been on the island for a while knew what the green toothpicks meant. To a party like tonight's, where there would be outsiders and children, he would likely bring something tasty but harmless, like wild mushroom risotto or poached halibut salad on bruschetta.

The party lasted until the smaller children fell fast asleep under layers of coats on Dale and Peg's bed and at least a few lifelong friendships, surreptitious love affairs, and seething enmities had either been rekindled or begun. Frankie occasionally joined in the singing, but mostly she lurked around the edges of the party with a mysterious, pleased smile on her face, taking everything in.

Jenny slowed the car and turned off Beaverton Valley onto her own dirt road. The mailbox door was open and she could see from the truck that Frankie must have carried whatever bills or school correspondence there had been to the house. There was a breeze picking up, enough to cause the line of firs to sway on the top of the ridge. Pulling up to the bleached driftwood log that marked her "parking space" in the front of the house, she made a mental note to bring a couple of blankets to Dale and Peg's, along with the lasagna.

She saw something glitter in the grass. Frankie's silver dolphin pendant. She turned it in her hand and then tucked it into the pocket of her jeans and went into the house. Frankie's backpack was splayed open near the door and her sketches were all over the table. The kitchen counter was littered with tiny pieces of egg white, and the bowl with the yolks, mayonnaise, and paprika was teetering on the edge of the sink. There was a thin film of steam in the air. Jenny heard splashing from the bathroom.

She scooped the last of the egg filling into her mouth

with the fork and placed the bowl in the sink. She called out, "Honey?"

"I'm taking a bath."

"Of course you are."

Frankie could lounge for hours in the claw-footed tub that David had given them the previous Christmas. Jenny dropped into a chair and listened to the splashing. David. There really was nothing wrong with him, she had been quite honest with her friend, at least about that. She thought about what Mary Ann had said about Jenny not feeling like she deserved a nice guy. The real problem was that she longed for something a little more exciting than *nice*. Jenny could barely admit it to herself, much less to Mary Ann, who had been there to pick up the pieces after Monroe.

The water started to drain from the tub, and before long Frankie appeared, steaming from her pores like a just-cooked dumpling. Jenny gave an exaggerated look at the skinny legs emerging from the bottom of her terry-cloth robe.

"From all that noise I expected to see flippers. Or a mermaid's tail."

"I wish." Frankie's eyes widened at the picture.

"You're perfect."

Frankie flopped onto her mother's lap. The damp ends of her hair flicked water onto Jenny's face.

"Ack. But you're too big for this."

"Phoenix *hates* going to Anacortes." Frankie laid her head against Jenny's shoulder. "And it's not even a real doctor her mother goes to see. He's some kind of *healer*."

Jenny tightened the knot on Frankie's bathrobe. "What does she need to be healed of?"

Frankie sighed. "Boredom."

Jenny couldn't help but smile. If you could divide children into observers and doers, Frankie would definitely be the first kind and Lilly the second. It seemed Jenny had once been like Lilly, at least that's what her mother and Sue reported. She could barely remember it. In any case, she had learned to be more like Frankie over time, but her watchfulness had been acquired the hard way, through experience. Frankie was observant out of sheer curiosity and often had the insights to match. Oddly, she had never asked much about her father. And Jenny, leaving well enough alone, had never volunteered. There would be a time for that, she had told herself often. The time did not ever seem to be right.

Jenny rested her chin against Frankie's damp back. "What kinds of things do you remember from when you were little, anyway?"

Frankie chewed her lip. "Like kindergarten?"

"Before."

"Didn't I used to sleep with one of those plastic trolls? With long blue hair?"

"You did." Jenny smiled. It had been years since she remembered Frankie's troll. Ludmilla. "Anything else?"

"I remember Lil making pills for me out of that white bread we got at the discount store. She'd line them up on the counter and watch until I'd swallowed each and every one."

Lilly. Of course. Frankie had been born into a world that had always had Lilly in it.

"What's she going to do next, do you think?" asked Frankie, as if she could read Jenny's thoughts. She tilted her head to look her mother in the eyes.

"Do you mean the next time she gets into trouble?"

So far there had been failing grades in high school, a shoplifting episode in Seattle, and more than one pregnancy scare. Jenny helped Lilly secure the landscaping job and made sure she was up on time in the morning. She grounded her after Seattle and got her put on the pill (the two things were unfortunately related), and mostly she told herself that Lilly would be fine if she avoided falling into one of the bigger holes over the next few years or so. She had managed to fall into every one she could find on their small island already. Jenny comforted herself with the idea that at least where they lived, the holes were not as deep as they could be on the mainland.

"No. I mean when she grows up. She's going to stay here, right? Stay with us?"

"Well, probably not forever," said Jenny, realizing both that it was true and how assiduously she had avoided reflecting on that fact until just then.

Frankie wrenched her head and shoulders free from Jenny's loose embrace and gave her a sudden scowl. "You're too strict with her, Mom. You know that, right? I mean, she's almost eighteen years old. She should be able to do what she wants."

The last part of Frankie's argument remained unspoken, but they both knew what it was: *You* change and *she'll* stay.

Jenny rolled her eyes. "Too strict? Is this Lilly Alexander we're talking about?"

"Well, you're too critical." Frankie made this last observation with her arms crossed over her bathrobed chest, peering down on Jenny in the chair with the air of a produce buyer sizing up a crate of tomatoes.

Jenny stared her down. "When was the last time I said something critical about *you?*"

Frankie appeared to think about that for a moment and apparently, finding no examples, tried a different tack. "I'll die if she leaves," she said fiercely. "I'll cry every single day."

Jenny refrained from pointing out that those threats were mutually exclusive.

Just six months before, Frankie would hold Jenny's hand walking down Spring Street. Now her younger daughter watched her carefully in public and from a distance, the way a bride might keep an eye on a drunk uncle. It shouldn't have surprised her that Frankie seemed to be approaching an adolescence that Lilly only now hinted at emerging from in one piece, but it did. Frankie had never been in any trouble. Jenny shifted under the girl's weight. Even at thirteen, she was the kind of child who would crawl in her mother's lap. In private, maybe, but still. Lilly hadn't sought refuge there since she was six.

"Remember how Lilly used to talk about being a teacher?"

"She would be a terrible teacher," said Frankie. "The kids would learn all the wrong things."

"Probably so." Jenny tugged at her T-shirt.

The front it had a wet spot on it the size of a grapefruit from Frankie's hair. Now she definitely had to change her clothes before the party. Her white tie blouse might look good on her tonight, she mused, wondering also if Lilly had replaced the hammered silver earrings she had borrowed. She wanted to look good but had to walk a delicate line. If she appeared too dressed up, for example if she dug through her things for that old black eyeliner pencil, someone who saw her daily in her Tevas and canvas shorts might notice. If it were Phinneas, he would wonder aloud who the makeup was for and tease her mercilessly until he figured it out. The fact was, she had no good explanation.

A lingering look from a stranger who might or might not be gay did not mean much after all. She sighed. Still, this was a stranger who traveled on jets rather than in the cab of old trucks, who ate in restaurants where he did not know both the kitchen and the waitstaff, who leaped at the chance of a summer adventure in a place he had presumably never been before. These were all things she had once done herself, with relish. Besides, she had always liked a man with the confidence to get up on stage.

"She's very good at landscaping, though," said Frankie. "I heard Mr. Edison say that she was better than anybody at grafting."

"Grifting?" said Jenny, and then when she saw that Frankie had never heard the word, she tapped her lightly on the nose. "It won't be long before *you're* seventeen. I wonder what you'll be like."

Frankie's eyes wandered past Jenny's face, to her future self, projected like a hologram in the narrow hallway. "Oh, probably like Lilly. Or the lead singer in a band." She looked back at her mother's face and added, "With big boobs."

Jenny raised her eyebrows, unsure as to which of those things seemed the least likely for her shy, flat-chested daughter. "I wonder if you'll be in love?"

"I hope so," answered Frankie.

Jenny had done her best to fill Lilly's ears with advice about the complicated dance between men and women, often braving the clear implication from Lilly that her own romantic track record disqualified her from giving any. She had told her how to recognize a respectful partner and impressed on her the importance of having enough cash to be able to leave if necessary. She wondered if she should say something to Frankie now but decided to wait. There was lots of time yet, and besides, the party was starting in just a few minutes.

She heaved Frankie's body off her own. "Get some clothes on, or we'll be late."

"And they're soooo punctual at Dale and Peg's," said her daughter, disappearing into her sister's room.

So, Frankie hoped she would be in love at seventeen, did she? Jenny didn't know why that should surprise her. Perhaps because it was the first time Frankie had betrayed any interest in the subject where she herself was concerned. She chewed the bottom of her lip in thought. Frankie, it seemed, was growing up.

Jenny began to look through the kitchen drawers for her big spatula until she remembered that she had left it at Dale and Peg's, along with her salad bowl and tongs, the last time she was there. Her stomach growled and she realized that, except for an apple around one, she had failed to eat lunch.

Frankie emerged from the back room in several layers of clothing that included at least two of her sister's T-shirts, a midcalf flowered dress, and a pair of faded jeans.

"Ready?" asked Jenny, lifting the lasagna.

"Almost." Frankie held a less than perfectly clean kitchen sponge under the tap and used it to apply the temporary tattoo of a flower to her left check. "Want one?" She held the sheet out to her mother.

"Sure."

Jenny chose a rose that reminded her a little of the cover of the Grateful Dead album *American Beauty*. She'd never admit it in mixed company, but the shows the band played in the outdoor amphitheater in Santa Cruz still popped into her mind whenever she heard the phrase *perfect happiness*. No matter how glum she was, the opening chords of "China Cat Sunflower" never failed to lift her spirits. She extended her arm to Frankie, who centered the small square of paper and applied the sponge.

Jenny looked at her daughter's head, bent in concentration, and smiled. After thirty seconds, Frankie peeled the backing away. The skin under the rose was taut and shiny. Jenny ran the tip of her finger over it and it did not smear.

"Looks good, Mom," said Frankie.

Jenny turned her arm in the light. "It does."

"Do you think Lilly will be there already when we get there? Should I bring one for her?"

"Sure. How about that snake?"

"Oh, Mom, that's so unfair," Frankie said, but she took it with her, running ahead of Jenny to the truck.

CHAPTER 3

A Strange Fish

There already was a handful of cars parked in the field when they pulled off the road at Dale and Peg's. Phinneas's dented Subaru sat on the grass alongside David's truck. Next to that she recognized the Volvo belonging to Stu Barnes, who owned the Peacock House Bed and Breakfast. Mary Ann's car was parked up in the actual driveway. Jenny guessed that was because Mary Ann brought too much food to carry from the pasture; she usually did. Jenny didn't see Elliot's car anywhere, but that didn't mean that Lilly wasn't around. She could have hitched a ride with any of the others.

"Hey, come back," she called to Frankie, who was halfway across the field and headed at a fast clip toward the flickering fire. Smoke filled the air, which was already fragrant with the smell of cut grass and pine needles and fog.

Frankie turned around reluctantly and dragged her feet back to the truck. Jenny draped the blanket around her shoulders and retrieved the lasagna. With her hip, she knocked the door to the truck closed and the two of them started in the direction of the house. She could already see people waving to them from the circle around the fire. The line of trees beyond the pasture looked almost purple against the darkening sky and high above a few birds of prey looked for field mice or rabbits in the tall grass of the hillside beyond.

"Hey, it's Beauty and the Beast," called Phinneas from a few feet away.

He loved teasing Frankie. He pulled off her cap as soon as she was close enough and held it up beyond her reach until she grabbed him around the waist and made him give it back.

"You're going to have to stop saying that, Phinneas," said Jenny, nodding hello to David, who was splitting wood and tossing it into the fire. "You'll damage her self-esteem."

Phinneas turned, his goatee and long face making him look like a hippie version of the god Pan. "How do you know I was referring to *her* as the Beast?" Seeing Jenny blush and look down at her boots, he came forward and gave her a kiss on the cheek. They had been a mismatched pair, the two of them, and their romance had been particularly brief.

He said, "It's your self-esteem we should be worrying about. Beauty."

Dale was huffing and puffing around the barn, dragging more chairs out into the yard. "Well, hello there." He stood up and put his hands on his hips. The scarf that he had draped rakishly around his neck had come loose and was flapping in the rising wind. His cheeks were rosy above his white beard and he resembled nothing so much as Santa Claus, though Jenny imagined he would welcome a more virile comparison.

"Your Lilly called a while ago and asked to have someone come get her at Snug Harbor," he said. "I sent Sally. Trinculo wanted to see the other side of the island, so she took him, too."

Trinculo, Jenny remembered, was the clown. He spent half the play drunk out of his mind, the sidekick of the butler, Stephano, who found a hidden cache of wine. She pictured a funny-looking character-actor type escorting Lilly back from Snug Harbor and smiled warmly back at Dale. Over his shoulder, Jenny caught a glimpse of a young woman coming out onto the porch. The house was made of rough wood beams and the porch was strung with lanterns and a variety of wind chimes that rang loudly now in the evening breeze. They would be tied up and silent during the rehearsals and readings of the play that took place over the summer in the barn.

Dale held his hands out for the lasagna. "Can I take that in for you?"

"That's okay, I'll get it. Peg in the house?"

He nodded. "Making mulled wine. We brought a bag of cinnamon sticks back with us from Sri Lanka. Formerly Ceylon." He leaned in close. "The American customs agents were very suspicious."

She laughed. "And they had every reason to be." Jenny shifted the casserole dish to her other side and started toward the house. "Watch yourselves around the fire," she called back to Phinneas and David, who were playing keep-away with Frankie's cap.

"Yes, Mother," called Phinneas, before being tackled onto the tall grass.

Dale and Peg's ancient dog, a half-paralyzed chocolate Lab named Alice, wagged its tail at her and struggled to rise as she walked by.

"Stay right where you are, old woman," she cooed, and set the lasagna on the grass for a moment so she could scratch Alice behind the ears. "*You* understand that some people have responsibilities to attend to," she said. "Not like some silly potters we know."

Alice thumped her tail and then laid her head back on the cool earth.

Jenny lifted her dish and approached the girl on the porch, who was looking out over Dale and Peg's property to the horses on their neighbors' pasture. Jenny guessed her to be about twenty-three or twenty-four.

"Hi, I'm Jenny. Are you Miranda?"

The girl nodded. "I guess I should be grateful you didn't guess Sycorax." Her eyes were pale blue and her skin was very fair.

"Or Caliban."

She laughed. "I know Caliban from New York. You should have seen him as Valmont in *Les Liaisons Dangereuses*. He was alluring. You won't believe it when you meet him. He's the pudgy one at the bar." She inclined her head toward the house. Several people standing around in the kitchen were visible through the large picture window behind Miranda. One of them appeared to be the willowy African American man from the grocer's.

Jenny felt her pulse quicken. She tilted her head slightly to see if she could see his companion from the store, but she could not.

Suddenly the front door opened and Peg emerged with her arms outstretched. "Jenny, darling. Come in. Come in. I see you've met Miranda. Let me introduce you to Caliban, Ferdinand, and our charming, charming Ariel."

Peg lifted the lasagna out of Jenny's arms with one hand and pulled her in with the other. She wore a green sari that appeared huge on her tiny frame and had a row of silver bracelets jingling on her arm. She was barely five feet tall and at fifty-something still had the body of a thirteen-year-old boy. Her nose was pointy and always appeared to be crinkled up in mirth or skepticism. The straight hair that reached to her shoulders was a red that no one would have believed was possible in nature if they did not know that Dale and Peg's grown daughter, a banker in Charlotte, North Carolina, had had hair that same color all her life.

Once inside Peg propelled Jenny in front of the small crowd in the kitchen with a little push to her behind. "Let me present the lovely and talented Jennifer Alexander. In addition to making positively wonderful creations on her loom, Jenny is an indispensable part of our stage set team. *And*, she is the mother of two equally gorgeous girls who, you will find this hard to believe, are almost grown." With this she cast a stern glance at a heavyset man of about thirty-five who leaned against the sink with a bottle of beer in his hand. He was wearing a sport coat and a skinny little tie. "Please note that I said *almost* grown."

He lifted the bottle to his lips without speaking. Was this Caliban, Jenny wondered, really someone who had been so alluring as Valmont in *Les Liaisons Dangereuses*? He seemed pretty uptight. Well, that was the magic of the theater, she supposed, that it could transform a pinched party guest into the uncivilized offspring of a witch and a demon.

A boyish blond beside him wearing a T-shirt that said *JC Rocks* lifted a hand from his side in a bashful wave. Clearly this was Ferdinand, who falls hopelessly in love with Miranda the moment he sees her. She made a note to herself to keep an eye on him around Lilly.

Jenny craned her neck to look behind him down the long hallway. She wondered if the man in the Nikes could be somewhere on the sunporch in back. It would be a level of self-deception that Jenny could not reach to try to convince herself that she had worn glittering earrings (that David had once referred to only half-jokingly as *lures*) for anyone else.

"In any event, you must be very kind to Jenny," continued Peg, "because she is a great favorite of ours."

"And particularly of Dale's," added Phinneas, who had managed to slip in unheard behind them. "But Peg, being Peg, forgives him for that."

"Don't mind Phinneas," said Peg, swatting at him with a dishtowel and missing as he ducked. "He hasn't gotten laid in who knows how long, and his sexual frustration gets translated into snarkiness."

"*You* know exactly how long. Or did I say something I shouldn't have," countered Phinneas, wisely dodging back out the front door with a beer in his hand.

The personage who Jenny had by now deduced to be Ariel shifted his weight against the counter. His hips were almost as narrow as Frankie's. "Well," he drawled, looking at the door through which Phinneas had disappeared, "I might be able to be of some assistance to that young man."

"I don't know about that," said Mary Ann, emerging from the back to give Jenny a quick squeeze with an arm around her shoulder. "Phinneas is a bit of a caveman under all that clay dust and glaze. I don't think they make 'em much straighter."

"A *bit*?" Peg chortled, and set Jenny's lasagna on the kitchen table next to platters of salmon, homemade banana bread, and pita chips with hummus. "He's the original Hetero Erectus." She leaned in and whispered to Ferdinand. "Get yourself a cup of that mulled wine, dear, and no one will be able to tell that you're blushing."

Jenny followed Ferdinand to the mulled wine and allowed the first sip to travel through her body on a warm current. She smiled at Ferdinand, who nodded at her shyly and ducked out the door.

Caliban raised his eyebrows and looked after him. "First show, you know. Ariel will have him on his knees in no time."

Jenny tried not to appear shocked by what he'd said. "You're from New York City?"

She could feel him sizing her up from half-lowered lids and got the distinct feeling that he was not impressed with what he saw. Well, let him gape. By July he'd be wearing fleece, too. Starlets who arrived at the dock in full makeup often left wearing Birkenstocks with their hair in braids. There was no telling what might happen to a guy, she thought as she cast a wry glance at Caliban's outfit, who would wear a tie to a bonfire.

He said, "I'm from Brooklyn, actually." He took another swig and added, unnecessarily, "Do you know where that is?"

She gave him a wide-eyed stare. "Near Manhattan, right?"

"Across the bridge. The Brooklyn Bridge."

"I've heard of that."

Any one of the island residents walking through the kitchen right then would have seen the look of mischief on Jenny's face and paused. She was well-behaved, was Jenny, except for those moments when she wasn't. Those were always worth staying around for.

Ariel pushed himself off from the counter and practically glided toward the front door. Jenny had taken ballet for seven years as a child and it had been three times that long since she'd seen a dancer's gait. "Mr. man here is from Tacoma. Double-you. A."

Caliban sighed. "I spent a summer vacation up here in the San Juans once, as a child."

Jenny took another sip. "Fond memories?"

He met her eyes. "Well, memories, in any case."

Frankie pushed into the kitchen on a cool draft, her hair wild around her face, and grabbed Jenny's hand. "We're singing 'Way Downtown' next. You *love* that song." Seeing Caliban, she ducked her head shyly. "Hi."

"Hello." From the way he looked at Frankie, Jenny deduced that children were not a regular occurrence in his world.

"All right, sweet pea," said Jenny. "Let me get a refill." She ladled more wine into her cup and smiled fondly at her baby. Her rescuer.

Frankie grabbed a corn muffin from the table on her way out the door. After the warm kitchen and Caliban's contempt, the evening air hit Jenny's face like a splash of water. A chorus of male voices rose over the snapping of burning wood.

> *Way downtown, foolin' around*
> *They put me in the jail*
> *Oh me and it's oh my*
> *Ain't no one to go my bail*

David was picking on the banjo and Phinneas, one boot propped on the plastic tub that formed the base of his instrument, was plucking away at the string. Dale sat on one of the kitchen chairs that had been dragged into the pasture and did the fancy guitar work he had become famous for, the product of what he liked to call his misspent youth. Around the fire and in clumps on the grass there were a couple more unfamiliar faces amid the neighbors, waiters, gas station attendants, librarians, and salespeople among whom Jenny and her daughters spent their days. But still no sign of the man she had seen with Ariel that afternoon. She began to doubt that he was part of the company after all. Perhaps he had just been standing next to Ariel by accident, waiting for a cut of beef to take home to his vacation rental. And his children. And his beautiful wife.

Frankie waited for Jenny to start on the next verse before she joined in, her voice tentative and yet truer than Jenny's would ever be.

> *Wishing I was at my sweet baby's house*
> *Sittin' in that old arm chair*
> *With one arm around this big guitar*
> *And the other one around my dear*

During the course of the song, headlights shone briefly on the circle of people, and in the pasture, car doors slammed. The people in the house came out with overflowing paper plates as the people outside went in. Hellos were shouted and chairs pulled away from the fire for private conversations. The sky grew dark and cigarettes, only some of which smelled like tobacco, gave the illusion of alien spacecraft hovering in the distance. Miranda stood with Jenny and Frankie and flipped through the songbook looking for something they all knew. They finally settled on "Will the Circle Be Unbroken." Dale strummed the first few chords. Jenny put her arm around Frankie, knowing that this song about a dying mother always made her tear up.

The bartender from Herb's held the last note a moment longer than everyone else, letting his voice warble on past Dale's last chord. Phinneas cracked a joke, and the guy sheepishly ad-

justed his knit cap on his head, mussing his shaggy hair in the
process. Dale handed him a beer and, with Mary Ann looking over his shoulder, flipped through the pages of a book for
another song. Jenny smiled. The island wasn't perfect, but she
could not deny that it was the best place she'd found.

Suddenly, Frankie pulled away and ran into the field after
a glow-in-the-dark Frisbee. Jenny turned back to the fire just
in time to see Lilly lean in to whisper something to an uncom-
monly handsome man in a turtleneck and Nikes. The man
from the store. Trinculo. Of course.

Jenny flushed, both delighted to see him and horrified that
he should be arriving at the party with Lilly, of all people.
She stole another glance at him. He was laughing in the fire-
light, turning to first one and then another person as he was
introduced. He had not, she was sure, noticed her yet. Perhaps
his arriving with Lilly was just a coincidence? He was at least
twenty years older than she was, after all. She turned her eyes
back to her daughter and her heart sank. Lilly stood draped in
an unfamiliar leather jacket, the light of conquest already shining bright in her eyes.

Mary Ann came up behind Jenny. A chill was spreading
with every star that popped into the sky and she edged in
to warm herself in the glow of the fire. A shout of triumph
traveled from the field, where Frankie must have caught the
Frisbee, followed by another teenager's whoop of congratula-
tion.

Jenny hoped Frankie wouldn't step into a crevice and break
her ankle. Half expecting to have to run to her in the dark,

she whispered in Mary Ann's ear, "What do you think of that one?"

Mary Ann glanced at Trinculo. "Very cute."

"Is he forty, do you think? Thirty-five?"

Mary Ann cocked her head. "Hard to say. He's way too old for Lil, in any case."

"Well, sure. Of course."

Mary Ann lifted Jenny's mug out of her hand and took a pull from it. Her graying hair was pushed back from her face with a headband and the wrinkles on her forehead were deep. "You're not thinking of getting involved in all that summer nonsense, are you? The intrigue? The late-night sex on the beach?"

Chad looked up sharply from the log on which he was sitting, warming his feet at the fire, and Mary Ann and Jenny both giggled. Mary Ann leaned in to Jenny and whispered, "And here he thought we didn't know about that night on Shaw last summer. Poor Chad." The song ended and she glanced at Jenny with a touch of concern. "They always leave, you know. After the play is over. Always."

Jenny raised her eyebrows. "And the bad news is?"

Mary Ann shrugged. "Don't say I didn't warn you."

They both watched as Lilly drank something mysterious from a cup and then held it up to the strange man's mouth. Lilly, who after escaping to a nightclub in Seattle at sixteen, returned home and regaled her sister with a story of how a man in his forties came up out of nowhere, wrapped his arms around her, and licked her face.

Jenny watched Lilly, and Mary Ann watched Jenny. This is so wrong, thought Jenny, in so many ways. She took a drink from her cup and the wine was unpleasantly tepid.

Jenny caught Lilly's eye and gestured to her to come over. Lilly stared defiantly back and then, glancing at Trinculo, must have decided that failing to obey might result in a more embarrassing scene than coming when her mother beckoned. She obliged, but in her most nonchalant way, shoulders rocking, arms swinging, as if every move she made was all her own idea.

Trinculo's eyes followed Lilly around the fire, and then suddenly, with a start, he saw Jenny, too. Jenny watched recognition cross his face, and when it did, warmth traveled up her spine. She had not imagined his interest at the grocery, after all. Perhaps he, too, had been scanning the crowd for her face. She reached for Lilly's arm and drew her close, noting that Trinculo was still watching.

Mary Ann said under her breath, "Probably the only man on this island who doesn't know the child is yours."

"What do you think you're doing?" whispered Jenny into Lilly's ear.

Lilly smirked. "Making friends."

"Well, stop it right now."

Lilly waved to Trinculo, who appeared not to see. "He's adorable, isn't he? I always like guys whose hair looks like they just crawled out of bed."

"Lilly!"

Jenny's eyes followed her daughter's. Trinculo was pretending not to notice either one of them now. He was nodding at something that Dale was saying and reaching for a cup handed to him by Sally, who couldn't stop being a waitress even when she was not working at the Backdoor Kitchen. Someone said something to make him laugh, and he threw his head back and flashed a row of teeth so white you could see the flames dancing in them. He ducked his head fetchingly and let a lock of sandy hair fall into his eyes. He glanced up briefly, fixing Jenny in his gaze, and then looked away.

Jenny smiled and then turned her head. Damn it, he was beautiful.

"Don't *do* that, Mom," hissed Lilly.

"Do what?"

"Make him like *you*."

"For heaven's sake, Lilly. The man is old enough to be your father."

Lilly narrowed her eyes. "You aren't even going to deny it then? That you just smiled at him?"

Jenny wiped a smudge of ash from her daughter's chin with the pad of her thumb. "Why don't you go inside and ask Peg if she needs any help."

Lilly brushed off her mother's touch. "God, I can't *stand* this anymore. I can't stand it." She stomped her foot then, which conveyed her anger well enough but did not exactly strengthen her case as far as being treated like an adult.

Jenny sighed. "So get a ride home."

"I'm not talking about Dale and Peg's," she tossed over her shoulder.

"What, then?" said Jenny, under her breath. "This planet?"

"This island! Where else in the entire world would you go to the most happening party in town and have to hang out with your *mother*? Living on San Juan is like growing up in an *elevator*. It's a prison!"

Jenny shook her head. "Poor Lil."

Frankie trotted by the fire carrying the Frisbee in her teeth like a dog. When she saw her sister she let it drop and ran over. "I was wondering when you would get here." She grabbed Lilly's arm and pulled. "Come meet Miranda. She is *so* cool. You're going to love her."

Lilly looked tempted but glanced again at Trinculo, clearly torn. "My bag is over there," she said, inclining her head in his direction.

Jenny said, "Go with your sister. I'll keep an eye on your bag." And on *you*, she wanted to add, but she let her go without another word.

Miranda sat on the stump of a tree that Dale had felled the year before after a big storm. Her hair and pale wrists shone like moth wings in the remaining light. A small clump of young island men stood around her talking, Jenny guessed, about fish they had caught, sheds they had built by hand, and cars they had repaired with nothing more than a pocket knife and gasket paper. The boys parted like the Red Sea to let the two girls through. They were used to doing that when Lilly arrived.

"Here's my sister who I was telling you about," said Frankie, pushing Lilly forward. "She just graduated."

"Hello." The one word was all the poor girl could manage,

though her smile was very convincing. She was an actress, after all.

Jenny felt sorry for her. She could imagine being a beautiful young woman headed to an outpost to star in a summer play and arriving to find someone like Lilly there, already reigning supreme. It would be quite a shock.

"Do you smoke?" asked Lilly. She reached into the pocket of her commandeered coat to pull out a pack of clove cigarettes.

Jenny found herself wondering if Trinculo, upon finding them in his pocket the next morning, might be brought to his senses. Surely the scent of cloves would be sobering enough to an adult man to clear any love-in-idleness elixir from his eyes.

"Sometimes." Miranda was clearly softening. She accepted a clove from Lilly's outstretched hand.

"God, you have such beautiful hair," said Lilly, lifting a plait of the other girl's pale tresses into her hand.

Lilly's hair had been just as pretty, Jenny recalled, before she had matted it and rolled it into a pile of snakes.

Frankie stood between them with the smug expression of a matchmaker at a wedding.

Miranda smiled, and this time the smile extended all the way to her eyes. It was done. They were friends. Jenny turned her attention back to the fire and to Trinculo, who was shaking hands with the boys' high school basketball coach.

Joined by several new masculine voices, the group around the fire broke into a chorus of "Rollin' in My Sweet Baby's Arms." *Gonna lay around the shack until the mail train comes*

*back, rollin' in my sweet baby's arms, arms, arms, rollin' in my
sweet baby's arms.*

Whenever a song ended or Dale paused to figure out the
key and adjust his cap, Jenny could hear the girls' voices murmuring in the background. At least she could hear Lilly's and
Miranda's voices. Frankie would be sitting there listening with
rapt attention. Without Phoenix, Frankie was even more attached to Lilly, it seemed. Jenny turned, and in the fading
light could still make out on Frankie's face the same starstruck
smile she wore at three when she used to follow her seven-
and-a-half-year-old sister around the garden in a nightgown
and rain boots. Jenny wondered if having Frankie shadow her
around the party all night would cramp Lilly's style. She hoped
it would.

Jenny was both annoyed that Lilly couldn't seem to get
through a single day without a hit of pot and grateful that she
took care to smoke it outside her sister's presence. She knew
it was wrong, but she couldn't help but take some comfort in
the fact that while Lilly smoked a lot of dope, her sister's children (one a freshman at Stanford, the other liberal arts college
bound) indulged, by all reports, in drugs both more addic-
tive and harder on the pocketbook. Sue would never say, but
according to her husband, who was quite fond of Jenny and
would refill her glass of Chardonnay without being asked, the
kids in Marin tossed random pills at each other at school all day
long. Jenny's brother-in-law had expressed relief that at least his
children had the sense to identify the pills on WebMD as Ad-

derall or Concerta before washing them down with a Caramel Frappuccino.

Jenny was weighing the relative advantages of interrupting Lilly's new clique with an admonition to behave when Trinculo suddenly appeared next to her at the fire. She shifted her feet and, catching her sandal on an uneven patch of dirt, nearly tumbled into Mary Ann's lap. Mary Ann reached out a hand to steady her and, seeing Trinculo, took on a look that was both amused and cautionary. Jenny ignored both and, crossing her arms over her chest, hoped the color in her cheeks would be easily missed in the low light.

Trinculo smiled. "You've got a nice voice," he said. Up close she could see lines in his face that had not been visible at a distance. Definitely over forty, she thought.

"I sang in church," she said. She was conscious of several interested glances from people around the fire. Dale was watching her, though pretending not to. Mary Ann, who had no use for pretending, was clearly keeping an eye on them.

Trinculo rocked on his heels and his shoulder knocked against Jenny's.

"Me, too. Every Sunday. Baptist?"

"Methodist."

"Lightweight."

She laughed. Surely she was not mistaking the undercurrent in his voice and in his eyes? Trinculo shifted, and the sense of solid warmth that radiated from him nearly made her swoon. One step closer and they would be hip to hip. A thin dusting of sandy whiskers glittered like powdered sugar on his neck. She imagined slipping her hand under the T-shirt that hung loosely to his belt. She swallowed. The pounding of his heart under her palm. Dale fished in his bag for his head lamp and fit it over his head before stepping away from the fire. She watched him go. Perhaps that was the difference this year, she thought. Perhaps this year she was merely unencumbered enough to wonder.

Trinculo stuck his hands farther down in his pockets and twisted his face into an expression of exaggerated dismay. Jenny could picture him in the jester's role all of a sudden. He would do well.

He said, "You're looking at one sanctified, certified, and now citified Holy Roller. Speaking in tongues. The whole bit. That's why I know what's in store for our poor young Ferdinand. My bet is that before the summer's end, he will either be giving up on prayer altogether, or praying for forgiveness."

Jenny pictured the blond young man in the kitchen. "Speaking in tongues?" she said. "Really? What about snakes?" Jenny wondered idly if Frankie had given her sister the tattoo that she'd stuck in her pocket for her.

He shot her a glance. "I wish I could say snakes, if that would impress you, but no. Alas, no serpents."

"And where did all this holy rolling take place, if I may ask?"

"You may. Colorado Springs."

She nodded. "I'm from Sacramento."

Not far from the tree stump Frankie called to Lilly and Miranda in response to a command that Jenny had not heard, "Something to drink, too, or just cookies?"

"If you can carry a soda," Lilly yelled after her, "we'll take that, too. Otherwise just cookies."

David tossed a new log on the fire and it sparked, but the cold still licked at their backs. Jenny wondered who among them had noticed Trinculo arriving at the party with Lilly. Probably everyone. As Dale was fond of pronouncing, *everyone knows everything*. As if on cue, she heard a loud guffaw from Lilly in the vicinity of the barn. She hoped that she and Miranda would have the sense not to burn it down.

"You're not from here, then." Trinculo swept his gaze over the people around the fire. "Though, I don't suppose many people are."

David broke a piece of wood over his leg. "She's been here long enough to break a few hearts."

Mary Ann headed in to get a jacket. "Stop putting on a show, David. Your heart will mend," she said.

He carried the ax to the woodpile for more logs. "Will not," he said, but he was smiling.

Trinculo raised his eyebrows at Jenny. "Old boyfriend?"

"Old friend."

"I see."

They watched the flames in silence.

When Frankie returned she came dragging a blanket from around her shoulders to the grass like a medieval robe. She carried a plate of cookies and had a Jones soda tucked under her arm.

"Have you seen Lil? She and Miranda asked me to get them some snacks, and when I came back out they were gone."

"I don't know, babe. Maybe they went for a walk."

"But I brought them cookies."

"I'll take one. Do you mind?" Trinculo plucked a cookie off the plate and gobbled it in one bite.

Jenny laughed.

He bugged his eyes out at her. "I'm starving."

Frankie was unimpressed by his antics. She leaned her head against Jenny's shoulder. "There's plenty of food inside the house."

Jenny pulled her daughter in to her side and adjusted the blanket so that it enveloped them both. The wind from the ocean had picked up a little and it was rustling the very tops of the pines.

Trinculo looked at them for a moment. "Okay," he said. "In the house." He glanced back at Jenny. "Can I bring anyone anything?"

"No thanks," said Frankie quickly, before Jenny could answer.

An hour or so later, Trinculo had not returned to the fire. Jenny, realizing that she had not heard Lilly's voice in quite a while, wandered off in search of her. She found a variety of people milling in the house around the snacks table, but no Lilly and no Trinculo. Peg was in the kitchen mixing baking soda into a glass of water.

She saw Jenny and nodded toward her concoction. "Bit of indigestion. This always helps."

"Have you seen Lil?"

Peg shook her head and drained her glass. "No. Have you

seen Chad? I ought to give that boy a good kick in the keister for bringing green-toothpick brownies to the welcome party. The place is swarming with mainlanders and children. He should know better than that."

"Frankie didn't?"

"I put them up there." Peg inclined her head toward the top of the fridge. "Frankie's in the back room watching TV. She told me that would be all right with you."

"It's fine. She'll just fall asleep in front of it anyway."

Jenny took a cracker off a near-empty tray and nibbled the edge of it thoughtfully. She grabbed a few more and headed for the deck. A number of people tried to draw her into a conversation, or a song, or an argument, but she shrugged off each effort and kept wandering around the house and the yard until her handful of crackers was gone. The absence of both Lilly and Trinculo was beginning to seem ominous. She ducked around behind the couch where she had tossed her bag and fished through it for her phone.

The light was flashing and she had several texts waiting. She knew they were from Lilly before the message even rolled across her screen. Lilly was the only one who ever texted her, and Lilly only ever did it when she needed something. Jenny crouched behind the couch reading her daughter's messages through the curtain of hair that fell around her face. *@Egg Lake. Trink hi. Pls. Cm.*

Trink high? Jesus. Jenny snapped the phone shut and, struck by a bolt of mother's intuition, grabbed the afghan off the back of the couch. She wove through the clumps of people milling in the house, past a couple kissing on the porch, and set out over the cool grass with only the full moon lighting her way. It grew dark on the trail from the pasture and the occasional root or rock caught her foot and sent her stumbling now and then, but she could see enough of the path to keep from falling flat on her face. The pine needles under her feet were damp with fog and the path held cold corners, like the pockets of chilled water in a sun-warmed stream. She wrapped the afghan around her shoulders and narrowly avoided walking into a broken branch. After a few minutes she began to hear voices. A girl laughing. Miranda. Lilly's voice chiming in after. She laughed, too, but Jenny knew her daughter well enough to detect the frustration in her tone. A man's voice. Then splashing.

Jenny burst out into the clearing to see three figures silhouetted in the moonlight at the edge of the T-shaped dock on Egg Lake. Only two of them were wearing clothes.

Lilly had her hands on her hips. "C'mon. You're going to freeze to death," she said. "Come *now*."

"Maggie," drawled a man's voice. "You are ruinin' my liquor."

Lilly threw up her hands. "Who the hell is Maggie?"

"It's from *Cat on a Hot Tin Roof*." From Miranda, "He played Brick."

"He's closing his eyes," wailed Lilly. "Oh God, we can't let him go to sleep."

"What have we here?" Trinculo waved his arms in the air above his body. "A man or a fish? Dead or alive?"

"Well, that's the right play, at least," said Miranda.

The dock shook with Jenny's footsteps. Both girls turned to look at her, their eyes reflecting the moonlight. Trinculo lay on the edge of the dock on his back, with his feet brushing the water.

"What in the *world* is happening?" Jenny reached for a pile of clothing and finding it sopping, let it lie. "Lilly, what did you *do*?"

"I didn't do anything," she cried. "I mean, I brought him some brownies. But they had green toothpicks in them, so it was obvious that they were hash brownies. And he didn't have to go eat *three* of them."

Jenny leaned over Trinculo's prone body to look at his face. He had a fine form, she could see that even in the dark. Broad shoulders. Narrow hips. Strong arms.

His eyes flew open and he stared at her with dilated pupils.

"Get up," she said.

He did so, wordlessly, and she wrapped him in the afghan. He began to shiver as soon as the blanket touched his skin.

"Where are his shoes?" Jenny practically barked the question at Lilly.

Her daughter, uncharacteristically docile, searched around for Trinculo's shoes and, finding them, set them by his feet so that Jenny could help him step into them.

"I think I'm going to throw up," he groaned, bending forward. He doubled over and retched off the dock into the water.

Miranda took a step backward. "Eww."

When Trinculo straightened Jenny put her arm around him and began to lead him back on the path to the house. She was aware of Miranda and Lilly standing guiltily behind. She could sense the looks of horror and excitement that passed between them.

"Bring his clothes, will you?" she called over her shoulder.

"Okay."

"Sure thing."

Trinculo's teeth were chattering as Jenny led him, naked except for his Nikes and wrapped in an afghan, up the path, toward the house. It was a measure of how interesting summers on the island often got that the sight of him in that condition warranted no more than a few raised eyebrows and the occasional call of, "Jenny? You need some help?"

"We're fine," she answered back, and led him up the stairs into the house.

Peg was waiting with her arms crossed over her chest. "Dale is moving Frankie from the back room." She shook her head. "That Lilly."

Trinculo lifted his head, which had been nodding with his chin against his chest. "Lilly." He repeated her name as if he were just now realizing that he'd left her behind.

"She's fine," said Jenny, giving him a push toward the back that was forceful enough to set him wobbling.

Once in front of the futon, she gave him a gentler shove until he was lying on the spot that was still warm from Frankie's body. She covered him with another quilt and then, before turning off the light, noticed a smudge of something on his cheek. She brushed at it with her fingers. A shred of temporary tattoo curled off and fell to the floor. A snake. Jenny shut the door behind her with a firm click.

· CHAPTER 4 ·

A Most Majestic Vision

It was one a.m. and the embers of the fire sizzled in the fog. Inside the warm house, Jenny, Lilly, Frankie, Dale, Peg, Mary Ann, David, and Miranda reclined in various positions on the couches, leather chairs, and floor cushions and polished off the last of the chips, grapes, and cookies that remained on the wide wooden table. Trinculo slept in the TV room. Ferdinand had gone home early and Caliban had begged a ride back to town with the owner of the harbor ice cream shop. Ariel was doing stretches in the corner and Jenny watched as Frankie, snuggled under a blanket with her head on a pile of coats, watched him under half-lowered eyelids.

"Not Gonzalo. But perhaps Adrian or Francisco," said Dale sleepily, after Peg had mused aloud whether or not Chad would be good to play one of the lords. He had done an excellent job as Le Beau in *As You Like It* and had been lobbying since May for a role in *The Tempest*. Before leaving again that evening he had pulled Peg aside to say how sorry he was about the brownies and how much he wanted to be in the play.

Peg had forgiven him. "They did have green toothpicks in them, after all," she'd said. "Trinculo could have at least asked what that signified before he ate *three* of them."

Now, Peg pulled both of her legs into the oversize chair and rested her chin on her fist. "I wonder if he could handle Stephano."

Jenny was only half following the conversation.

After putting Trinculo to bed she had waited on the porch with a glass of wine until Lilly and Miranda emerged from the woods. The girls arrived whispering and holding Trinculo's dripping clothes away from their bodies. They were roughly the same slender shape, but Lilly was clearly Lilly from her lumpy dreads. They were almost to the house before they noticed Jenny on the porch. Lilly saw her and froze. Miranda took a step or two more and then she, too, stopped and stood still. It was almost comical, thought Jenny. Almost.

"Get up here, Lilly. March."

Miranda reached for the wet clothes in Lilly's hand. "I'll put these by the fire."

Jenny glanced from Miranda back to her daughter. One leg of Lilly's long underwear had ruched up to just below her knee, exposing a slice of sun-browned calf. The other disappeared into the fuzzy, ankle-high Ugg that had consumed a third of Lilly's first paycheck. Pine needles clung to her sweatshirt. From the very way she held herself as she slunk up the stairs, Jenny could see that Lilly was wavering between launching some kind of offensive claim of her own innocence to seeking quick absolution through immediate and contrite capitulation.

"This may all seem like a big joke to you," said Jenny softly. "But giving someone drugs without their consent is a violation. It can feel, to the person who got them, like an assault."

Lilly glanced up from the chair she had settled into with genuine shock. "I didn't *give* him the brownies. I had gotten some for me and Miranda and *he* snatched them. All three."

"Did you tell him that they were hash brownies? Or did you allow him to eat them without telling?"

From the look on Lilly's face it was clear which of the two alternatives had occurred.

"But they did have green toothpicks in them," protested Lilly weakly.

"Lilly."

"I'm sorry." Lilly sounded on the verge of tears. Her eyes held genuine confusion. "I guess I was thinking because, well, he is a *grown-up* and all . . ."

Jenny sighed and took a pull from her wine. There was Lilly in a nutshell. Confident she was old enough to seduce the guy but not mature enough to take responsibility for what might happen.

"Lilly, you're going to be eighteen any day now. It's time you started acting like a grown-up, too."

Lilly had taken a clump of matted locks in her hands and squeezed it thoughtfully. Then she had ducked her chin and looked at her mother with the mischievous half smile that males of all ages found so fetching. "I'll try to make it up to him," she had said.

Jenny frowned at the memory, even as she looked at her older daughter now, who was curled up on the same sofa as Frankie and looking markedly unrepentant. Trinculo snored in the back room unmolested, but the rest of the snake tattoo, ragged and patchy, clung to the skin of Lilly's throat.

And then there was Frankie. After Lilly and Miranda had ditched her, Frankie had been more shy than usual. But whenever Jenny had thought to look for her she'd found her in the penumbra of Ariel, whether he was aware of her presence or not. She hovered about the youthful actor like a bird with her eye on a bit of lost bread, as if she had only to wait and watch and an opportunity would come along for her to dart in and claim it. It was clear that she wanted to be noticed by him, but Jenny could not figure out why. He was beautiful in his way, lithe and fey and sarcastic. Talking with him around the fire, she had learned that he was from Detroit. The only child in a family named Wilcox.

"The beloved son of the Wilcoxes," said Jenny, smiling.

He had looked at her for a moment and then added drily, "Beloved by whom?"

Jenny glanced at Frankie now, her skinny limbs folded under the blanket. Perhaps she saw what she hoped was her future self in the way he held his body. He made his lankiness work for him. He turned gangliness into grace. Jenny wondered if she could find some dance instruction for Frankie on the island. It might provide a diversion for the inevitable heartache when Phoenix left. It might boost her confidence. They didn't have a lot of extra money, but Jenny decided she could scrape together enough for a lesson or two, just to see if Frankie took to it.

She rubbed her lower back through her shirt and wondered how long she could allow herself to entertain this little romantic sizzle with Ariel's friend before making herself completely ridiculous. It was clear that Lilly would not give Trinculo up easily, and the idea of vying with her own teenage daughter for the affection of a professional actor was absurd. It was morally, ethically, and spiritually wrong. Besides that, it was impractical. Lilly was seventeen years old and adorable. What forty-two-year-old mother of two could compete with her? Jenny unfolded herself from her chair and tottered to the bathroom to splash cold water on her face. Her skin still dripping, she pulled back her hair with one hand and bent to drink from the faucet. She toweled her face and bared her teeth in the mirror to check for any stray pieces of potato chip or carrot.

Dale had once pulled her into a wet kiss at the Roche Harbor after-party. Though he'd apologized and she, embarrassed, had never said a word, it was a reminder to keep on her toes in the midst of all this enchanted storytelling. She could understand how Lilly, of all people, might be susceptible. She could understand, but she didn't like it. She slipped back into her chair with a frown.

"Are there any parts for girls?" asked Lilly suddenly.

Peg snorted.

Dale pulled himself into an upright position and looked at Lilly with incredulity. "You haven't read the play?"

"Not yet." Lilly blushed and shot a quick furtive glance toward Ariel.

Ariel strolled toward her. "Prospero, my dear, is a big cheese in Milan." He stopped just short of the couch and leaned against the wall. "A duke. Until his naughty, ambitious, betraying brother has him banished to an island where he is served by an uncouth toad named Caliban and an enchanting, chameleonesque spirit named Ariel." He took an almost imperceptible bow. "Conveniently, one day, a boat carrying his old enemies, as well as a luscious young prince named Ferdinand, sails by and Prospero conjures a storm." Here Ariel waved his hands around in front of her face. "That wrecks the boat and brings them all to shore."

"An interesting interpretation," murmured Peg.

Ariel turned away and resumed his stretching. "Oh, and Prospero has a daughter."

"Miranda," breathed Frankie, just before drifting off to sleep. She had burrowed her face under the blanket for warmth and darkness.

"Yes, Miranda is a *girl part*, as you say. But that role's taken." Dale cupped his hand over the top of Miranda's head as if he were her actual father and not just her theatrical one.

"I didn't mean any *main* parts," continued Lilly. "I'm talking about a smaller role that a girl could play." She was silent for a moment and, perhaps reflecting on the marijuana that had made her last year in high school so challenging, she added, "with not too many lines."

"You're persistent," sighed Dale, "but would you be *reliable*?"

Persistent was a *very* good word for Lilly, Jenny thought, and it was unsurprising that Dale should find just the right one to describe her.

Ariel padded back over to the couch and leaned his pelvis against the back of it, looking down at Frankie and Lilly with interest. "Iris? Ceres?" He shifted his gaze to Jenny. "Juno?"

Dale straightened his back against the chair. His eyes traveled from the girls on the couch, one sleeping, the other tousled and eager, to Jenny and then back again. He tugged at his beard like an Old World rabbi. "Iris, Ceres, and Juno," he repeated. *"This is a most majestic vision, and harmonious, charmingly. May I be bold to think thee Spirits?"*

Peg came to stand by Dale's chair. Her sari was coming undone and she had a small twig clinging to her hair. She said, *"Spirits, which by mine art I have from their confines call'd to enact My present fancies."* There was more than a spark of interest in her eyes. "All three of them?"

"Oh, yes," said Dale, "absolutely." He reached for his wife's hand and drew her close.

Jenny was suddenly wide awake. They were talking about putting them *in* the play? Jenny and her daughters?

"You should only give Lilly the part if Jenny and Frankie will be players, too," said Dale to Peg emphatically. "We want all three."

"Please, Mom?" The cool that Lilly cultivated so assiduously was gone. She wanted this. Badly.

It didn't help that Jenny wanted to be in the play, too. Even without the blue-eyed Trinculo, in years past she had longed to burrow deep down into the center of the theater magic. To be one of the players.

Miranda tucked her hair behind her ears and looked at Jenny with curiosity. "Will you do it?"

In answer, Jenny found herself looking square in the face of Ariel, who gazed back with curiosity and perhaps, if she was not mistaken, a touch of naughtiness. Did he have any idea of the mischief his suggestion might have set in motion, she wondered. She narrowed her eyes at him, not in an unfriendly way, but her scrutiny was clear. He glanced demurely to the side and began a new round of stretches, a smile playing at the corners of his mouth. Jenny chewed the inside of her cheek and sighed. She suspected he knew quite well.

· CHAPTER 5 ·

Opportunities. Challenges. Ideas.

The last school bus of the year was due in ten minutes and Frankie was still in the bathroom. She stuck her head out of the door. "Maybe there's a part for Phoenix?"

"I don't know," said Jenny. "Maybe."

"I'll ask Dale tonight at the . . . *what* was it called?"

"The table reading."

"The table reading." Frankie nodded with satisfaction and closed the door.

Jenny stirred the honey in her tea and closed her eyes to take her first sip. Now that the actors were on the island, she mused, the most ordinary places, the post office, the bowling alley, the Whale Museum, all crackled with new possibility. She would have allowed herself to be drawn and quartered before admitting to Lilly that she scanned the avenues of Friday Harbor for one particular sandy-haired man. The northern light always gave her a touch of insomnia in late spring and early summer, but this year it was worse than usual. Though it was past eight in the morning, she would have liked nothing better than to climb back under the covers and listen through the window for geese and ospreys, hawks and oystercatchers.

"Hurry up, Franks," Jenny called. "The bus is going to be here any minute."

Frankie emerged from the bathroom with a spot of toothpaste on her chin. "Or me'n Phoenix could play the same part." Her eyes were bright with the genius of it. "Like with an understudy. Or twins, you know, on TV shows. Like the Olsen twins."

"I remember the Olsens." Frankie's room had once been plastered with pictures of them. She motioned for her to wipe her face and Frankie did so with her hoodie, before putting it on.

"Depending upon the costume, we might look exactly alike. We're almost the same size, except for she's about three pounds heavier than me." Frankie giggled. "And that's all up here," she said, cupping her hands under imaginary breasts.

Jenny stood and stretched her hands toward the ceiling. She had been out of school for more years than she could count, but even she had that summer vacation feeling. She hoped the play might turn out to be one of her better decisions. It was, after all, Shakespeare, and an enriching activity for her and her girls to do together. Perhaps, in spite of all her mistakes and misjudgments, it suggested that she hadn't been such a bad mother after all.

She kissed Frankie on the cheek and pushed her toward the door. "Do you know what you and Phoenix are going to do when school gets out?" The last day was always a half day.

"We're going to the art store. Phoenix wants some new colored pencils." Frankie grabbed the charms that she'd attached to the end of her zipper and pulled her hoodie closed up to her little pointy chin. "I can't wait till she meets the cast," she said, backing through the door as her mother flapped her hands in a brushing sign, sending her out. "She's going to love Ariel."

"Call if you need a ride home."

"Okay."

Jenny pulled the door shut and Frankie, standing on her tiptoes, made a kissy face against the glass. Jenny tapped at the glass with the tip of her finger and Frankie disappeared.

Five minutes later a truck bumped over the ruts toward the house and stepping back to the window, Jenny could see Elliot sitting in the front seat. This early in the summer his neck was as pink as a newborn mouse. He honked twice, loudly. She waved. He sat up straight and waved back.

Lilly emerged from her room tying her dreads back with a bandanna. She had slipped a pair of army shorts over long johns.

"I might be just a hair late to the meeting tonight. Would you let Dale know?"

"Why?" Immediately, Jenny realized the futility of that question: Whatever answer she would get was likely to be tempered with varying shades of the truth. She followed her daughter to the pantry. "No. Lilly. I will not. We're going do a read through of the entire play, and that's going to take a little while. Dale said you had to be present at this meeting if you wanted to be in the company."

"I didn't say I wouldn't be *present*." Lilly's exasperation was hard on the banana and granola bars she was tossing in her bag for lunch. "Just late." She slung her lumpy woven bag over her shoulder and gave her mother one last look of persecuted innocence. "Okay?"

"It's not my permission that you need Lilly. It's Dale and Peg's. Call them yourself."

Lilly scowled. Her bag buzzed and she flipped open her cell phone, no doubt receiving and then replying to a text from Elliot, who sat within shouting distance in the yard. She flipped the phone shut again and pirouetted toward the door with her back to Jenny. On the way out she called casually over her shoulder, "Oh, and I forgot to tell you. Auntie Sue phoned the other day and she invited me to come down."

"Just by yourself? To visit?" Jenny followed Lilly through the door out onto the concrete step in front of the house. She could feel the chill coming up through the wool of her socks, but the sun was bright on her face. She shaded her eyes with her hand so that she could see her daughter bending to get in the passenger side of the truck. "When did she say you could come?"

"Not to visit. To stay. She said maybe I could go to that community college that they have there. College of Marin? Marin College? Whatever it's called." Lilly's voice faded as she hopped in next to Elliot.

"She invited you to *live* with them? Lilly? What did she say exactly?"

Elliot began backing the truck toward the road and Lilly

stuck her head through the window and yelled over the sound of the engine, "We'll talk about it later, Mom. Okay?"

In a moment they were already too far to hear from Jenny whether or not it was okay. Lilly go to Marin? To *live*? She had known that Lilly would probably go somewhere, sometime, but this was too soon. Barely two weeks had passed since her high school graduation. And to Jenny's sister's, of all places?

She went back into the house with a sigh. The top was off the sugar bowl, the dishes were still in the sink, and a handful of tried-on and rejected garments lay draped over the backs of chairs and on doorknobs like the limp forms of exhausted ghosts. In the mornings after the girls had gone, the house always seemed doubly empty. Triply so.

Jenny began humming to break the quiet.

Cornbread and butter beans and you across the table. Eating beans and making love as long as I am able. She finished the verse and then headed toward the four-harness jack loom in the corner of the porch, determined not to spend the hour or so she had before work on petty chores like straightening up the house. This was a simple weave she was working on, a tapestry for a baby that was due in the fall, and as she pushed the treadles she knew she ought to take a few moments and phone her sister. A chickadee called outside the window (*chickadee-dee-dee, chickadee-dee-dee*) and the angled sunlight coming through the glass scattered rainbow fragments on the wall. She decided she would call from work in an hour, enough time to compose herself so that she would be able to discuss Sue's offer without sounding defensive and ungrateful.

As girls, the best Jenny and Sue could muster was tolerance. At worst, they fought. In the pacifist, nuclear-power-no-thank-you days after leaving home Jenny preferred to pretend that the hair-pulling and shoving parts of their fights never happened. Sue, however, with her French-manicured fingernails and perfectly applied Estée Lauder makeup, was not above claiming over a glass of Chardonnay that she could still kick Jenny's butt if it came to it. Jenny beat the weft with the shuttle, drew it across the warp, and beat it again.

By lunchtime Jenny had sold two fifty-dollar hand-painted canoe paddles, new but made to look old by an island resident who claimed to have a sliver of Skagit in his otherwise German background, and a genuinely antique silver tea set. She popped a sign on the door and headed out to pick up some lunch. It was warm enough to walk down to the market in just her tank top. There was couscous salad on special, one of her favorites. She lingered at the counter deciding whether or not she wanted a roll. In the end she grabbed her carton without the roll but with a boysenberry soda sweating in her hand. The cashier offered her a bag, which she politely refused, and a fork, which she accepted. She turned toward the sun and headed straight through the door into Trinculo.

"Oh, shoot. Sorry. Did I . . ."

"No. Ooops. I . . ."

They looked into each other's eyes and laughed.

Trinculo was wearing khaki shorts with lots of pockets

and a T-shirt that said, *Save the Drama for Your Mama.* Jenny looked at his shirt and then at his face.

"It's from a show I was in, it . . ."

She stepped out of his way. "Going shopping?"

He glanced at the carton and soda in her hand. "Can I join you for lunch? Or did you want to be alone?"

Jenny was often alone, but she rarely wanted to be. She uncapped her soda and took a swig. "I'll wait here."

They walked down the hill toward the harbor and sat on a bench near the turnaround. The gulls started circling before they had even unwrapped their food.

Trinculo regarded his cheese sandwich. "I owe you an apology after the other night. It was so stupid to gobble up those brownies without thinking." He looked up sheepishly. "Apparently, green toothpicks are the universal signal for *proceed at your own risk.*" He grimaced at the memory. "I'm here to play the fool, I know, but I hadn't planned to make a fool of myself before the rehearsals even started."

Jenny touched the back of his hand. "If anyone should apologize, it's Lilly."

"Lilly?" He looked momentarily perplexed.

Jenny scooped a bite of couscous into her mouth and waved her fork to signal lots of hair.

"Oh. *That* Lilly." Trinculo's eyes widened. "The gorgeous girl with the dreads. Man, the word *TROUBLE* flashes in neon over her head. You people on this island have your hands full with Lilly, I imagine. People in *Seattle* would have their hands full with Lilly."

Jenny swallowed. She allowed her eyes to follow a family with two little children exiting the ice cream store down by the ferry slip. The smaller child, a boy of about three, took a forceful lick of his ice cream and sent the ball rolling off the ledge of the cone to the pavement. She blinked her eyes shut before his look of outrage turned to tears.

"What? What did I say?"

Jenny found her throat was a bit parched and took another swig. She smiled her most understanding smile. "Lilly is my daughter. And she *is* a handful, truly."

"She's your *daughter*?"

Trinculo brought both his hands up and pushed them through his hair in distress, smearing mayonnaise on one eyebrow. "I can't believe . . . Well, I should have known, really. I mean, you're both gorgeous and . . ." He looked at her in such panic that she couldn't help but burst out laughing. Still, she wondered if something more than the partial transfer of a temporary tattoo might have occurred that night.

"It wasn't," he said, as if reading her thoughts. "I mean, we didn't . . ."

Jenny held her finger to his lips. "Shhh. It's okay. I seem to recall that you were not completely of sound mind."

Trinculo covered her hand with his. She gave it a gentle tug, but he resisted letting it go.

"I should tell you, however, that she's seventeen."

"Oh, geez." He dropped her hand and reeled back against the bench as if he had been staked through the heart.

Jenny pressed the plastic lid back on the top of her salad

and eyed Trinculo with a thoughtful tilt of the head. Life as the mother of two teenage girls often seemed to call for the pantomime looks of slack-jawed surprise and elaborate double takes that he made so naturally. Too bad he was only on the island for the summer.

ᘓ

Jenny held the phone against her ear with her right shoulder and began braiding a chunk of the long black hair that fell forward into her face. She could picture the ring bouncing off the granite countertops and recessed lighting in her sister's kitchen and echoing through the large family room with its energy-efficient windows and view of Mount Tamalpais.

"Hello?" Sue finally answered.

Jenny sat up straight, letting her braid fall and unravel. "Hi. I hear you called."

"I call all the time, Jen. Thank *you* for calling back." Her tone was light and teasing, but her point was taken.

"Hey, thanks again for the laptop you sent Lilly for graduation. She really wanted her own computer."

"Ed and I were very happy to do it. She's a bright girl, our Lilly."

Jenny felt a rush of warmth hearing her sister describe her child as "our Lilly." She pictured that good feeling as a deer trail she could follow in the conversation, one that would lead them both to friendly, neutral ground.

"I hear Walter is doing great at Stanford," said Jenny. "And Katie is applying where? Oberlin?"

"She hasn't decided yet. We're going to go look at a couple of schools this fall. She still has another year."

"Right. She's a junior."

Katie was on the plump side with unruly curls and a gravelly voice that made her sound like a woman with a two-pack-a-day habit. Sue and her family had visited Jenny one summer when Katie and Lilly were about eight. They had rented a vacation house on the east side of the island, and upon visiting Jenny and the girls in their cabin, Katie had tugged on her mother's shirt and whispered audibly in her ear, "Where's the rest of the house?"

Jenny had been embarrassed but oddly satisfied, too. Unlike Katie, her girls would never take a roof over their heads for granted.

Sue cleared her throat. "Lilly should really be in school this fall, Jenny. Don't you think?"

A motorcycle revved its engine near the back window of the shop and Jenny's mind followed its fading growl around the corner. "I don't think it's a bad idea for her to work for a year or so," she said. "It might help her get a better sense of herself."

"Oh, Jenny." Sue sighed, and as she did she sounded exactly like their mother used to when Jenny was a teenager. *Oh, Jenny, don't you want to do something this afternoon besides listen to rock music? Oh, Jenny, that outfit makes you look like a foundling. Oh, Jenny, is a C in English really the best you can do?*

What was left of lunch twisted in Jenny's stomach. She poked at her fingernails with an unbent paperclip and braced herself for the criticism to come.

"Of all people," continued Sue, "you should know how hard it is to go back to school once you stop."

No one in Jenny's family had approved of her dropping out of college after her sophomore year, and in spite of her promises she'd never gone back, just as they'd all predicted. Nor could she convincingly argue, *Well look at me, I've done all right.* Not as long as she bought her rice and beans in bulk and drove a truck that you could hear coming from half a mile away.

"This is a good place for my girls," she said, as firmly as she could. "They have friends here. It's beautiful. It's clean." She was unaccountably near tears and wondered if her sister could tell. "It's safe."

"I know how important safety is to you, Jen," said Sue in a gentle voice. "But think of Lilly. She's *seventeen years old.* She needs opportunities. Challenges. Ideas."

"The College of Marin isn't exactly Harvard, from what I understand," said Jenny. She sounded way too much like Lilly herself for her own peace of mind.

"Did she apply anywhere else?"

Neither of them spoke for a few moments after that. Of course Jenny had gone through the college brochures that Lilly had brought home during her junior and senior years, first with Lilly and then later, alone at the kitchen table late at night. She had even offered to help Lilly with an application or two, though in the end Lilly had not asked and Jenny had not followed up. The colleges that Lilly liked, with their tree-shaded quads and big brick student unions, were all so far away. And so very expensive.

The clock tapped against the quiet in the store, and outside the window, the wind rustled the trees. The inter-island ferry, chugging in from Shaw, let out a long, wavering blast of its horn.

"She'd stay with you, then?" asked Jenny at long last. "In your house?"

"Walter said she could have his room."

Jenny ran her fingers through her hair. "I don't know, Sue. I think it might be too soon."

"Too soon for you, maybe, but for Lilly . . ." As usual, Sue pushed just a little too far.

"Well, she's not going anywhere before July, that's for sure," said Jenny. "We're all going to be in the Props to You version of *The Tempest*."

"So I heard." Sue's voice, too, had snapped back into its combative range. The deer trail had vanished and now, damn it all, they were in the thicket. "Lilly seems quite taken with one of the actors. A grown man, I gather."

Jenny twisted a chunk of her hair around a finger and her gaze drifted out the window to the bench by the harbor.

Trinculo had walked her to the door of the shop after lunch. They stood there in the bright sun, smiling, each of them reluctant to say good-bye. With each of her most recent boyfriends, Jenny had felt warmth and desire, but at the end of the day she had still felt like, well, Jenny. Trinculo shifted from foot to foot with his hands in his pockets, and for a brief second, glimpsing herself through his eyes, she had almost been able to see Juno.

Jenny adjusted the phone at her ear. "Lilly's quite taken

with everyone," she said. The bell on the front door rang and Jenny nodded to Mary Ann, who was making her way to the back. "Look, I have to get going. We can talk about this later, okay?"

"Okay. Love you."

"You, too."

"Big sis?" asked Mary Ann. She slung her bag over the back of the chair and handed Jenny her alpaca shawl.

"That obvious?"

"Mmmm. Oh, hey, I think I saw Frankie down the street by the ferry landing."

"With Phoenix?"

"By herself. I'm not sure, though. But I think it was her. See you later?"

Jenny walked down the hill toward the harbor until she saw her daughter pacing on the corner of A Street and Nichols. It wasn't just the fact that Frankie's hat was gone, or that she was running her fingers through her hair in the way that Jenny did when she was distressed or even that she was alone, as she so rarely had been all the years of her life. There had always been Phoenix by her side, or Lilly, or Jenny herself. It was the startling tautness in the way her body moved, a coiled-up anger and despair so at odds with the girl who filled the quills of scavenged eagle feathers with ink that made Jenny stop and stare.

She lurched toward Frankie, who, seeing her mother, stumbled forward and fell into her. Frankie's sadness spread like an electric charge from her body to her mother's. Jenny took the current like a tree in a thunderstorm. For long minutes they stood locked together, startled by the bright light of surprise. The inevitability of it did not lessen the pain.

Jenny did not tell her daughter, *Shshhh*. She held her until Frankie, gulping, found the ability to speak.

"Phoenix is moving to Mount Vernon. In *three weeks.*" The looming deadline brought forth a new round of sobbing. "Theresa wants her to go to high school in Mount Vernon, with her cousins. She wants her to *get to know all kinds of people.*" This last part was singsonged with an acidity born out of pure bitter rejection.

"Oh, baby. Sweetheart." Her arm firm around Frankie's shoulder, Jenny turned her toward the harbor. "Let's go sit down."

Frankie let herself be led to a bench by the playground on Tucker Avenue.

"Theresa's already rented out their house to someone," wailed Frankie, "so she can't even change her mind. They have a *lease.*" She pronounced the word with the dread a condemned man might use to refer to the noose.

"Poor Phoenix," whispered Jenny. She tried to smile reassuringly at a small boy who had stopped swinging in order to rubberneck.

Frankie lifted her damp, splotched face up to look her mother in the eyes. It was at that moment that Jenny realized that the deeper pain had not yet been revealed, the pain that so far, alone, Frankie had been afraid to even glance at. Jenny wrapped both her hands around her daughter's bony fingers to warm them. She did not need to ask herself what she would do to protect this child from harm. In the real world you did what you could and the harm came anyway.

Frankie could do no more than whisper, "She *wants* to go."

Jenny's eyes filled with tears. She pulled Frankie close and pressed her head against her chest so that she would not see her mother cry.

Frankie's words spilled out wetly against Jenny's shirt. "She says she's sad about moving but she's *lying*. I can tell. All she wanted to talk about was the Appaloosa that her cousin rides and the high school gymnastics team that she's going to join. She even bragged about the fucking *Tulip Festival* that they have in Mount Vernon. As if I could care."

Jenny allowed herself a brief, wry smile and a glimmer of hope at that *fucking*. It was that fighting spirit that might get Frankie through to the other side, if she could hold on to it. If Jenny had been able to muster more fight herself, she might not have stayed with Monroe as long as she had.

"I would never drop a friend I'd known since I was a baby for some dumb Appaloosa and a chance to do gymnastics," said Frankie, hiccupping. She was bent forward over herself like a busted hyacinth, dripping tears and snot into her lap.

"I know, honey. And I know that Phoenix loves you. But people are different. They want different things."

"I would *never* do this. I never would."

"I know, baby. I know you wouldn't."

· CHAPTER 6 ·

Brave New World

The tables in the barn were arranged in a square with a hole in the center. Dale and Peg sat at one end with their heads together, whispering furiously, only pausing in their talk to refill their coffee cups from a large carafe that sat in front of them. The binder in Peg's lap was open to the middle, and from years previous Jenny knew that the bag at her feet was packed with a variety of items she or anyone else might need during the two-hour reading of the play, including tissues, Sharpies, safety pins, paper clips, eyedrops, and Advil.

For the past three years Jenny had been present at the table reading as an assistant costume designer (with a strong emphasis on the assistant part, since the ideas were mostly Peg's), but this was her first time as one of the actors. And it was also the first time attending with her daughters, one of whom stood red-eyed at her side. The other was nowhere to be seen, though it was already past the time they were to assemble. So far Dale and Peg had not noticed Lilly's absence, however, and Jenny had to restrain herself from slipping out the door to call her on her cell. It was important for her oldest daughter to have an opportunity to make her own mistakes, she reminded herself, and suffer the consequences. She imaged her sister, Sue, saying something similar about letting Lilly go to Marin and she felt a twinge of discomfort. All she was risking here, she imagined replying, was getting yelled at by Dale. She continued the argument in her mind until Peg stood abruptly and began clapping her hands for their attention. An elf-size woman, she had the voice of a giant.

"Okay, people! Take your seats. It's time to begin."

Jenny pulled out a chair for herself and one for Frankie, as silent and still as a photograph. Mary Ann smiled at Jenny from across the room and began heading toward the chair on her other side. She had gained some weight in the past few years and her body now had the round, rolling heaviness of a country cook. She and Jenny had gotten used to conspiring on the costumes and set pieces and they had learned to mix gossip and speculation and planning seamlessly into the details of running the store and setting out inventory. The chair next to Jenny scraped against the concrete floor and Trinculo, rather than Mary Ann, dropped into it with a nod.

Mary Ann paused and took in the scene with an appraising glance, then found a chair next to Ariel, who appeared to be wearing a bodysuit made out of plum-colored velour.

Trinculo leaned in to Jenny. "Hi again."

"Hey."

She looked down at her hands and then glanced up again,

quickly, when Frankie shifted beside her. Peg was shuffling her notes and preparing to speak. There was no time to explain to Trinculo that since they'd seen each other at lunch she'd become preoccupied by what was happening with Frankie. If she seemed distracted, she wanted to say, then that was the reason. Trinculo had worn a canvas shoulder bag to the reading, and bending to pull a notebook from it, he brushed against Jenny with his arm. Skin to skin. She flushed, and looking around the table at all the people packed into the old barn, both familiar and unfamiliar, realized that the problem was, she was not distracted *enough*.

Caliban was seated directly across from Jenny and Trinculo, wearing dark sunglasses, though the light in the barn was dim. As soon as Peg spoke, he began unloading his own small supply cabinet's worth of stuff onto the table: colored pencils, throat spritzer, small Post-it notes, and a bag of peppermints. Ferdinand chose the seat closest to the door. The rest of the chairs were filled with the handful of island people who were either musicians or had been chosen for one of the smaller parts, including Chad, who had indeed won the role of Stephano. With a look of undisguised delight, he sat next to Miranda, who wore a low-cut T-shirt and bicycle shorts. Still no Lilly.

An owl hooted in the eaves. Frankie breathed softly through her mouth, her nose plugged from nearly an hour of solid crying. Peg laid her hands palms-down on the table and leaned toward the company, scanning people's faces with all the intensity she could muster. If she noticed Frankie's distraught state, she did not reveal it.

"This is what I see." She closed her eyes and tilted her head back toward the ceiling. "Darkness. A howling wind. Thunder like big bass drums." She opened her eyes and turned her face toward David, who jotted something down in a notebook. "The spirits in black costumes, but layered." Here she turned her attention to Jenny and Frankie. She frowned. "Where the fuck is Lillian?"

"Here I am."

The barn door swung open and Lilly appeared in her trademark long underwear, under a short skirt this time and topped with a tie-dyed University of Washington sweatshirt. Jenny hoped that for Lilly's sake Peg would not notice the cookie crumbs on her chin. She would have bet anything that Lilly had commanded her chariot, driven by Elliot, to stop at the Roche Harbor ice cream shop on the way, for snacks.

Peg narrowed her eyes in a look that would have made Frankie cry. Lilly simply dragged a chair from the back of the room and began pushing it into the narrow space between Jenny and Trinculo. There was not enough room for both mother and daughter in that spot. Conscious of Peg's glaring, Jenny moved her chair toward Frankie's and let Lilly in.

"Five o'clock, Lillian. I said five o'clock."

"I'm so sorry everybody, really, but the thing is, the Edisons, you know, who live out on Wold, are having this complicated irrigation system put in, to, you know, water their. . . ."

In a matter of seconds Lilly had buried the entire company under a blizzard of teenage excuse-speak.

Even Peg looked cowed. "Okay," she said. "Enough. Take your seat and close your mouth."

Lilly shifted toward Trinculo and grinned. Jenny turned to give her daughter an admonishing glance and instead found herself watching Trinculo watching Lilly. He seemed unable to avert his eyes from her, no doubt finding Lilly in the flesh a hundred times more compelling than the hash-fueled Lilly of memory. He gaped and then, without noticing Jenny's eyes upon him, he blushed a deep, crimson red. Jenny quickly turned away. Somehow, on the bench that afternoon with the salt breezes and the circling gulls, she had managed to convince herself that whatever had happened between her daughter and this man that night was unimportant. What, she asked herself now, had she been thinking?

Caliban gazed at Lilly also for a long moment over the top of his sunglasses and then carefully selected one of his colored pencils. He scribbled something in his notebook, applied a Post-it note to the same spot, and then unwrapped a peppermint and placed it on his tongue as if he were giving himself communion, or more likely, thought Jenny, taking a hit of LSD.

Peg took a draft of her coffee. "Act one. Scene one," she said. "A tempestuous noise of thunder and lightning heard. Enter a Ship-Master and a Boatswain."

Sally Muller had been chosen as the Ship-Master. "Boatswain!" she called.

"Here, master," called back Stu Barnes. "What cheer?"

"Good' speak to th' mariners. Fall to't yarely, or we run ourselves aground. Bestir, bestir. Exit."

Everyone laughed at Sally's inclusion of that *"exit."* Everyone except for Frankie, who sat bowed over her copy of the play, her hair falling forward, abject misery still visible on her face. Jenny placed her hand reassuringly on Frankie's leg, but she did not stir. From the corner of her eye she saw Ariel reach into Caliban's bag of peppermints and pluck one out. Caliban glowered and Ariel crossed his eyes at him in response. Then, with remarkable accuracy, he shot the peppermint over the table to Frankie. She sat up straight, gave him a grateful, puppyish look, and put the candy in her mouth.

On Jenny's other side, Lilly turned her face in Ariel's direction and smiled winningly. He stared back and then, without changing his expression or reaching for another peppermint, he looked down at the play on the table in front of him and began to read.

Within a week all of their lives had been reordered to correspond to Peg's call sheets. Scene stagings, costume design and fittings, music and transitions were all central to their existence. Everything else became secondary. Work, outside friends, and spouses receded into their shadow lives. As a group they began to develop habits (the nonsmokers kicked a Hacky Sack while the smokers smoked), favorite snacks (sunflower seeds and Mary Ann's home-baked intergalactic bars), and self-referential in-jokes that circled back in various permutations (Miranda's cleavage at the table reading, Lilly's tendency to disappear when needed—did she have a studio apartment hidden somewhere? Did she hold office hours?). Still, by the second week of rehearsals, not all mysteries had been solved.

One morning Frankie stirred her oatmeal carefully, watching the brown sugar dissolve with intense concentration, and mused aloud, "What if the naked rehearsal is really, you know, *without any clothes on?*"

"It is." Lilly scooped up a handful of raisins from the box and shoved a chair back from the table with a foot that sported, to Jenny's horror, toenails so long they curled.

"No, it's not, Franks. Don't worry," said Jenny, wishing she were sure. "Lilly, your *toenails.* If you don't trim them this instant, I'm going to lose my breakfast."

"I'm eating." Lilly lifted her spoon by way of demonstration. "And by the way, I don't know why you are telling your own offspring things that aren't true." She raised her eyebrows in reproach.

"I always tell you the absolute truth." Jenny plopped down next to Frankie and reached for the raisins. She'd eaten at five when the girls were still sleeping, and it was almost nine-thirty now. She figured as long as she didn't look anywhere in the vicinity of Lilly's knees or below, she could manage a bowl of oatmeal. She poured soymilk on the raisins and stirred, adding, "At least as far as I know it."

Lilly dropped her bowl on the table. "You're lying now. When you say that."

"When have I ever told you something that wasn't true?"

"Omission is lying."

Jenny flushed. "Omission. Nice word. Is that what you were up to all those days you skipped class then, during senior year? Vocabulary?"

Frankie looked back and forth between them, a speck of oatmeal clinging to her cheek. "Stop it, you guys. Just stop it!"

Jenny focused on a row of jars containing dried beans and rice and millet and black-eyed peas and tried to remember the yoga she'd taken for six months before the prices had gone up and she'd had to quit. Breathe, release, breathe, release, breathe. Maybe she should have continued the class, she thought, because the exercise would have helped to hold back the tears that were pressing against the backs of her eyes. Instead of this harsh, hurtful stranger, she forced herself to picture Lilly as she had been at four. They had a ratty old green couch then, with sagging cushions and a rip in the back that they covered up by pushing the couch against a wall. Jenny had collapsed onto that couch, leaving the broken crockery all over the floor, and held her breath while Monroe backed out of the gravel driveway toward the road.

Little Lilly, in a boy's striped T-shirt and tights (Lilly was so attached to her three pairs of tights back then that Jenny used to wash them by hand at night), crawled into her lap with a dirty kitchen sponge and a pack of Sesame Street Band-Aids to tend to the cut on her mother's jaw. "Daddy hurt you on accident," she'd said, patting Jenny's tears away with the smelly sponge. For all her righteous indignation now, Lilly had been a skilled liar for a very long time.

"Telling the truth is good," said Jenny slowly. "But that doesn't mean you have to be as mean as a badger when you do it."

"Sorry." Lilly carried her bowl to the sink. "It's just that I happen to be someone who finds stuff out."

She paused to give Jenny a look that could have been merely dramatic—proving her appropriateness for the stage, as it were. But it also could have been intended to convey to her mother the worrying notion that she knew even more than she was telling. About what? Jenny found herself wondering. Monroe?

Lilly continued, "See, a little bird told me last year that the super-secret naked rehearsal is just that. Butt naked." Her own butt was covered thinly in tie-dyed long underwear that had holes in the knees. She shook it for emphasis. "In front of God and the world." And though she loved her sister, she couldn't help adding, "In front of *Dale*."

Frankie grew pale. She looked like she might throw up.

Jenny placed her hand on the back of Frankie's. "Nobody's going to make you take your clothes off," she said firmly. "And if for some reason that's a condition of being in the cast, you won't have to be in it."

She did not think it was the right time to point out that both girls cavorted naked in front of half the island on various hot summers when they were little or to remind Frankie that most of the grown-ups she knew, including Dale and Peg, thought nothing of a naked soak in the tubs on Doe Bay. Worn-out hippie norms meant nothing when you were a thirteen-year-old girl who had had her period for less than a year.

"But I want to be in the play," breathed Frankie. She sounded like she was three.

"We'll work something out," said Jenny firmly.

Her children had no idea how precious they were. Neither of them.

"C'mon, sweet pea. Get the brush and I'll help you fix your hair."

Frankie didn't move. It was clear she was still picturing herself stripped bare and offered up like a piece of freshly caught halibut.

"Chill out." Lilly gave her sister a half-tender, half-annoyed tap upside the head on her way into the bathroom. "Dale isn't going to be looking at *you*." She eyed Jenny slyly. "He's going to be looking at Mom."

Jenny shot Lilly a glance. "Gee. Thanks, Lil."

Lilly smirked. "The human body is beautiful in all shapes and sizes," she said, parroting back to Jenny the words she had repeated to her daughters over the years. "I couldn't care less who looks at *me*."

Jenny supposed if she still had a body like Lilly's she might welcome the opportunity to show it off, too.

Frankie did not appear to be listening. "But . . . Well . . ." She took a deep breath and looked at the wall in panic. "Ariel."

Lilly circled back to stare at her sister in astonishment. Jenny set down her spoon. The glance that passed between her and her older daughter when they met each other's eyes surpassed understanding. It was a cosmic blend of experience, love, dawning awareness, and incredulity that only women of the same family, living under the same roof, could muster. Lilly spoke first, with her usual careful reticence.

"Are you blind or something? Ariel plays for the other team, Frankie."

"What?" She looked to her mother for confirmation. "He's gay?"

Jenny nodded. "I think so, hon."

"Of course he is," said Lilly. "You could smear your boobs with chocolate sauce and hold a cherry in your teeth and he wouldn't notice." She shook her head and held her toothbrush under the faucet. "Of all the guys in the world," she growled around the plastic in her mouth, "how funny that Frankie would go for a gay guy."

Red-faced Frankie looked down at the table as if she might cry.

Jenny brushed her hand over the back of Frankie's head before beginning to gather the dishes. "He *is* very beautiful," she said softly.

Frankie looked around wildly, jumped up from the table, and then suddenly Jenny was watching the hunched figure of her daughter trudging down the dirt road. To the bus stop, no doubt, and then to Phoenix's. The two girls had achieved some kind of tentative, polite peace ever since Phoenix had promised, on her dead dog Bear's grave, that she would be there for the San Juan opening of *The Tempest* in July.

Jenny pulled her alpaca sweater close around her pajama

top. It still didn't get her warm, so she walked across the room and stood full in a shaft of light coming in through the window. She rubbed her toes together in thick socks and watched the dust float in circles. It might be funny to Lilly, perhaps, that Frankie would fall first for someone who wouldn't love her back, but it should not have been altogether unexpected. Frankie was an island girl. What did she know? There weren't enough people of any particular type to allow for broad categories and generalizations. They were just individuals up there, each as quirky and unique as the next. Jenny sighed and touched her fingertips to the still, cold glass of the window.

Finally, Jenny left her spot of warmth to begin piling the dishes in the sink to do later, after work. Also in socks, Lilly padded up behind her and began, unexpectedly, to help. Jenny thought about pressing her hand to her daughter's head to check for fever, and instead moved aside and began wiping down the counters. Lilly turned the faucet on and ran water in the sink.

"Speaking of love," said Lilly. She filled a bowl with water until it overflowed and then tipped it, grimacing, into the sink. "Or not love, actually. Well, I don't know. Crap." She wiped her hands on her sweatshirt.

Jenny watched her curiously. It was rare to see Lilly thrown into this kind of confusion.

Absentmindedly, Lilly poked a knife in the water. "It's always been pretty easy to tell, in the past, whether a guy liked me or not." She met Jenny's eyes and then looked away with an embarrassed smile. "Well, cause they did, mostly. Like me. But those were island guys, you know. It's so different with him. He's not from around here. He's older and stuff. Sophisticated." She said the last word with self-mocking, as if she were simultaneously aware of her relative innocence but hoping that her own awareness of it took the edge off.

Jenny's heart began to pound. "Who do you mean?" she asked, buying time.

"Duh. Trinculo." Lilly examined her own jagged fingernails with great interest. "Trinculo is all I can think about these days, practically. And I'm thinking maybe, well if it's not too conceited, that maybe he's thinking about me, too?" She got the sly look that was more characteristic of the Lilly that Jenny knew. "Didn't you see how he blushed when I sat down next to him at the table reading?"

Jenny found herself looking anywhere but at her daughter. She felt like the hummingbird that had found its way into the cabin a week or so before. Its little frantic body revving the engine while it scanned for a way out.

Lilly did not appear to notice. "The other day when we were alone in back of Dale and Peg's barn, you know, during the long scene with Alonso, Sebastian, and all those guys? When they're going on and on about the wedding in Afric? Well, I just went for it and kissed him and I could *tell* he liked it. I could tell. The thing was, he didn't really kiss me back or put his arms around me or *anything*. I mean, what's *that* about? I'm going to be eighteen in two months, so it can't be the age thing. Can it?"

Jenny could not speak. Here she'd been dreaming of kissing Trinculo and Lilly (Lilly!) had been *doing* it. Her chest was a tangle of emotions. She couldn't tell whether she was furious with Trinculo, protective of Lilly, embarrassed, or just plain jealous. She could remember sitting with Frankie on the grass during that scene and wondering where Trinculo was.

Finally, she sputtered, "He's too old for you."

"I *knew* you were going to say that. You're so predictable!"

"I'm looking out for you." Jenny did not need to press herself to know that it was a bit more complicated than that. Still. Lilly was *seventeen*.

"He *does* like me, though. He's just trying not to." Lilly stretched her arms toward the ceiling to reveal a flash of breasts and the glint of her silver belly-button ring. "He won't be able to hide it at the naked rehearsal, though." She smiled. "*Everything* will be out in the open then. And you know guys . . .'"

"That's enough!" Jenny pulled her hair back and twisted it like a rope behind her head. "Geez, Lil. Give it a rest, will you? And look at this." Jenny began frantically tossing silverware, dishes, and even kitchen towels toward the sink. "Pick up after yourself for once, okay? None of us is a wife here, you know."

Lilly looked at her with injured surprise. "Okay. Sorry." She tipped dish soap onto the sponge and began, tentatively, to clean the dishes.

Jenny stood and watched her for a moment and then, pulling herself together, reached for a towel to dry.

They worked in silence until a horn sounded in the drive.

Lilly dropped the sponge and ran past Jenny to the front

door. She slipped through it without a word. Jenny watched her tromp down the drive toward where Elliot would turn in, stuffing her phone in her back pocket. She had failed to close the door in her hurry, and it swung back open, wide on the brightening morning. Jenny gazed out in the direction her daughter had gone and without realizing what she was looking at, slowly focused her eyes on a fawn, standing in the woods. She stood still for as long as she could and then, when she shifted, the fawn bolted.

She sighed and pushed the hair from her face. In the now familiar play that was consuming their attention and their imagination, the chronology was clear. Prospero conjured a storm and a company of men was washed ashore. In the experience of her little family, it was just the opposite. The men had brought the storm.

The empty house seemed stunned and sleepy after the morning's racket. Her loom called to her from its tranquil, sunny corner, its threads as poised as guitar strings waiting to be plucked. Yet she did not move from the window looking out onto the yard. It occurred to her that she and her girls were, all three of them, in a new way now in a world of men.

Poor shipwrecked Miranda had seen just two such creatures, her father and Caliban, before Ferdinand arrived, reflected Jenny. And then suddenly, it seemed that the entire island was full of them. "*O brave new world,*" she had exclaimed. "*That has such people in't!*"

Jenny doubted that the Neapolitans, even Ferdinand, were as different as all that, really. Men were men, after all. It was

Miranda who had changed. Jenny could well understand what it was that Prospero had said to his daughter then, to this girl looking out onto a world no more fresh and new and, yes, even brave, than the one that her own daughters had just disappeared into. What he had said, this father who had raised her, alone no less, from babyhood was, *Tis new to thee*.

· CHAPTER 7 ·

Lowering the Flag

A new wine bar opened in Friday Harbor. Jenny and Mary Ann closed the shop early so they could get there in time to get a table near the door. Peg had been called away to Vancouver, where her aged mother lived, and had given them all the weekend off from rehearsals. A bunch of the actors rode the ferry to the mainland to spend the weekend in Seattle. Phoenix had taken Frankie with her to visit the cousins in Mount Vernon. Now that the move was in the works, even Theresa had been onboard with that plan.

The new bar was called Swirl and it was decorated in light maple, with bamboo on the floor and large windows that let in the early evening light. It was only five-thirty, but the tables were already filling up with tourists and a few locals. Jamie from the gas station stopped by to chat before heading toward the back where the owners, a tech couple from Northern California, had put up some ping-pong tables. Jenny and Mary Ann sipped Chardonnay from delicate glasses and munched on candied pecans and walnuts from a little ceramic bowl.

Jenny tapped the side of the bowl with a fingernail. "I wonder if Phinneas made these."

"I think Ivy made them. You know Ivy? From Lopez?"

Jenny popped another nut in her mouth. "Oh, sure. Well, that's good then. She has kids and all. Unlike Phinneas."

Mary Ann poured them each another glass. "That he knows about," she added drily, and they both cracked up. "Oh, God, poor Miranda," sighed Mary Ann. "I think Phinneas was the one who put himself in charge of 'showing her around' Seattle."

"He wouldn't!" Jenny's eyes widened over the rim of her glass. "What is she, Lilly's age? Not much older, in any case."

"You'd have to watch him around Lilly, too, if she weren't your daughter." Mary Ann plucked the appetizer menu from between the salt and paper shakers and spread it on the table carefully.

"I'd have to watch Lilly."

Jenny peered at the room through the gold liquid in her glass. The wine was cold and a bit sweeter than she was used to. She could tell her cheeks were getting rosy. She felt good. As Iris, Ceres, and Juno, she and her daughters had few lines, but she was finding that there really was a difference being *in* the play, rather than just supporting it from the outside. Whenever the actors lounged around on the grass in the sun, she lay around with them and listened to the gossip about New York and L.A. and Seattle. Miranda and Lilly would giggle together or start up a game of Ultimate Frisbee on the pasture by the road, and one of the others, usually Trinculo, would pull Jenny to her feet and urge her to play. She'd acted modestly surprised that first game when Caliban gaped at her ability to leap in the air and catch a long pass.

"Clearly you haven't spent enough time around hippies," she'd said, bending into a low toss.

He'd smiled. "Clearly not."

Everyone had noticed the change in Caliban lately. He'd begun to sing along with what they'd taken to calling the Egg Lake Jam Band and even beat out a percussion rhythm with a couple of sticks. He hadn't worn a tie in weeks.

Now, Jenny raised her hopeful eyes to Mary Ann. "Lilly decided to stay on the island this weekend, can you believe it? Instead of going to Seattle with the others. I grounded her a few weeks ago, but if she'd begged, I probably would have let her go. She said she wanted to stay home this weekend and work." Jenny tapped her glass lightly against Mary Ann's. "It could be we've turned the corner with Lilly."

What she didn't tell Mary Ann was that Trinculo, at rehearsal the day before, had asked Jenny if *she* was going. Jenny took a sip of wine and let it trickle down her throat. She could imagine the kinds of women that Trinculo was surrounded by in the city. Gorgeous, stylish, professional women. Young women. And still, he had asked *her* if she was going to Seattle.

"Nah. I go to Seattle all the time," she'd lied. The truth was, she hardly ever went. The deeper truth was that she was afraid.

The bustle, the noise, the homeless, and the strangers all made her feel lost and anxious.

"She's a good egg," said Mary Ann, about Lilly. "She'll be okay." Mary Ann waved to Kelly, who'd hopped from her job at the craft store to the new bar just as soon as it opened. No tips on felt pieces, she'd pointed out.

"Hi, girls." Kelly was wearing a tight white T-shirt and a jeans skirt on which she had appliquéd a variety of multicolored birds. "What can I getja?"

Mary Ann pushed her glasses down on her nose and peered at the menu. "Veggie tempura?" She looked at Jenny. "That sound good?"

"Sure. Whatever."

"And the cheese plate," added Mary Ann.

Mary Ann had recently begun taking pills for her blood pressure, and it occurred to Jenny to say something about her friend's heart, but she decided against it.

"My sister has invited Lilly to come live with them and attend college in Marin."

Mary Ann popped her glasses back up on her face so she could see Jenny clearly. "That's wonderful, Jen. I hadn't realized that Lilly wanted to go to college."

Jenny sighed. "I'm not sure that Marin County will be such a good place for her."

Mary Ann pretended to find a spot on the table that needed burnishing with her napkin. "But you can't say the same thing about school, can you? Surely that would be a good thing?"

Jenny didn't answer. She gazed out the window at a couple

strolling by, hand in hand. They were about her parents' age, she thought. Mid-sixties. They looked happy and well-fed and confident in each other's presence. The wish to have someone with whom she could discuss these matters of her children—not Mary Ann, but a real partner—pierced her so sharply that she winced.

Mary Ann caught the gesture, and her features softened with sympathy. Her husband had died within six months of being diagnosed with bone cancer. It had been more than ten years since then.

"It's weird having Frankie gone," said Jenny, after a long silence. "I think this is only, like, the second time she's been away from me since she was born."

"That angel." At the mention of Jenny's younger daughter, Mary Ann patted the palm of her hand against the top of her blouse, over her heart.

Someone yelled "good shot" from the back of the room, and a couple people sitting at tables around the women swiveled in their chairs to look. Jenny stood up and peered into the back of the bar in time to see Jamie chasing a little white ball through the swinging doors into the kitchen.

When Jenny turned back around she was just in time to see Dale striding through the front door. His face lit up with delight upon seeing Jenny and Mary Ann.

"If it isn't the two loveliest women on the island," he said. He kissed them both on the cheek, but the kiss he gave Jenny lingered a bit longer and was slightly closer to her mouth. "Which is a statement I make with impunity only because my own dear bride is on another northern isle." He pulled a chair back from the table and plopped into it. He looked like a sea captain in his windbreaker and battered deck shoes. He crossed his legs at the thigh. "She has left me alone, alas." His face contorted into a comic mask of grief.

"How's her mom?" asked Mary Ann.

Dale's expression reverted back into its normal wry contours. "The old gal will live forever. I promise you." He leaned forward and lifted the wine bottle at an angle so he could assess its contents. "I see you've gotten a head start on me." He tilted the last sips of wine directly into his mouth from the bottle. "Looks like it's time for another."

Dale carried the empty bottle to the bar and returned a few moments later with a full one and a dish of nuts commandeered from another table. "These are good," he said, tossing a few pecans into his mouth. "So . . . how do you think it's all going so far?"

Jenny smiled. "I'm having the time of my life."

Dale looked into her eyes and beamed.

"It's going to be great," said Mary Ann, "though I think the part where Caliban appears is a bit dark, still. We should consider another flashlight."

Dale waved her comment away with his hand. "Oh, you'll have to talk to Peg about that," he said. He turned back to Jenny. "What do you think of Miranda? She's a beauty, isn't she? And Trinculo?" He rolled a swig of wine around in his mouth before swallowing. "Trinculo is what we used to call a fox. If I were a man of certain proclivities. . . ."

Mary Ann snorted. "I've never known you to be someone who limited his proclivities in any way," she said.

Dale burst out laughing. "Well said."

By the time they finished the next bottle, the ping-pong in the back had given way to music. Dale had pulled both Jenny and Mary Ann into a dance in turn. The band was playing *Turn on Your Love Light* and Jenny was being dipped dangerously low when the cell phone in her pocket started to vibrate. It might have been the wine, or maybe it was the swinging, but as soon as she felt the phone go off she was gripped with a sudden wave of nausea and panic. The music and voices and faces were blocked out with images of car crashes on Highway 1, the road to Mount Vernon. One word entered her mind. A plea. A prayer. An appeal to whatever gods might be listening. Frankie, she thought. Please let it not be Frankie.

It was Lilly. "Hi, Mom. Hey, where are you? What's all that noise?"

"I'm in a bar, Lil. The new one. With Mary Ann."

Dale held his hands palm upward to protest his abandonment on the dance floor. Jenny grimaced, holding a finger in her ear, as she headed for the table.

"Is Mary Ann the only person there?" asked Lilly. "From the play?"

"Well, Dale's here, too. Why?"

"Nothing. Just wondering."

Lilly rarely asked what Jenny was up to, much less called her to keep tabs, so that wondering set Jenny wondering, too.

She tried to remember what Lilly had said she was going to do after work. She had been typically vague.

"Do you need something?" asked Jenny now, making her way back to the table.

"Nah." Lilly did not hang up immediately. "Trinculo isn't there by any chance, is he?"

"He went to Seattle." Jenny leaned against the doorway. How many glasses of wine had she had? She had lost count.

"Mmm. Miranda did and Caliban did. But Ariel and Trinculo decided not to go." Lilly paused. Faint music played in the background. The radio in Elliot's truck. "Or at least I think they did."

At least she thought they did. Ah-hah. So that was it. Jenny raised her eyes to the ceiling, where a fan spun lazily. She would have to be quite a bit more soused than she was not to recognize what she had failed to grasp earlier: Lilly's staying behind was most assuredly *not* a sign of restraint and responsibility. Quite the opposite. She was scheming on Trinculo.

"Look, Lil." Her voice was clipped. "I'm going to hang up now. I can't hear a thing in here."

"Okay, okay. Sorry to *bother* you."

"You're not bothering me," said an exasperated Jenny into a phone that was already dead.

"Not bothered?" Dale had come up behind her and rested his chin on her shoulder. His breath smelled flammable. "Well, that's too bad."

He grabbed her hand and pulled her back toward the music. Jenny did not want to think anymore, and she let herself be pulled. She dropped her phone back into the pocket of her cotton skirt and tried to keep her balance in the face of Dale's exuberant lead. Mary Ann was dancing with Ellen from the bookstore and David, who'd shown up without Jenny noticing, was jamming with the band on his harmonica. There were several couples Jenny had never seen on the floor now, clearly reveling in their vacation from office cubicles and endless e-mails. When he swung her around this time, Dale had to pull her close. The turn ended and he kept holding her there, clutched against his damp chest. It wasn't unpleasant, but it was a little awkward, particularly with David eyeing them over his harmonica. She tugged herself loose. Dale suddenly pressed his cheek against hers and said abruptly into her ear, "Peg wants an open marriage. She says she's feeling trapped."

Jenny pulled her head back to look him in the face. Had he really just said what she thought she heard? Dale spun under her hand and did not look her in the eye. The song picked up tempo, merging without interruption from "Turn on Your Love Light" into "Hard to Handle." Dale dropped her hands and shook himself as if he were trying to elude a stinging insect that had flown into an opening in his clothes. David's harmonica whined in her ear. Jenny let her body slow like a top winding down. Sweating and bouncing and spinning, no one around her appeared to notice.

Peg wanted an open marriage? She pictured Peg in her sweatpants and batik top, chewing on the end of her pencil. Looking sharply at Dale, she was suddenly suspicious that he was misrepresenting the situation by a cool one hundred percent. He gave Jenny a mischievous smile, which practically confirmed it. Of the two of them, he seemed the more likely to want an open marriage, in spite of what had happened with Puck that first summer and, well, okay, there was also Jacques from *As You Like It*. Still, that was more than three years ago. Dale flirted outrageously all the time. Jenny put her hand to her mouth, remembering how he'd kissed her on Shaw the summer before. Stepping forward, Dale lifted her hand and pulled her close again, then dipped her.

"You can't just . . ." she started to say, once she was back to the vertical, but the words died in her mouth.

Ariel and Trinculo stood in the doorway scanning the room for familiar faces. Ariel was wearing yoga pants and a tank top that was thin and tight enough to show exactly how little fat there was on his lithe body, how much unexpected muscle. His hair was covered in a purple bandanna. Trinculo was wearing black jeans, boots, and a leather jacket. He looked like he was ready for a night on a town considerably bigger than Friday Harbor, San Juan.

"I have to go to the bathroom." Jenny slipped from Dale's grasp and wove through the crowd toward the dim, narrow hallway in the back.

She tried the door with the androgynous stick figure and found it mercifully unlocked. Luckily, she did not wear any makeup and could splash her face with cold water without messing anything up. But maybe she should wear makeup? She stared at her dripping red-cheeked face in the mirror. She was drunk. This was ridiculous. She wanted to cry. She laughed out loud. What was Trinculo *thinking* in his black leather and boots? She looked down at her home-dyed cotton skirt, with pockets no less, and at her well-worn Tevas. The only boots she owned were made by Redwing and they had soles caked with mud. She wished she knew what was in his mind. He had said more than once he wasn't interested in Lilly, he had been attentive and polite and always sidled up to her after rehearsal, and yet . . . he had never kissed *Jenny*.

Someone banged on the door. "Hel*lo*?"

"Coming."

Jenny tucked her hair behind her ears and dried her hands. She smiled at the woman in the hallway, an impatient-looking tourist in a killer whale T-shirt, and stepped back into the light and sound of the bar. The band was taking a break and, as she made her way back to the table, she saw Dale and Mary Ann laughing at something Ariel had said. Trinculo was talking to the waitress and gesturing at the menu. The curator from the sculpture park, along with her husband who was, like Lilly, a landscaper, had joined them and there were two empty chairs at the table. One, she assumed, was for David, who would be smoking on the patio. The other was for her.

"Speak of the devil," said Ariel sweetly, as Jenny sat down.

Trinculo's eyes flicked to her from the menu and he finished his order.

"Hardly," said Jenny, giving Ariel a whack on the shoulder. "I thought you were in the big city this weekend."

"Seattle is *not* the big city."

Trinculo patted Ariel's hand. "Ariel here decided to stay and keep me company."

"Seattle is a bore." Ariel yawned elaborately and allowed his leg to fall casually against Trinculo's. "And *I* decided not to go first, by the way. Trink here is keeping *me* company."

"What*ever*," said Trinculo.

"You would have had fun," said Mary Ann. "There's a big farmers' market on the weekend in Pioneer Square."

"The tacos at Aqua Verde are worth the trip alone," said Dale, returning with a couple of extra wineglasses.

Ariel glanced around the table and Jenny could have sworn that his gaze lingered extra-long on her. "Our friend Trink isn't interested in having fun. He thinks he's going to burn in hell."

Trinculo laughed and reached for a glass. "I don't *think* I'm going to burn in hell, sweetheart. I *know* it." He drank and set the glass down again, and without meeting her eyes, he let his hand trail briefly along Jenny's elbow.

She started and then glanced around to see if anyone had noticed him do that. All Trinculo had to do was brush against her and her skin rose up to meet his touch like yeast dough in a bowl.

"So are we all," said Dale, draining his glass. "In the meantime, what if we take this bunch of mainlanders over to Roche Harbor for the colors ceremony?"

"Oh, no. Not really!" Mary Ann laughed. "It's so *corny*."

"It's perfect. Everyone loves it when they come."

"The first five times, perhaps," said Jenny.

"I'm game," said Trinculo. "Do you dance around a fire and roast mainlanders on a spit?"

Mary Ann shook her head. "It's the lowering of the flag at Roche Harbor, is all. With a little pomp and circumstance."

"Sounds charming," drawled Ariel.

"I'll drive then," said Mary Ann.

"Jenny and I will ride with you," said Dale. "I get to sit next to Jenny."

"You can sit in the back," said Mary Ann, with a stern look. She glanced at Trinculo. "Do you want to follow us?"

"Sure." He drained his glass and stood up.

They arrived at Roche Harbor as the sun was lowering itself toward the water. Tourists, boaters, diners, and strollers were all assembling on the dock and the hillside. The crowd shifted and suddenly there was Lilly running up the hill to meet them, her dreads bouncing against her back, her bright smile and slightly overlapping front teeth on full and glorious display. The sight of her stopped Jenny in her tracks. Sometimes it took her glimpsing her older daughter from a distance to see how grown and beautiful and *ready* she was. Keeping Lilly on the island would be like trying to hold back the tide, Jenny realized. This was Lilly's moment, and before the night was through she knew she would give her permission to go to California. She would give her blessing. In her mind she could already hear her daughter's yelp of delight and feel her arms, stronger and browner but not so very different than when she was a little girl, flung around her neck.

Still, how had she known to meet them there, wondered

Jenny. She cast glances at Ariel and Trinculo, who were unfolding themselves from the Mini Cooper that they had borrowed for the summer. Had Trinculo called her? In any case, there she was, coming toward them. Jenny spied Elliot at the bottom of the hill standing shyly with his hands in his pockets, and she waved. He waved back. In minutes, they had all joined up into one boisterous group and were headed down the hill together.

The islanders knew what came next. There would be the lowering of the flag, the playing of national anthems from the boats in the harbor, and the hilarious finale, in which color guards and honored guests jumped from the pier into the water. Meanwhile, the harbor master would be reminding the swimmers of incoming tide drifts and pointing out the fact that Canadian boats seldom had holding tanks for their waste, so keep your mouth closed in the water.

They passed Our Lady of Good Voyage Chapel and continued down toward the glittering bay. The sun set. The flag fell like a fainting woman into the arms of the color guard. The color guard jumped. Ariel jumped. Lilly and Jenny were pushed. Trinculo leaped after, and in just a few moments they were all treading salt water among the anchored boats.

· CHAPTER 8 ·

An Unexpected Visitor

Jenny, Lilly, Frankie, and Phoenix rode their bikes to American Camp and back for a picnic. They arrived at Jenny's turn-off sweating and red-faced. Their legs, after working the pedals hard, were slick and itchy. Each passing car—and there were relatively many of them at this time of the year—had left a cloud of exhaust that lingered in the air just long enough for them to ride through it single file.

They dropped their bikes onto the yellow grass and looked up to see Ariel sitting comfortably on the front step, reading a novel in a patch of shade by the flowerpot. A plastic shopping bag was tucked up next to him. He was wearing a tank top, shorts made out of some extremely high-tech-looking material, and gladiator sandals that Jenny immediately coveted. He smiled pleasantly and waited until they were close enough so that he did not have to raise his voice to speak.

"Ladies."

Frankie was less cool by a mile. "Ariel!" She ran forward and plopped down next to him.

Phoenix approached warily, her face displaying equal parts of curiosity and envy. The truce, Jenny suspected, was now officially over.

Jenny stepped forward. "Would you like a glass of iced tea? We've got some chamomile in the fridge."

"That would be lovely." Ariel lifted himself from the step and fanned at his face with his book. "It's scorching."

Frankie tugged him into the house by the arm. "What's in the bag?"

He smiled down at her. "A present for you, actually. But don't peek."

Phoenix followed behind, momentarily forgotten.

Jenny scooped the pile of yarn off the table and tossed it into the basket on the floor. She pulled the pitcher from the fridge and surreptitiously swept a trail of crumbs into the sink with a frayed towel. Then she tucked the towel in her back pocket.

Ariel pulled out a chair. Jenny kept a collection of chopsticks in a mug in the center of the table. Ariel plucked one out and used it to stir his tea.

Frankie perched beside him. "Do you want some sugar? It's just raw sugar, unfortunately," she said, giving her mother a disapproving look.

"Raw is fine."

She leaped up. "Lemon?"

"Absolutely."

Phoenix was on the phone by the window, calling her mother to come pick her up.

Lilly, who was foraging in the fridge, had her back to them all. She emerged with a package of tortillas and a jar of peanut butter. She pulled a chair back at the other end of the table, and before sitting she held them up in her hands. "Peanut butter wrap?"

Ariel wrinkled his nose. "Thank you. But no."

Jenny poured herself a glass of tea. "Have you been enjoying the day off?"

"It's been incredibly boring, to tell the truth. Trinculo is in a sulk, and the last thing I want to do is hang around the apartment with his mooning." He swung the plastic bag in front of Frankie's face like a ball of yarn before a kitten. "So I went shopping."

Jenny looked up sharply. Wasn't mooning a word that necessarily carried an object with it? Kind of like, well, lusting? The private thoughts she'd been having about Trinculo brought heat to her cheeks. How pathetic to think that her imagination provided the most intimacy she'd experienced in months.

Lilly brightened. "He's mooning?"

"Perhaps he was just waiting around for an invitation to a tea party," said Ariel. He looked at Lilly, who was smearing bits of tortilla with peanut butter and folding them into little packets before popping them in her mouth, with distaste. "Foolish to wait around," he continued. "If you want something," he lifted his glass, "you should just go get it."

"What do you mean?" Lilly stopped chewing.

"Well, like I was saying to a friend just this morning," he glanced over at Jenny. "Where would Romeo be if he'd never declared himself to Juliet?"

Jenny narrowed her eyes. Was this friend he was talking about Trinculo? And why, for heaven's sake, was he telling this to *Lilly*? And had he really just winked at her? She stabbed at the ice in her glass with a chopstick. "Well, he might be alive, for one thing."

Lilly groaned. "God, Mom." She looked at Ariel. "My mother does not have a romantic bone in her body. She is the original buzz kill for romance."

Jenny sat back in her chair, stung. "I quit school to follow a rock and roll band, Lilly. If that isn't romantic, then I don't know what is. And look where it got me."

Frankie glanced up. "It got you us," she said.

Jenny softened. She reached across the table to touch Frankie's cheek. "Yes it did, sweetie. It got me you." She turned to Ariel, eager to change the subject. "Why don't you show us what's in the bag?"

Ariel pulled the bag back and rested it on his lap just as Frankie reached for it. "You all know what's coming up on Tuesday, don't you? Peg's famous rehearsal au naturelle."

Frankie covered her face with both hands and groaned. Phoenix hovered in the doorway, watching from a distance.

Jenny's forehead wrinkled as she looked at Frankie. "Peg seems to feel it's very important, though I don't know why. The other day she went on and on about stripping off your id and blah de blah." She looked at Frankie with sympathy.

"But you know you don't have to do it if you don't want to."

Lilly pressed the tortilla bag against the table with her palm to reseal the zip-locking edge. "*You'll* only be naked for like thirty seconds," she said. "Peg just wants the nude-o-rama for when you're on stage. When you're not acting you can wear your clothes."

Ariel leaned forward. "What our illustrious director said was, and here I quote, *I want to look at the stage and see flesh, not T-shirts and tank tops and modern waterproof sandals.* He reached into the bag and pulled out a piece of fabric. He shook it so that they could see what it was: a flesh-colored body-suit made out of a very thin material. It was the size a slender thirteen-year-old girl might wear. It had two bright red dots drawn on it where the nipples would be.

Frankie clapped her hand over her mouth.

Lilly reached for the suit and shook it out before all their eyes. She peered at the nipples and then her eyes traveled farther south. "What about the pubes? Frankie has pubes, you know."

Frankie and Phoenix locked eyes. Their shared horror overcame the distance between them.

Ariel gazed coolly at Lilly for several heartbeats before saying, "Pubes aren't really in fashion now, darling, are they? I would expect you're bald down there. Or am I wrong about that?"

Lilly turned bright red and hopped up from the table. "I'm going to go take a shower."

Jenny watched her bend to put the tortillas back in the fridge and thought, not without admiration, that it was quite a feat to have made Lilly blush. She turned back to Ariel. "Can I get you something to eat? We have some tabbouleh in the fridge. It's nice and cool on a hot day."

Ariel put his hands on his thighs as if prepared to hoist himself up from the chair with great effort. It was a funny gesture, thought Jenny, for a man so unusually light on his feet.

"I should really get back to town," he said. "Trink will eventually stop sulking and want to begin drinking. I should be there to support him."

"Did you walk?" she asked, trying to picture him trudging alongside the hot shoulder of the road.

"I do what I have to do, sugar." The look that he gave her then, half-mocking and half-sympathetic, seemed to imply that he knew all she had been thinking and more. It was odd. They were so different in so many ways, and yet it had been a long time since anyone on that island, with the exception of Mary Ann, had seemed able to read Jenny so easily.

She turned. "Phoenix, honey? Did you call your mom?"

"Yeah. She's coming to get me." Phoenix's reply was unusually soft for such a bold girl. Bold, perhaps, only in comparison to Frankie.

"You might want to walk back," she said, turning to look at Ariel once more. "But if not, we can ask Theresa to give you a ride." Jenny was curious to see what Theresa would make of Ariel.

He sipped his tea. "I wouldn't turn down a ride back to town."

&

Theresa came too soon for Phoenix, who had overcome her shyness and was sitting at the table with Frankie and Ariel, gossiping about various TV and film actors whom Ariel had met in New York and Los Angeles. They didn't hear her truck and so she appeared in the doorway suddenly.

Jenny stood up from the table. "Ariel, this is my friend Theresa. Theresa, this is Ariel."

Phoenix broke in, "It's not his real name."

Theresa glanced down at her grime-stained clothes before shrugging and holding out her hand to Ariel. "I bet this seems like the total sticks for you. Are you from New York City?"

Jenny smiled. This was the Theresa she remembered from all those years ago. The one who would show up at Jenny's place with a pack of cigarettes and a bottle of wine and sit on the porch with her while the girls climbed around on fallen logs.

Ariel shook his head. "Seattle."

"Oh." She looked disappointed.

"I do go to the Big Apple quite frequently," he added. "When I'm in a show there I usually stay with a friend in the Village. Are you familiar with Greenwich Village?"

Theresa's eyes shined. "Oh, sure. I mean, I've heard of it. I haven't been able to get out there yet."

The Big Apple? Jenny gave Ariel a sharp look to see if he was making fun of Theresa. There was no mockery in his face that she could see.

"Have you been in a lot of shows? And TV and movies, do you do that, too, or mostly just the theater?"

"I had a small part in *Two and a Half Men*. And I've done some commercials." He drained his glass and set it delicately back on the table. "I'm primarily a stage actor." He turned to Jenny with a mild but lingering look.

She straightened. "Theresa, would you and Phoenix mind giving Ariel a ride into town?"

Theresa beamed. "We'd love to."

Phoenix pulled herself reluctantly away from Ariel and Frankie and went to get her things. Just as he was about to get up, Frankie spontaneously grabbed Ariel in a hug. She looked surprised at herself, but delighted when he did not pull away. Jenny, too, was surprised at how easily he seemed to sit with Frankie's obvious affections. He was snippy with almost everyone else, even Trinculo, but he was enormously gentle with her.

"Thank you," she said softly, not meaning just for the leotard, but for everything.

He patted Frankie on the head and extricated himself gracefully from her grasp. He lifted the leotard off the table, tucked it into the bag, and slipped it to Frankie like a spy handing off the secret papers. "I figure you're naked enough as it is, at thirteen," he said.

Lilly had clearly been waiting for Ariel to leave before coming out of the bathroom. She emerged with a faded towel wrapped around her body. "Is he gone?"

Frankie looked at her sister as if she could not believe her ears. "Ariel?"

"Yep," said Jenny, clearing the glasses off the table.

"Good." Lilly sent drops flying from her dreads as she swung her head. "He can be such a bitch."

Frankie ran past her. "God! If there's anyone who's a bitch around here, it's you!"

Lilly watched her go and then turned to Jenny with her eyebrows raised. "Is she still crushed out on him? Poor thing."

Jenny grabbed a handful of grapes from the fridge and dropped into the soft chair by the window. "I think she's just fine, actually. Better than fine."

Lilly shrugged. "You always take her side."

It didn't bother Jenny, really, that the afternoon's peace and cooperation had frayed. She had long since learned that when you were raising children, no phase lasted for long, either good or bad. At about six months old Lilly had begun to make a sound like a cat in heat. She howled and screeched whenever she opened her mouth, and Jenny and Monroe had looked at each other in horror and amazement. Just when they were beginning to think there was something wrong with her and that they would have to spend their lives listening to that sound, she stopped. By the time Frankie began to exercise her vocal chords in the same way, Jenny was no longer looking Monroe in the eye. It didn't matter, though. She knew that all she had to do was wait. This, too, would pass.

Lilly disappeared into the back room to get dressed and then, apparently having second thoughts, reappeared in her bathrobe. She perched on the edge of Jenny's chair.

"I want to ask you something." She waited for Jenny to meet her gaze.

"Okay."

"Just this one time, will you put aside the mom thing and give me your honest opinion? Please?"

"I'll try." It took every ounce of self-control Jenny had for her not to laugh out loud. The *mom thing*? Is that what Lilly thought these last eighteen years represented to Jenny? A *thing* that she could just *put aside*?

"Should I just come out and tell him directly that I'm in love with him? Do you think that's what Ariel was trying to say this afternoon? That I should declare my feelings for Trinculo so that he knows it's okay to, well, you know . . . ?"

"No. Don't." The words jumped out of Jenny's mouth before she even knew she was thinking them.

"Why not?"

Lilly looked at her with interest, apparently convinced that Jenny was speaking to her as a woman now, instead of as her mother. Jenny cringed inwardly. If she only knew.

"I don't want you to get hurt."

"Oh, great." Lilly stood up and looked down at Jenny with disgust and something very much like pity. "That is so you. Typical. As if getting hurt was the worst thing in the world. I feel sorry for you sometimes, Mom. I really do."

Lilly headed for her bedroom, shaking her head in disbelief.

Jenny buried her face in her palms. In less than a week, she was going to strip naked in front a group of people that included not just this girl, but also her friends and neighbors and a man she might well be in love with. In light of that fact, Jenny had two questions for herself, and she thought it might not be a bad idea to take Lilly's advice and put aside the *mom thing* while she searched for the answers. The first? Was she utterly out of her mind? The second? Was it too early for a glass of wine? She stood up and headed for the kitchen. Only the second, she decided, could be answered definitively.

CHAPTER 9

Wild Waters

On the day of the naked rehearsal, the cast assembled at the dock in Friday Harbor as instructed. Peg had arranged for them to be ferried somewhere, she didn't say where, by Leroy Jones, who captained a whale-watching boat out of Deer Harbor, on Orcas. Apparently he, like they, had been sworn to secrecy about where they were going (but unlike the rest of them, he would actually know where it was before they arrived). Lilly scoffed at the idea that they would be followed by paparazzi, if that was what Peg was afraid of. Jenny suspected that Peg, her face lit up with expectation while she chatted on a bench with Caliban, simply liked the intrigue that the whole thing interjected into the middle of their summer preparations. In Dale and Peg's world, after all, drama was to be embraced rather than avoided.

It was bright and windless, but the heat had broken from the previous week. Along with lunches and thermoses filled with iced tea and lemonade and the random bottle of white wine, they had sweaters and jackets and hiking shoes. Peg had hinted that they might all go on a walkabout after the rehearsal. Chad had brought his guitar along and he sat on the bench playing it while everyone waited for the boat. Frankie and Lilly had rediscovered through the play how much they liked singing together and they provided harmony for him and a few of the other deep-voiced *O*s on "The Needle and the Damage Done." Trinculo had borrowed David's harmonica and was screwing around on it tunelessly.

Frankie wore her flesh-colored leotard under her clothes, a fact that Ariel, now stretching elaborately at the railing as if it were a balance bar, had confirmed with a quick lift of her T-shirt.

Jenny listened for a while and then stood up and wandered over toward the edge of the dock. She took her sunglasses off to polish them with the hem of her T-shirt and was momentarily blinded by the glare off the water.

"I'll tell you where we're headed, if you want." For a large man, Dale had an uncommon ability to sneak. His breath was hot in her ear.

She turned. "Blakely?"

He whispered. "Stuart. Peg has a friend with property on the east side."

"Oh." She looked back out at the water. An oystercatcher hopped onto a rock near the water's edge, close enough so that she could see its scarlet beak and gleaming red eyes.

Dale stood by her so close that their bodies touched from

the shoulder to the elbow. "I feel like you've been avoiding me," he said.

Jenny sighed. "How are things going between you and Peg?"

Dale turned to face her. His hair was windblown and the sunburn on his nose and cheeks made him look like he'd been drinking. "She doesn't mind, I told you. She wants an open marriage."

"Geez, Dale. You and I are old friends . . ."

Dale looked despondently at his hands on the railing. His fingers were thick and sprinkled liberally with the white hair that covered his chin and head. "You're hot for that jester, eh? You, Ariel, Miranda, and even, I suspect, my own sweet Peg. Well, good luck is all I can say." He smiled sheepishly. "Actors are a notoriously unhinged bunch."

Jenny leaned against the wood railing, picking at its flaking paint with her fingernail. Water lapped against the rocks below to make the steady pat, pat, pat sound of a baker kneading dough. A seagull cried and then landed nearby, looking at them carefully in case they might be holding food. The description of Peg as sweet was a bit incongruous (generous, brilliant, unconventional all worked, but sweet?), but the more important fact was that Dale thought she was interested in Trinculo. Is that what all this randiness was about? He was threatened by the new guy?

Finally she said, "He kissed Lilly."

Dale appeared to think about that. "*I've* kissed Lilly."

Jenny turned and punched him in the shoulder. Hard.

"Ouch." He rubbed his arm. "Just once, okay? I was inebriated and it was late and, well, she reminded me of you."

"God, Dale. You are such a jerk."

He looked out at the water. "Sorry."

Jenny said, "You should be."

A forty-something-foot twin outboard motorboat chugged into the dock. The seagulls scattered into the air and the wake churned up the water against the rocks. The captain cut the engine and came out on deck to toss David a rope.

"Our ride is here, people," called Peg from her perch standing on a bench. "Get ready to load up."

Jenny searched for her girls and finally saw them jogging back from the ice cream shop holding cones. Frankie's T-shirt was so thin and worn that in a certain light the nipples that Ariel had inked on to her bodysuit were visible. Jenny hoped Lilly would keep her mouth shut about that and resolved to pull her aside before boarding to make her promise. The boat was large by whale-watching standards, but with the whole cast on it, it would be crowded to capacity with no opportunity for a private conversation. She shouldered her bag and saw first Trinculo's Nikes, then his brown legs.

She said, "I think Peg wants us on the boat."

He touched her lightly on the arm and her eyes were drawn, damn it, to his face. His frown was so elaborate it might have been painted on.

"Juno? Oh, Juno? Have I done something to displease you?"

"Watch yourself around Lilly, please."

Trinculo glanced toward the boat, where Lilly bent her knees to catch the drips from her ice cream cone with her open mouth. "I am doing my very best. She's a persistent one, though, isn't she?"

Jenny had to smile. It was exactly how Dale had described her. Apparently it didn't take ten years living with Lilly on the island to figure her out.

Trinculo caught her smiling and his eyes flashed. He bowed low. "As you wish, goddess."

Peg stood on a bench and put her hands on her hips. "Hurry up, you two!"

A number of other stragglers looked for misplaced articles of clothing, topped off water bottles, took last-minute trips to the bathroom, and generally spent more time than could be anticipated preparing to depart for a twenty-minute hop from one island to another. Trinculo bounded toward Prospero, calling him Skipper in the way of Gilligan and lamented that neither Mary Ann, nor Ginger for that matter, was joining them (like the Waldron trip, this journey was only for the actors and Peg). Caliban popped a Dramamine and offered one to Miranda, who, busy smearing sunscreen on her face, declined. Sally the Ship-Master, who actually did know her way around a ship, caught the rope that the captain tossed to her and tied it to the dock. Finally they were all on the craft, crammed into the cabin, sitting on the benches and coolers in the back, standing at the railing, and, in the case of Lilly and Frankie, sitting with their legs stretched out in front of them on the bow.

This was the first time they had gone anywhere together, and the sound of excited chatter was audible over the engine until they hit the open water and the captain pushed down the throttle. The wind picked up their hair and whipped it around their faces and they leaned into each other and shouted in each other's ears, all except for Lilly and Frankie, who were visible through the windscreen laughing in the spray and holding tight to the metal railing. Peg stood inside next to the captain, looking pleased, and Jenny thought, okay, so maybe this togetherness before the first performance is a good idea, but why do we have to be *naked*?

It soon became obvious to the islanders where they were heading. Stuart Island loomed ahead of them. The boat slowed into Reid Cove and they began telling the newcomers about the lighthouse and lovers' leap and the dangerous rocks in the channel. The company was quicker getting off than it had been getting on, and before long they were standing on the shore watching the boat chug back out the way it had come.

"See you this evening," the captain called.

Peg waved back and the actors stood around her in a windblown group, clutching their sweaters and water bottles and hiking boots.

Jenny stood near enough to see the face of Caliban's watch when he turned his arm to look at it. It was ten-thirty in the morning. The boat disappeared and they all looked at one another and then Peg with the same question on their faces: What now?

"This way," said Peg. She turned and began walking.

Suddenly much quieter, the company followed.

"Down with the topmast! Yare! Lower, lower! Bring her to try with main course."

"Ahhhhhh."

"A plague upon this howling! They are louder than the weather, or our office."

Tossed about on their imaginary boat, the men formed a loosely linked amoeba of arms and hands. Crashing into each other on the pitching deck, they were naked as the day they were born. Poor Ferdinand's face had been as pink as the tip of his penis since he stepped out of his shorts and onto the sand. The wind rustled the tops of the trees and the rest of the actors stood in mortified silence on the sidelines. Frankie sat on a rock with her knees pulled up against her chest, peeking through her fingers.

"All lost! To prayers, to prayers. All lost!"

"Mercy on us!—We split, we split!"

"Fairwell, my wife and children!"

"Farwell, brother!—We split, we split, we split!"

"Wind!" called Peg.

Jenny and Lilly and Frankie almost missed their cue. The spirits, doubling as the gale, made the sound of the raging storm. In the play they would be wrapped loosely in torn sheets, dyed gray and blue. Their only lines might be "Woooo, wooooo, woooo," at this point in the play, but they were lines nonetheless. According to Peg's rules, they were expected to perform. Naked.

Lilly had worn a sundress with nothing underneath, and she shed it easily, strolling forward like Venus emerging from the waves.

Frankie pulled the T-shirt over her head, and when Peg saw her suit she frowned but said nothing. Jenny wished she had declined more tortilla chips and done more sit-ups in the previous weeks, but there was no altering the past. She stepped out of her shorts and tossed her shirt on a rock, and before she made her first loud wail as the wind, she grabbed her younger daughter's hand and squeezed it tight. All she could do now, she figured, was do her best to model grace under pressure.

Lilly was already circling the men, woo-wooing in her scariest voice. She darted close to Trinculo, barely missing his arm with her shoulder, a lock of her hair whipping his cheek.

Jenny tried not to peep, but she couldn't help it. First his eyes. They locked into hers with a look that she had, in fact, exchanged with a naked man on occasion but in circumstances that were quite a bit more private than these. Then, his chest, as Lilly's hair, striking him, slid down his body like a snake, before falling away. His eyes followed Lilly's hair, and Jenny's eyes, though she tried, Lord how she tried not to let them, sunk lower on Trinculo's body. The flat stomach. The thin trail of hair pointing south. She flushed. Lilly was right. The body did not lie.

Jenny was happy that the scene called for her to make a loud and terrible noise. She obliged. It might be telling too much, that brown and agile body of his, but the specific thing that she wanted to know most it could not reveal. What exactly, or more pointedly, *who*, had produced the response that he, within the limits of his role, now tried to hide from the cast?

Jenny and Lilly and Frankie howled together like a pack of hungry wolves.

Gonzalo cried, "Now would I give a thousand furlongs of sea for an acre of barren ground, long heath, brown, anything." The imaginary boat split into pieces and sent them all flying in different directions, and he called out one last time, "The wills above be done! But I would fain die a dry death."

The men fell into the sand or draped their bodies over the boulders and logs that littered the beach.

"Well done," yelled Peg. She wore a lime green tunic over black leggings, and the hair that rose with each gust around her head was the color of a blood orange.

Down the beach a bit, Prospero stepped out of his robe for his first scene with Miranda, who, with her perfect breasts and carefully manicured pubic hair, looked like she had been waiting for just this moment for most of her life.

Without looking in Peg's direction, Trinculo, still naked, walked toward the sea. He waded waist deep into the water and let the cold do its work. Peg shifted her attention to the scene underway.

Jenny threw on her clothes and leaned against a gnarled Madrona tree watching Trinculo. Her stomach was churning. She could tell how furious he was from the set of his shoulders and the veins in his neck. Anger in men—even in gentle men—made her nervous.

Her first thought was that he was angry at Peg for putting him, and his manly lack of control, on display. But even Peg, with her love of drama and tendency to cling to a nostalgic flower-child sensibility, could not have predicted what had happened with Trinculo. Jenny glanced around to locate her children, one of whom crouched in as close to a fetal position as you could get without lying down, under several layers of borrowed clothing. The other basked in the sun on a rock, still nude.

"Lilly, get your clothes on, for God's sake!" Jenny hissed at her.

Lilly languidly reached for her dress and pulled it over her head.

Trinculo stood near the quietly lapping shore in his shorts, hands on his hips. She could feel his eyes on her, but she could not meet his gaze. What about that look he had given her on the beach? What about the fact that he had kissed Lilly? How in the world had she allowed herself to be in the ridiculous and appalling situation where it mattered to her who he had been thinking about when he got that erection? She glanced at Frankie, who had her legs drawn up to her chest. That's whom she *should* be worrying about, she told herself. She looked out toward the Sound, in the direction their boat had gone, and saw nothing but glittering water, distant sails, and the mountains beyond. For the first time that morning, she realized that they were on this island with no way off, until Peg said they were done. They were trapped.

The rest of the cast was standing in uncomfortable silence looking at the horizon, the woods, or the mixture of wave-polished rocks and seaweed around their feet. Looking anywhere but at each other. She turned her head again to see Peg, murmuring to Prospero and Miranda and pot-bellied Caliban, who was just off-stage but close enough to be audible to the watching cast when he spoke. From a distance she could appear to be a child among adults, but no one who knew Peg doubted for a moment that she was in charge.

Perhaps Peg had *wanted* them to feel trapped, thought Jenny, exactly as Ferdinand and his fellows had felt on *their* island. She had to acknowledge that there was genius in it, if it was true. Evil genius, perhaps, but genius nonetheless.

Prospero and Miranda were speaking, Jenny realized suddenly, and leaned her head against Frankie's to listen. Trinculo's feet made a crunching sound on the sand as he inched toward them from the shore. She remained firmly focused on the action of the play.

"Tis a villain, sir, I do not love to look on," said Miranda, her hair long enough to cover all but the undersides of her breasts.

Dale-as-Prospero nodded and then looked off into the distance meaningfully, toward where Caliban stood, hunched and hairy, by a log. "But as tis, We cannot miss him. He does make our fire, Fetch in our wood, and serves in offices That profit us. What ho! Slave! Caliban! Thou earth, thou! Speak."

Caliban, though off-stage, was visible to all. He leered in the direction of Prospero. The sweep of his gaze took in the rest of them, coming to rest on Trinculo. His line was familiar, but the emphasis, today, was new. He said, "There's wood enough within."

Ariel stood in the wings behind him, preparing to be called by Prospero. "You can say that again," he muttered.

Peg shot him a hard glance, and he pretended not to notice.

Prospero turned, ever so slightly, away from the audience. "Come forth, I say, there's other business for thee. Come, thou tortoise, when?"

Jenny was conscious of Trinculo breathing behind her and she stared resolutely forward.

Peg called out, "Actors! Get your clothes on and come to the beach. We need to process the scene."

They picked up their jackets and water bottles and found somewhere to sit on the smooth driftwood logs and rocks that formed a half circle on the beach.

Ariel groaned, "Process, process, process. Why didn't I go into something less complicated? Like dentistry."

Jenny sat on the sand between Sally and Frankie. Ariel perched nearby on a log. Lilly moved to find a spot next to Trinculo, but he got up to scratch a pretend itch, at least Jenny thought he was pretending, and plopped back down on the other side of Caliban. He sat cross-legged, with the straight back of a yogi, his eyes studiously fixed on the branch above Jenny's head.

Peg began, "We have had this naked rehearsal for ten years now. The purpose of it, as you may have guessed, is to allow you to inhabit the person of the role for one last time before you appear on the stage. Without your play costumes or even the costumes that you wear every day in the roles you call your regular lives. It is," and here she looked around at each of the cast members in turn, "a *secret* that we keep among ourselves. Like any family, we have things that cannot be spoken of in public and those things tie us more tightly together."

Ariel muttered under his breath, "As if we didn't all have enough family secrets already."

Dale cleared his throat. "What Peg means to say," he said, "is that our Ceres is a beautiful young woman, and it is very natural that a man would . . ."

Trinculo had been drawing lines in the sand with a stick. He looked up sharply. "Ceres . . . ?"

"What I *mean* to say," Peg shot him a look, "is that the laws of nature are paramount in this, what the esteemed literary critic Northrop Frye referred to as the *green* world." She waved her small pale hands around to encompass the beach, the water, and the sky. "We are not governed by the rules of the city here. This world is other, it is feminine, it is unbounded."

As far as Jenny was concerned, the feminine world might have different rules than the masculine one, but *unbounded* was taking it a little too far. And it might have been natural for Trinculo to respond like a man when Lilly flipped her hair in his face, but that didn't mean she had to like it.

Trinculo glanced once furtively at Jenny. The blood rose in his cheeks. He said, "Look, this had nothing to do with Lil . . . I mean Ceres . . ." He caught Lilly looking at him with hurt and added, "Damn this whole thing is just too . . ."

Peg held up her hand to silence him. The loose sleeve of her tunic swayed in the breeze. She turned her small face to each of them in turn, wrinkling her nose and fixing them in her stare one by one. "We shall not speak of this again."

Frankie kept her clothes on for the rest of the afternoon and Peg did not protest. In spite of the process circle, or maybe even because of it, the members of the company were all newly awkward around each other in the breaks. They spoke softly and offered each other portions of their lunches, which were, as likely as not, politely refused.

The sun rose in the sky and they approached the play's epilogue—where Prospero asks the audience to fill his sails with their gentle breath and set him free, not as people who had spent weeks together but as virtual strangers once again. Rather than sweep away the last of their secrets, seeing each other naked had highlighted how little they knew of each other still. Peg's crazy scheme had introduced a bit of danger and mystery into what, as recently as that very morning, had begun to seem like summer camp.

After they had finished all their snacks, the company left their extra sweaters and jackets on the dock where they would be picked up and began the hike to the lighthouse at Turn Point. The trail began in the woods and then spilled onto a country road at the northwest point of the island. A lighthouse perched there, overlooking the treacherous Haro Strait. It would take them about two hours to hike there and back.

When they returned, the boat would be waiting. Frankie ran ahead to join Ariel, Ferdinand, Lilly, Miranda, and Sally; all the youngest actors with their strong young legs led the way.

Dale and Peg were in deep conversation with each other at the back.

Jenny walked alongside Chad for a while, who complained about the quality of fish that he'd had to choose from for the last three dinner services at the restaurant. The tourists don't notice the difference, but *he* did and the reputation of the restaurant rested on *his* shoulders . . . Jenny nodded and murmured her sympathy when necessary, but mostly her attention was on the bellflower blooming on the side of the road and a group of spotted towhees gorging on a juneberry bush. The sun was warm on the back of her head and the voices of the others, and their feet crunching small twigs on the trail, made a soothing accompaniment to Chad's good-natured fussing. She pretended not to notice that Trinculo had jogged to catch up with them.

"Hey, man," said Chad to Trinculo.

Trinculo showed his palm like a Hollywood Indian. "Hey."

Jenny acknowledged his presence with a quick nod in his direction but did not meet his eyes. They walked with their gaze straight ahead while alongside them, Chad segued into a rant about the dishwasher, a boy who had come down from Canada that summer and couldn't find his ass with his own two hands. Both Jenny and Trinculo pretended to listen, neither one of them hearing a word that he said. To Jenny it no longer seemed that her arms and legs were working together and she sensed that her gait was awkward and self-conscious. She looked at the backs of her children, hiking in front of her, but then, aware that Trinculo's eyes had followed hers to rest on the girls, she quickly glanced at the tops of the pines. He cleared his throat. A flutter rose in her chest.

The company left the trail for the dirt road and the gang in front began kicking up dust. Trinculo coughed and Jenny glanced at him sharply. She had her answer ready. They were *her* girls. They were *fine*.

"About what happened earlier . . ." Trinculo started to say.

Jenny blanched. "Sorry, you'll have to excuse me, but I. . . ." Her hand flew to her chin as if she had forgotten something. Chad and Trinculo stopped and looked at her in confusion. "Sorry!" she said again and ducked back toward Dale and Peg.

"Hi Jen. Good job today." Peg approached her with a smile. The wrinkles alongside her little nose were particularly deep and her eyes sparkled.

"Goddamn it, Peg." She waited with her hands on her hips. "Did the girls really have to be naked? *Frankie?*"

Jenny felt a stab of guilt. She could speak her mind to Peg, a woman who had been her friend for more than ten years and who would never, intentionally, harm either her or her children. But a sandy-haired man with a strong jaw and smooth brown wrists? Never. What a wimp.

Peg shifted her backpack on her shoulder and moved her walking stick from one hand to the other. "She wasn't naked. Or did I miss something?"

Jenny chewed her lip. "But you wanted her to be."

Dale slipped his arm through Jenny's. "Cute suit she had on," he said. "Was that your handiwork?"

"Ariel."

Peg said, "What I *wanted* didn't seem to be paramount in the end, did it now?" She put her arm around Jenny and gave her shoulders a quick squeeze. "Look, stop brooding, Jen. If seeing an accidental boner is the worst thing that ever happens to Frankie, she'll be one lucky girl." She caught Dale's eyes over Jenny's head and smiled. "Though I think Lilly rather enjoyed it."

Jenny groaned and then couldn't help laughing helplessly because, of course, Peg was absolutely right.

Peg smiled. "You know that Mary Ann is prepared to step in for Frankie on Thursday night if she wants out. She's learned the lines for all three of you."

"No, no. Frankie is determined to be in this play."

"Okay then."

Thursday night. In just three days they would be riding the ferry to Orcas with their costumes and props, their sleeping bags and their tents. From Orcas they would be taken by private boat over to Waldron, where the entire population of the island, all one hundred or so people, would come to the show. Afterward they would have a bonfire and spend the night. The following week they would perform on Shaw, in an actual community theater, for several nights, and everyone would be there: the design people, the costume people, and all the musicians. Lopez Vineyard followed and then, finally, the first of a series of big performances on San Juan Island. Frankie couldn't wait. Theresa had promised to deposit Phoenix at Anacortes for the big opening on San Juan. Jenny and Frankie would pick her up in Friday Harbor that afternoon and then she would stay the night at their cabin.

The trees thinned as they approached the lighthouse. Yellow grass covered the tip of the island, from the last stand of trees to the cliff. At the edge stood a small, white, clapboard building with a red roof and then, perched just beyond, was the short tower of the lighthouse itself. The sun was beginning its approach to the water and the slight breeze from earlier had kicked up into an actual wind.

Jenny chugged from her canteen and offered water to Dale and Peg, who each took a swig before handing it back. She set it on the ground at her feet and slipped into the long-sleeved T-shirt she had tied around her waist. By the time she had slung the strap of her canteen back over her shoulder, the group in front (Lilly, Frankie, Ariel, Miranda, Ferdinand, and a few others) had broken into a run. Trinculo and Chad jogged after them.

"Whales," exhaled Jenny.

Dale brightened. "I heard J pod was back in the Sound."

"Well, let's get a move on then." Peg lifted her walking stick up onto her shoulder and the three of them picked up their pace.

The last part of the trail sloped downward toward the drop-off and so from hundreds of yards away Jenny, Peg, and Dale could see the others spread out along the cliff facing out to sea. Beyond were the whales themselves, cresting and diving and expelling air in echoing fountains of spray. Peg, Dale, and Jenny joined the others on the edge of the cliff and the group rippled like one organism in response, shifting their bodies to make room. Nobody spoke. There were twenty-five individual orcas in this pod that lived between the Sound and the sea and there were twelve awestruck humans watching them from the shore.

"That's Ruffles," said Dale, pointing at a large male swimming on the outside of the pod, on the shore side.

"Shhh," scolded Frankie.

Dale zipped his lip with the exaggerated wide eyes of a mime.

A midsize whale leaped out of the water and the splash carried for yards.

"Ahhh."

"Ohhh."

They were like a crowd watching fireworks on the Fourth of July. The intermittent echo of the blowholes was soothing and seemed to come from every side of them at once. Most of the large animals made no sound at all as they circled each other in the water. Jenny glanced at the people beside her, taking in the row of faces bathed in golden sunlight and wonder, the smooth cheeks and bright eyes of her children and Trinculo's lock of windblown hair. Frankie seemed fine. She relaxed and turned her attention toward the orcas in the water.

She wondered if the summer visitors knew how something like seeing a family of whales at sunset could draw you in for life. How it could lead you to sell your house in the city and whatever possessions would be cumbersome and take up residence in a hillside cabin warmed by a woodstove, within walking distance to a ridge where you could see the beach.

Suddenly, as if sensing her presence beside him, Trinculo turned his head and let his eyes meet hers. His face was full of joy. She felt it, too. They stared at each other for a long moment before each of them, smiling, turned back to the sea.

On the hike back, when Trinculo saw her walking alone and lingered to fall into step beside her, Jenny made no attempt to get away.

He ran his hand through his hair nervously before speaking, doing the last of the job the wind had started. "Jenny, I . . . About the whole naked thing. With the girls . . . I don't know what to say other than . . ."

"You don't need to say anything," said Jenny.

The orange light of the setting sun and the graceful falling leaps of the whales had reminded Jenny that sometimes intuition could guide you where logic and rationality could not. She didn't know what the future would bring, but then who could have ever imagined that she would have ended up living the life she led, in a northern world so very unlike the broad, hot streets of Sacramento?

"I really think I do." A look of embarrassment flitted over his face. "Getting excited around a teenage girl requires some kind of explanation, in my book."

Jenny smiled. "Two teenage girls, actually."

Lilly glanced over, but instead of hanging back to join them as Jenny might have expected, she jogged forward to catch up with the others.

Trinculo winced. "Damn, Jenny, I . . ."

Jenny raised her hand to graze his cheek.

He tilted his head toward her palm and closed his eyes. "I just didn't want you to think that I . . . Lilly is a great kid, but . . ."

Jenny let her hand fall and Trinculo opened his eyes.

"Do you think I'm a bad mother?" she asked.

He reached for her hand again and pulled it in between both of his own. "Are you kidding? I think you're a fantastic mother." He tugged her toward him until their faces were just inches apart. The salt on his skin mixed with the salt in the air and his breath had just the faintest hint of cinnamon. "I think *you're* fantastic."

Down at the dock the captain blew his horn to signal he'd arrived. Jenny stood with Trinculo on the path and did not move. She might not be as young and peachy as Lilly and Miranda, but her body was strong and healthy and it fit her well. She was standing on the rocky path of a tree-covered is-land, under a bright summer sky, and an interesting man was holding her hand.

"Do you think I'm a cad?" he asked her.

She shook her head. "You're beautiful."

He touched her lips with the pad of his finger. Ever so slightly, she opened her mouth. His fingers slipped inside and then gently, very gently, spread the wetness to her lips.

The horn blew again and she took a step back and turned

toward the harbor. Her heart was pounding and she was al-most panting. She took off in a jog toward the boat.

Trinculo ran after. Jenny was a good hiker and was used to the trail. It was all he could do to keep up.

Jenny made sure the girls had their hoodies and canteens and climbed onto the boat. She was aware of Trinculo watching her and she was aware as well of new undercurrents traveling between the players, like the ripples on a pond after a thrown rock has disappeared. There were electrical charges between Chad and Miranda and Dale and Peg and Sally and David and yes, even between Ferdinand and Ariel, as Caliban had predicted. Their time on Stuart Island had altered their little dynamic in a number of subtle and not so subtle ways; Wal-dron would likely alter it still more.

The boat bobbed on the open water and most of the com-pany huddled inside to stay out of the wind. Jenny lingered out back and watched the wake fade into bubbles behind them. Sporting a sunburn on her shoulders, Lilly made her way to the rail beside her mother.

"I saw you guys talking on the trail," she said. "You and Trinculo."

Jenny reached for the rail. It was cold and wet with spray. Her pulse beat in her throat. Had Lilly seen him holding her hand? She remembered the taste of Trinculo's fingers in her mouth and her knees almost buckled.

"Were you talking about me?" asked Lilly. She looked up hopefully into her mother's face.

Jenny shook her head.

Lilly zipped her jacket and glanced quickly toward the cabin where Trinculo and the others were listening to an explanation of the GPS system. "Did he say whether he liked me?"

"Oh, Lil."

She reached out and pulled her daughter close. She knew she should tell Lilly what had happened between her and Trinculo, but something more than the fear of hurting her oldest daughter held Jenny's tongue. It was the fear that Lilly's knowing might somehow *prevent* what might happen still. And she wanted Trinculo. She was ready to acknowledge this finally to herself, if not to Lilly. She wanted him so badly that it made her ashamed.

Lilly shivered and Jenny rubbed her hands up and down on the girl's back to warm her. It was her job, she knew, to keep Lilly away from Trinculo and Trinculo away from Lilly, but what, exactly, was her obligation beyond that? Was she supposed to keep him away from herself, as well? She imagined what Sue would say, or Theresa, or any number of other mothers if she asked them: *It would be best.* The engine kicked into gear and the two women rocked on their feet. The wind whipped around the cabin and howled past their ears.

CHAPTER 10

Waldron: In Three Acts

Captain Jack	The captain of the boat that takes the company to Waldron
Peg	The Director
Frankie	Daughter to Jenny, Iris in the play
Jenny	A single mother, Juno in the play
Lilly	Daughter to Jenny, Ceres in the play
Ariel	An airy Spirit, kind to children
Dale	Husband to Peg, also Prospero in the play
Esme Burton	Waldron Island resident, host
Sally	Waitress at the Backdoor Kitchen, also Ship-Master
Trinculo	A Jester, in love with Jenny
Caliban	A savage and deformed slave, yearning for TV roles
Ferdinand	Son to the king of Naples, sexually questioning
Miranda	Daughter to Prospero, growing bored
Alonso	San Juan Island man

Sebastian	San Juan Island man
Antonio	San Juan Island man
Gonzalo	San Juan Island man
Adrian	San Juan Island man
Francisco	San Juan Island man
Winifred Calloway	Resident of Waldron
Chad	A horny chef, Stephano in the play
David	An honest carpenter, in love with Jenny
Jim Burton	Waldron Island resident, host
Arthur Calloway	Resident of Waldron
Luke Anderson	A Waldron boy with a boat

The Scene: [The dock on Waldron] The boat carrying the company arrives. Late June.

ACT I, Scene I

A small boy in swim trunks runs the length of the pier and cannonballs into the water.

Boy 1: Geronimo!

Boy 2: Watch this. Bombs away! (*Splash.*)

Captain Jack: Look out kids, we're coming in.

Peg: Listen up, everyone. As soon as we dock you can fan out and find a place to sleep tonight. The beach will be available after the performance. There's a pasture on the east side of the house and then the Burtons have offered a pull-out sofa and a guest bed.

Frankie: I call the bed.

Jenny: Your sister will sleep there with you.

Lilly: Mom! You're even going to micromanage where I *sleep*?

Jenny: Yes.

Lilly: Typical.

Jenny: You both brought your toothbrushes, right?

Frankie: Sure. But oh, crap. I can't believe it.

Lilly: What? What did you forget?

Frankie: The plastic garlands. For Miranda's and Ferdinand's hair during the wedding scene.

Peg: We'll just have to use real flowers. We have about an hour and a half before we need to assemble on the beach. Esme will give you some string.

Jenny: Why don't you look in your bag, Lilly? Could you have them?

Lilly: No. Oh, shoot, I . . .

Peg: What now?

Jenny: Did you forget something, too?

Ariel: Like your diaphragm?

Lilly: Very funny. And it's none of your business anyway.

Dale: If it's your weed, Lil, no need to worry. They have plenty of pot on the island. Or didn't you know that Marcus has a hydroponic greenhouse?

Lilly: Wow. You're all so nice and helpful. I'm really looking forward to being trapped on a barely inhabited island with you for the next twenty-four hours.

Captain Jack: Esme! Take the rope?

Esme: Sure!

Ties up boat.

A small boy comes racing down toward the end of the dock.

Boy: Duck and cover!

Lilly: Bryce! You got me wet!

Ariel: Point me to the nearest café and I'll see you all in an hour.

Sally: Ha. That's very funny.

Trinculo: No services on Waldron at all, right? No electricity or garbage collection or police?

Jenny: No crime.

Caliban: Now this is the life for me. Far away from the backbiting of New York. No smell of urine on the pavement. No honking horns.

Ariel: No black people.

Ferdinand: What if someone gets hurt? Are there doctors on the island? Is there a clinic?

Dale: Clinically speaking, we'll be in isolation.

Peg: All right. Here we are. Watch your step everyone. Take a look around, actors. This beach will be your stage.

Miranda: So where do I hide before coming out the first time?

Ariel: Oh, coming out is a bitch that first time, no doubt about it. Right, Ferdinand? But the good news is that once you're out, you're out.

Peg: You'll be behind this rock, Miranda. And Caliban, you'll hide over there, behind that one. Ariel, over here.

Frankie: (*Lifting a piece of driftwood up to Lilly.*) What do you think of this as a loaf of bread?

Lilly: I'm not eating it.

Frankie: For the Spirits' Feast, silly. We can use seaweed for a salad. And some cedar bark for pasta.

Trinculo: The audience sits where?

Dale: They'll bring blankets and chairs and pillows and sit on the sand.

Peg: With their backs to the water.

Trinculo: With the tide coming in, they might wish they went back-to-the-land.

Esme: Welcome everyone. Who wants to come up to the house? Some neighbors brought snacks over and I can show you the various places to sleep. Remember when choosing a spot that the moon will be full tonight. It will be bright enough to cast shadows out in the open.

Lilly: (*To Trinculo.*) Do you want me to take you up to the house?

Jenny: Go with your sister, Lilly. Put your stuff by the bed.

Sulking, Lilly heads off with the rest of the company toward the house. Jenny and Trinculo meander slowly on the path through the woods.

Trinculo: Wow. Look at that.

Jenny: What?

Trinculo: That tree over there. It's been broken in half somehow. Lightning maybe? And there's a round boulder balancing on top.

Jenny: It's Raven's. He has sculptures all through the woods here.

Trinculo: And check this out. A mobile of driftwood and clamshells. How cool. What a place! Waldron Island.

Jenny comes to look over his shoulder. He turns abruptly and kisses her.

Jenny: Don't.

Trinculo: But we're all alone, Jenny. In the deep dark woods.

Jenny: I know, but . . .

Trinculo: You act as if it's wrong of you to want to be with someone. You're an adult woman. You're single.

Jenny: Lilly is in love with you. Or hadn't you noticed?

Trinculo: Lilly is a kid. You don't think I'm interested in her, do you?

Jenny: You wouldn't be the first.

Trinculo: I like women a little older than that. Late thirties. (*Raises an eyebrow at her, questioning.*) Forty?

Jenny: (*Smiling.*) Forty-two.

Trinculo: (*Leans in to kiss her again.*) Forty-two. Exactly. (*Steps back.*) You don't trust me.

Jenny: Well, you are an actor.

Trinculo: Hmm. So if I were, say, a carpenter, I'd have a better chance?

Jenny: Stop that. David is just a friend.

Trinculo: Is it Monroe then? Is that the reason? I guess a guy like that might ruin a woman's trust in men.

Jenny: (*Stands still and stares at him.*) What do you know about Monroe?

Trinculo: Just what Lilly told me. That he was an asshole.

Jenny: Lilly told you that? What else did she say?

Trinculo: That she went to see him once. In Seattle.

Jenny: She went to see him? She went to see Monroe?

Trinculo: She said he was living in a dingy apartment downtown. And that he asked her for money.

Jenny: She's confiding in you, and Lilly doesn't do that often, believe me. This is a big deal, Trinculo. This is serious. (*She places her hand on his shoulder.*) And you have to put a stop to it right now. Tell her, in no uncertain terms, that you are not interested in her. She won't believe me. She just thinks I . . .

Trinculo: You what?

Jenny: (*Resumes walking.*) Never mind.

Trinculo: You like me?

Jenny smiles.

Trinculo: (*Twirls.*) She likes me. She really likes me.

Jenny: Talk to her.

Trinculo: If I do, will you sneak off with me tonight? After the show?

Jenny: (*Blushes.*) We'll see.

Trinculo: I'll do it. I'll do it tonight.

ACT I, Scene II

The Burtons' private beach on Waldron. An hour before sunset.

Enter Caliban, Stephano, and Trinculo.

Stephano: Tell not me. When the butt is out, we will drink water—not a drop before; therefore bear up and board 'em. Servant-monster, drink to me.

Trinculo: Servant-monster? The folly of this island! They say there's but five upon this isle; we are three of them; if th' other two be brain'd like us, the state totters.

Stephano: Drink, servant-monster, when I bid thee. Thy eyes are almost set in thy head.

Trinculo: Where should they be set else? He were a brave monster indeed if they were set in his tail.

Laughter from the audience. Peg steps out.

Peg: (*To the audience.*) I'd move your stuff a foot or two if you don't want to get wet.

More laughter.

Peg: Don't say I didn't warn you.

Stephano: My man-monster hath drown'd his tongue in sack. For my part, the seat cannot drown me; I swam, ere I could recover the shore, five and thirty leagues off and on. By this light, thou shalt be my lieutenant, monster, or my standard.

Trinculo: Your lieutenant, if you list, he's no standard.

Stephano: We'll not run, Monsieur Monster.

A surge of water hits the beach.

Audience members: Damn!

Get the blanket!

My pillow!

I thought that was part of the play!

Trinculo: Nor go neither; but you'll lie like dogs, and yet say nothing, neither.

Jenny: (*Whispers to Lilly.*) Did Trinculo speak to you earlier?

Lilly: About what?

Jenny: He said he wanted to talk to you.

Lilly: Tell me you didn't ask him to.

Jenny: Did he?

Lilly: Sure.

Jenny: Are you okay?

Lilly: Why wouldn't I be?

Peg: Shhhh!

Stephano: Lead, monster, we'll follow. I would I could see this taborer; he lays it on.

Trinculo: Wilt come? I'll follow Stephano. *Exeunt.*

Enter Alonso, Sebastian, Antonio, Gonzalo, Adrian,
Francisco, etc.

Gonzalo: By'r lakin, I can go no further, sir. My old
bones aches. Here's a maze trod indeed through forth-
rights and meanders! By your patience, I needs must
rest me.

Trinculo (*To Jenny.*) I was worried about the tide! Did it
ruin the scene?

Jenny: No, not at all. (*Whispers.*) So you talked to her?

Trinculo: To her, with her, and now, about her.

Jenny: What did you say, *exactly*?

Peg: Jenny! You're on in two minutes.

Offstage, a man with a long braided beard lifts a
three-foot wood tube to his mouth and begins to
blow.

Ariel: What the hell is that noise?

Peg: Not so loud, the audience will hear you! It's a didgeridoo. An ancient aboriginal flute made from the branch
of a eucalyptus tree and hollowed out by termites.

Caliban: I love it. It makes me want to dance naked in the
moonlight.

Ariel: Lord deliver us.

Trinculo: It sounds like a moose. Or a plane taking off. A moose bellowing in the hold of a prop plane while it's taking off. On gravel.

Peg: I told Raven he could play. It's eerie.

Ariel: If by that you mean my ears are going *Eeeeee*, then I would have to agree with you.

Alonso: What harmony is this? My good friends, hark!

Gonzalo: Marvelous sweet music!

Peg: Jenny! Lilly! Frankie! You're on.

Enter several strange Shapes, *bringing in a blanket; and dance about it with gentle actions of salutations; and inviting the King, etc. to eat, they depart.*

ACT II, Scene I

A bonfire on the beach after the play.

Captain Jack: Who needs their brewski topped off? Got a pitcher comin' round.

Ferdinand: I guess I'll try some after all. I don't want to be a party pooper. You said the beer was homemade?

Esme: Pretty much everything is, on Waldron.

Winifred: Brewed with real chocolate. Twelve percent alcohol.

Sally: I can tell. I'm seeing two Calibans. And one is enough for anybody.

Chad: Who's our designated driver, anyway?

Winifred: There are no traffic cops on Waldron.

Miranda: No clubs, either. And I always go out on opening night.

Dale: You are out, my girl. Way out.

Lilly: What are the cast parties like in New York?

Miranda: Crazy. One time I was dancing with this guy to . . . you know that song by King Arut? Jolly Rancher?

Lilly: (*Sings.*) She know I do anything that she tell me.

Miranda and Lilly: (*Together.*) So I say, suck me like a Jolly Rancher.

Peg: Girls! You're ruining a perfectly glorious night. After a wonderful performance.

Ferdinand: I liked the part where you told the audience to move their pillows and blankets because the tide was coming in.

Winifred: My pants are still damp.

Captain Jack: The lanterns were spooky at the end. That was a good touch.

Sally: It was beautiful.

A howl echoes toward the fire, followed by hysterical laughter and several loud thumps.

Chad: (*Calls out to the dark.*) What's going on out there, you burnouts?

Miranda: What *is* that?

Chad: Caliban and some local boys are having an excellent adventure. Jasper has some blue veil growing in bark mulch on his property.

Miranda: Magic mushrooms? Aren't those dangerous?

Chad: Only to us, if they come near. Would you like to try?

Lilly: Yes.

Chad: I wasn't asking you.

Miranda: Hmmm. I don't think so.

Peg: Chad, you should have told me. Don't you remember what happened to Puck that first year?

Chad: Caliban won't get lost here. No matter how often we tell him to.

Peg: He better not.

From deep within the woods comes the sound of the didgeridoo. A low moan growing high and echoing like a metal spring.

Captain Jack: You better hope that Raven abstained or we'll be hearing that racket all night long.

Dale: It was great for the show tonight, though. The Spirits were wonderful also, with their bare feet on the sand.

Peg: I'm thinking they should go shoeless from now on. Lilly, Jenny? What do you think?

Lilly: Whatever. Sounds good.

Peg: And the others? Spirits, speak!

Dale: Frankie went to bed about an hour ago.

Chad: I thought I saw Jenny here a while back.

Lilly: Where's Trinculo anyway? Wasn't he here a few minutes ago?

Dale: He might have gone to bed also. He seemed tired.

Lilly: Don't be ridiculous. C'mon, Miranda. Let's go find him and take him skinny-dipping.

Chad: (*Scrambles after them.*) Sounds like a plan!

Exit.

Sally: Well, that was a pretty good try, Dale. But Trinculo can probably look after himself.

Dale: It's not Trinculo I'm worried about.

Peg: I'm not sure about that scene when the girls pretend to be dogs. I thought it worked in rehearsal, but to-night I didn't like it at all. I think they need to be more ferocious.

Dale: I'll be sure and point that out to Jenny when she returns from bonking Trinculo in the woods.

Peg: It's none of your business whom she bonks, old man.

Dale: Ouch.

Ariel arrives from the house with a towel draped around his neck, his skin still damp from the shower. Followed by David, rubbing his eyes.

Ariel: Hello, fellow tricksters. (*Sits down on a log.*) Ahh, the lonely ones, around the fire. The poor souls who are not getting laid.

Captain Jack: I must've missed something. Who's getting laid?

Ariel: I'll never tell. (*Leans over and stage whispers.*) Lilly.

Ferdinand: But wait a second. Lilly . . .

Dale: Hi there, David. Take a nap?

David: Until Raven started blowing that damn horn again.

Captain Jack: (*To Ariel.*) Lilly was just here by the fire.

David: Yeah, she and Miranda just passed me on the path. (*Turns to Jack.*) It looked like they had one of your growlers with them, full of brew, in case you want to go get it back.

Captain Jack: (*Rises.*) I doubt there's anything left by now.

Ariel: Well, then maybe it was *Jenny* sneaking off behind the boathouse. She had long black hair and was making out with Trinculo, why wasn't I to think it was Lilly?

David: Hand me that pitcher, Ferdinand?

Ferdinand: Sure. I think there's a clean cup around here somewhere, too.

David: I don't need a cup. (*Drinks directly from the pitcher.*)

Peg: (*Looks at Ariel.*) Was that absolutely necessary?

Ariel: Don't blame me. You people are not always that easy to tell apart in broad daylight.

Yelling and loud laughter can be heard from the beach.

Lilly: (*Sings loudly.*) Scarcity and want shall shun you.

Lilly, Miranda, and Chad: Ceres's blessing is upon you!

Lilly: Are you out there somewhere listening? I looooove you!

Sally: I wonder if that means they found Trinculo?

David: It's more likely they found the bottom of the growler.

Peg: (*Sighs.*) Actors.

ACT II, Scene II

In the woods near the boathouse. A lantern swings from a tree. Two people lie on a blanket, bodies entwined.

Jenny: (*Giggles.*) You knocked over my beer.

Trinculo: *We* knocked it over. I'm not doing this alone, am I? Are you perhaps a figment of my imagination? (*Kisses her.*) A spirit?

Jenny: Oh, God.

Trinculo: That's what I like to hear.

Jenny: I shouldn't be doing this.

Trinculo: Doing what?

Jenny: Letting you slip off my tights, for one thing.

Trinculo: Letting me?

Jenny: (*Raising her hips into the air.*) Helping you.

Trinculo: There you go.

Jenny: Wait! Did you hear something?

Trinculo: Like what?

Jenny: An animal?

Rustling in the trees and leaves crunching. The long low tone of the didgeridoo can be heard in the distance.

Trinculo: No. Listen. It's that godforsaken instrument again. Wa wa wa.

Jenny: (*Singing.*) Woke up this morning with a wineglass in my hand.

Trinculo: (*Joining in.*) Whose wine? What wine? Where the hell did I dine?

Jenny and Trinculo: (*Together.*) Waaa waaa waaa.

Jenny: Wait. I heard it again. Shush.

Silence. Jenny sits up, her eyes shining wide in the reflected light of the lantern. Suddenly they are looking into the face of Caliban. He is shirtless, with wild hair and widely dilated pupils.

Trinculo: Caliban?

A branch snaps and Caliban *disappears. Minutes later the silence is broken by the sound of yelling from on the beach.*

Jenny: That was Lilly.
Trinculo: Are you sure?

*The yelling continues and suddenly, loud and clear,
they can both hear I LOVE YOU, TRINCULO!*

Jenny: I'm sure. (*Tugs her tights up past her waist.*) I'm sorry. I can't do this.

Trinculo: No, wait. I did speak to Lilly, Jen. Just like I promised. I told her I was way too old for her. That it would never work.

Jenny: Okay, then what did she say? You never did tell me that.

Trinculo: She'll get over it, Jenny. I promise.

Jenny: What. Did. She. Say?

Trinculo: (*Drops his head to stare at the ground.*) She said that guys always said that to her. At first.

Jenny: Terrific. (*Grabs her sweater from the ground and pulls it over her head.*) I'm going to put my kid to bed. I'll see you tomorrow.

Exits.

ACT III Scene I

Bright morning sunlight. Jenny is lying in the Burtons' guest bed where Frankie *and* Lilly *were to sleep.*

Frankie: Mom. Wake up! Lilly disappeared.

Jenny: (*Groggy.*) What? Did I fall asleep? What time is it?

Frankie: *Mom.* This is serious. None of the search parties could find her. The grown-ups are talking about having a Community Meeting. Winifred told me to wake you up.

Jenny: Search parties?

Frankie: Well, me and Dale looked all over the beach. Trinculo, Ariel, and Ferdinand went through the forest, and Jim Burton and Jack hiked all the way up to Point Hammond. Even Miranda hasn't seen her, and they're best friends.

Jenny: Well, she has to be somewhere, right? We're on an island that's only 4.5 miles around.

Frankie: We have a ton more shows! Why would she hide? Is she mad at Peg? Or Dale?

Jenny jumps out of bed and heads for the door, still wearing her costume from the night before. She grabs her bag on the way out.

Jenny: Where is everybody?

Frankie: (*Runs after her.*) By the fire pit.

Ten or twelve adults are talking in a group on the beach. Children of varying sizes are running around them, playing tag or pushing each other toward the water.

Jim: There are still a couple of houses on the east side of the island that we don't know about. The Strohs tend to be pretty late sleepers, though, and their place was still dark. I doubt she would have ended up there, though, since they have the new baby. No one answered at the Andersons and it looked like Luke had gone out fishing early.

Arthur: What about Marcus up near Disney Point?

Winifred: Oh, that seems unlikely. I love Marcus, but he is a little strange.

Jack: About Disney Point. She would know better than to go swimming around there, I hope? (*Turns.*) Oh, Jenny. Good. Lilly wouldn't swim in President's Channel or anywhere around there, would she? She knows about those currents, right?

Jenny: (*Slowly.*) She knows how treacherous the currents are.

Peg: Jenny, honey. You look like you've seen a ghost. This is Lilly we're talking about, remember? She'll turn up.

Dale: Probably in some boy's bed.

Jenny takes her cell phone from her bag and begins punching buttons.

Miranda: I've tried texting her about ten times already.

Trinculo: Did anyone look on Jack's boat yet?

Chad: I looked. She's not there.

Sally: She's not in the boathouse either.

Ariel: Or in the bathhouse.

Jenny: (*Snaps her phone shut.*) I'm going up to Disney Point.

Frankie: Wait a second. This is a mystery and we should do what any good detective would do, which is try to discover a motive. What does Lilly want?

Peg: Frankie, stop.

Silence.

Frankie: (*Looking around.*) What is it? What are you guys not telling me?

Arthur: Mmm. Jen? (*Clears his throat.*) When you're ready, I can walk you up there. To Disney Point. We can stop by Marcus's place on the way, just in case.

Jenny: I'm ready now.

Trinculo: Me, too.

Jenny: No. You stay here. Please. (*Turns to Frankie.*) And you, too. I've got one daughter missing, the last thing I need is to lose another one.

Ariel has been standing outside the circle, next to a tree, watching everything.

Ariel: I'll come.

Jenny: If you want to.

Arthur: This way.

Exit.

At Disney Point there is a cliff, covered with shrubs and jagged stones, jutting out over the sea. Jenny,

*Ariel, and Arthur stand looking down at the water of
the strait.*

Arthur: I'll call everyone to the schoolhouse, then. For a
meeting.
Jenny: Yes.
Ariel: You're sure that Marcus guy doesn't have her tied up
in a back room somewhere now? He was an odd one.
Arthur: He's harmless. (*Looks hard at Ariel.*) We're not big
on judging each other, here on the island.
Ariel: Touché. (*Brushes Jenny's arm with his fingertips.*) I
was just making light. I'm sure she's fine.

Arthur heads down the hill the way they'd come.

Jenny: What makes you think so?
Ariel: She's the original survivor, that girl. Stronger than
Frankie. Even stronger than you.
Jenny: Survivors get depressed, don't they? They get their
hearts broken.
Ariel: She didn't do it, Jenny. She's no Ophelia.
Jenny: (*Staring at the water.*) But how do you *know*? How do
you know which ones would and which ones wouldn't?

Pause.

Ariel: Because I was one of the ones who would. Tried, in
fact. More than once.

Jenny: (*Turns to him.*) Really? That doesn't seem like you.

Ariel: It doesn't seem like me *now*. (*Looks back out at the sea.*) The first time was when I was Frankie's age. Washed an entire bottle of aspirin down with Tang—do you remember that stuff? Had my stomach pumped.

Jenny: Oh, I'm so sorry.

Ariel: You're sorry about a whole lot of stuff, and only some of it has anything to do with you.

Jenny: I didn't mean . . .

Ariel: It's okay. I'm just a bitch. (*Gives her a sidelong glance.*) I'm not sorry about it, though.

Jenny: (*Smiles.*) Well, okay then.

Ariel: Okay.

Jenny: Shall we head back down?

Ariel: Yes, we ought to.

Back at the Burtons' a circle has formed around a young man in a knit cap, a long underwear shirt, and a pair of raggedy and patched canvas pants. He has a scruffy beard and earrings in each ear. The circle breaks open when Jenny and Ariel approach.

Peg: Mystery solved, Jen! It was Luke Anderson. He took Lilly to San Juan early this morning on his boat.

Winifred: Your parents thought you had gone fishing.

Chad: Lilly was the release, but what was the catch?

Luke: She asked me to. Was I supposed to say no?

Esme: You could have told someone.

Luke: So, I'm supposed to tell someone now, every time I go fishing?

Sally: You didn't *go* fishing.

Luke: Whatever. Anyway, it was barely even light.

Peg: Okay, people. Thanks to Lilly, we're about two hours behind schedule. Captain Jack has the boat ready. As soon as the first group loads up we can run them over to Orcas.

Trinculo: Can I do anything to help?

Dale: You've done enough, Tiger. Don't you think? And been done enough, as well, I should imagine.

Jenny: (*To Luke.*) You brought her into Friday Harbor? Did she say anything?

Luke: (*Glances from Jenny to the ground.*) She said a whole lot of stuff.

Jenny: I'm sure she did, knowing Lilly. But did she say she was going *home*?

Luke: She said she was going to make a bold declaration.

Jenny: A bold declaration? What does Lilly have to declare?

Luke: Her love.

· CHAPTER II ·

Ceres Loves Trinculo

The wind had picked up on the ride from Waldron to Orcas. When the second group arrived at the ferry terminal they found the first cupping paper coffee cups in their hands and huddling around the entrance to the Orcas Village Store. Peg got a table inside to go over her Waldron notes and Dale snapped the buckles on his guitar case open and hoisted himself, with a fair amount of huffing and puffing, onto a low stone wall that bordered the small patio and outside tables. Ferdinand and Ariel walked up the hill to look around. Chad pulled a Hacky Sack from his pocket and he and David and Sally proceeded to kick it around in the street. Each time it hit the ground they all would pause for sips from the coffee cups that they had lined up along the wall. Dale sat strumming the guitar and trying to remember the lyrics to "Wake Up Little Susie."

"We both fell sound asleep, wake up little Suzie and weep . . ."

"Wake up, little Suuuusie, waaake up!" sang Miranda and Frankie.

Dale frowned. "No, wait. Not yet. First it goes, it's four o'clock something something and we're in trouble deep . . ."

Trinculo came up beside Jenny, who was standing apart from the others watching the ferry make its way across to them from Lopez.

He inclined his head toward Dale and the girls. "They sound good together."

Jenny glanced at Miranda and Frankie and smiled. Frankie was clearly enjoying having the older girl's undivided attention without her sister around. Jenny avoided looking directly at Trinculo and pulled her phone from her pocket to check, once again, for messages. Nothing.

Trinculo brought his coffee cup up to his mouth with both hands. "Caliban, on the other hand, looks like he could use some sleep."

Caliban hunched in a plastic chair with a sweater wrapped tightly around his shoulders, staring off into the distance. An untouched powdered donut sat on a paper plate on his lap. He was wearing sunglasses though the morning was still shrouded in fog. His skin had a sickly green tinge.

Jenny stirred her coffee with the plastic straw. "Peg will be furious if he blows the performance tomorrow night."

Trinculo said, "Oh, no. Don't worry. He's a professional. He may have forgotten how to tie his shoes last night, but come tomorrow he will know his lines."

Jenny kept her eyes in her cup, watching her coffee settle back into a smooth, black disk.

"I'll talk to her again, Jenny," said Trinculo softly. "Whatever it takes."

She shook her head. "No. It should be me who does it." The coffee was cold, but she swallowed a mouthful of the bitter liquid anyway. "You know, I was standing here remembering the first real broken heart that Lilly had. She was sixteen."

Trinculo's expression was pained. "It doesn't get easier."

Jenny met his eyes for the first time since Waldron. "No. It doesn't." She looked from his face back out to the water. The ferry was close enough to see people standing on the deck outside. "She was crazy in love with this boy at school. A senior. And he loved her, too, I think. For a while. He was her first . . ." She kicked a small rock down the hill with the toe of her boot. "God, I shouldn't be telling you this. She would *kill* me if she knew I was telling you this."

The fog was breaking up in chunks, like snow melting off a car. Trinculo set his cup by his feet and fished his sunglasses out of his pocket. "Look. I don't want to come between you and your daughter, but I will say that you've both seen me naked and in, well, a somewhat compromised position."

"Shhhh," said Jenny and she touched her finger to his lips. She then added, in a pretty good imitation of Peg, "That is not to be spoken of."

Trinculo laughed. "I was just sayin.'"

Jenny continued, "The thing was, it was so *Lilly*. We went

to Marin to visit my sister, and while we were there she got an e-mail from the guy saying that he'd met someone on vacation with his parents. He didn't say he wanted to break up with her, what he said was he thought he might be in love with both of them at the same time." Jenny smiled. "And Lilly, being Lilly, knew right away that this was bullshit. She sobbed in my arms for maybe five minutes all out, and then she looked up at me and do you know what she said?"

Trinculo waited.

"She said, 'He couldn't go without sex for *two weeks*?' "

They both laughed.

"No one is going to pull anything over on that girl," said Trinculo, shaking his head.

"No." Jenny touched his arm. She could feel the warmth of his skin through the fabric of his waffled cotton T-shirt. "We should go down."

Trinculo looked at the back of her hand and then raised his eyes to her face. His look had such desire in it that she blushed.

"When will I see you next?"

"Tomorrow night. At Peg's."

"I meant alone."

Jenny chewed her bottom lip. "I don't know," she said. "Let's play it by ear, okay?"

The ferry captain let out a long, loud blast. The cars in line started their engines and from the Village and the market and the parking lot and the edge of the cliff, each of the Waldron travelers began to make their way down the hill toward the boat.

The actors followed the line of tourists off the ferry in twos and threes, separating at the landing as if an invisible string binding them together had been cut. They called out their good-byes to each other on their way to the market, to a restaurant for lunch, or in the case of Caliban, home to bed. Jenny and Trinculo touched hands so briefly before parting, and said so little, that it was unlikely that anyone noticed but themselves. Frankie climbed into the truck with her backpack clutched to her chest and her hair wild around her head. She had packed her toothbrush, Jenny thought, but it was unlikely that she had used it.

"You tired?" Jenny started the engine and looked over her shoulder, backing up and then out of her spot on Second.

Frankie nodded and leaned back against the seat. "It was great, wasn't it, Mom? The show?"

Jenny smiled. "*You* were great."

Frankie looked out the window. "Do you think Phoenix will be jealous?"

"I imagine she will." Jenny started to turn on Argyle to get to Cattle Point, their normal way home, but then on a hunch she kept going straight on Beaverton Valley Road. On the ride from Orcas to San Juan she had taken what Luke had said and turned it over so many times in her mind that it was polished smooth, like beach glass or a witching stone. A declaration of love?

"We have the Shaw and Lopez shows first," mused Frankie. "Maybe by the time we open on San Juan she'll have heard so much about it from everybody . . ." Her eyes were shining at the thought. "She'll have read about it in the paper even by then, and well, maybe Phoenix will be so used to the idea of me as an actress that it won't bother her. As much." She sat up straight in the seat. "Hey! I thought we were going home."

"Your sister told Luke that she was going to make a declaration of love. It just occurred to me where she might do that."

"Who is she in love with now? Elliot?" Frankie followed their progress past the neat rows of the apple orchard that produced hard cider in fall and winter. She turned to look at Jenny. "Are we going to the Big Rock?"

Jenny nodded. For fifty years the huge granite boulder on the corner of two heavily traveled roads had served as a kind of community billboard with ever-changing painted messages of loss, longing, love, and celebration. It was there that the Friday Harbor High graduating classes of many years in a row marked their passage. One year it had held a farewell message to the island from a German exchange student named Henrike and another time it had memorialized a young man who had died of AIDS. For one week it had sported a finely drawn portrait of a salmon. The American flag painted on it after 9/11 was painted over within twenty-four hours with a giant peace sign. The images might last for a week or six weeks, but sooner or later someone would always sneak over there and paint something new.

And it was always done in the middle of the night, thought Jenny grimly, pulling her truck onto the shoulder of the road.

Frankie leapt out of the passenger side before the engine died. She ran to the rock and stood in front of it, her mouth hanging open. "She loves *Trinculo*?"

Jenny took a few steps toward the rock, her boots crunching in the dried grass. It was about twice as tall as she was and ten times as wide and it was covered with dark green paint. There were just three words spelled out in white, and they were drawn in the bubble-shaped letters that Lilly had once used to advertise a car wash for her junior high softball team. *Ceres Loves Trinculo*.

Frankie turned with a look of disbelief. "But he's *old*!"

Jenny reached her hand out to touch the rock and pulled it back with green on her fingers. The paint was still wet.

"Where'd she get the paint, do you think?" breathed Frankie.

"It's from the shed." Jenny held her fingers up so that Frankie could see the color. "Remember?"

Frankie took a few steps back and crossed her arms over her chest. She stared at the rock with a mixture of admiration and dread. "*Everyone* is going to see this."

Everyone was right, thought Jenny, hopping back in the cab and waiting for Frankie to buckle up before she started the engine. Beaverton Valley Road was one of about twelve major roads on San Juan and it cut straight through the heart of the island. The rock was on the corner of Beaverton Valley and Egg Lake Road, where Dale and Peg lived. Where they were scheduled to meet the next night to review the Waldron performance and make some last-minute changes before the play opened on Shaw. Jenny did not know how long it would take the news of a mysterious new message on the rock to spread around the island, but by tomorrow night, at least, everyone who mattered to Lilly would have seen it.

Jenny chewed on the nails of her left hand and held the steering wheel with her right. She drove as fast as she thought safety permitted around the curves on Egg Lake and Wold, which in summer was about half as fast as you would think because of those damn scooter cars the half-blind tourists rented from the moped shop. Trinculo was right, heartbreak *always* hurt, no matter how old you were. But when you were almost eighteen, humiliation was even worse.

She turned onto their gravel road so fast that Frankie's backpack slid from the seat to the floor. In the settling dust of her own driveway, Jenny could admit to herself that she had been afraid of Lilly's wrath and that she had been afraid that exposing this new thing with Trinculo (Lilly might be prepared to call it love, but Jenny was forty-two and for her it was too soon to even think that word) would kill it, and that her fear had led her to do things that she was not proud of. She could admit all that, but what she could *not* do was let it continue.

She hopped down to the ground and headed for the house without even waiting for Frankie to collect her backpack and her jacket. She flung open the door and tossed her pack onto the floor by the coatrack. Her T-shirt was damp with sweat and she was grimy and exhausted from the events of last night and this morning. The muffin she had eaten with her coffee on Orcas was long gone, and her stomach growled. She ignored all that.

"Lilly!"

Seeing the words in Lilly's handwriting had clarified Jenny's purpose for her in a way that all her daughter's flirting and speculating and attention-seeking had not. She would tell her the truth about Trinculo. She would deal with her anger and disappointment. And then she would help her paint over that rock.

"Lil! Where are you?" Jenny flung open the door to Lilly's room.

"Waa? Oh. Hmmm. Hi." Lilly's head emerged from her bed in a tangle of blankets. Outside the fog and the breeze and the sun had given the morning air the freshness of spring, but all Lilly's windows were closed tight and her room smelled like patchouli, unwashed clothes, and ripe fruit. A bowl with a crust of leftover granola teetered on her night table along with a pack of clove cigarettes, a silver-threaded Indian scarf, and a book of Far Side cartoons, which apparently was what she'd been reading instead of *The Tempest*. She stretched a bare arm up toward the ceiling and peered at Jenny with sleepy eyes. "I didn't think you were home."

"We are now." Jenny stood with her hands on her hips. She fought the urge to ask Lilly what she thought she was doing leaving Waldron at the crack of dawn without telling anyone and how she had gotten out to Beaverton Valley without the truck. She reminded herself what she had to do. "Frankie and I took a little detour on the way home," she said, and sat down on the edge of the bed.

"Oh, yeah?" A smile played on Lilly's lips. She sat up, clearly proud of herself.

She was, thought Jenny, dancing happily toward a cliff. And it was Jenny who had to push her over.

"We saw what you wrote about Trinculo," Jenny said. She reached a hand out to push a lock of Lilly's hair off her face. The texture of the dreadlocks still surprised her when she touched them. It was so unlike the silk that fell from her baby's head when she was small. "I think you might want to paint it over. Before everyone else sees it, too."

Lilly fell back against the pillow. "You mean *you* want me to paint it over."

"He doesn't love you back, sweetheart."

"How do *you* know?" Lilly narrowed her eyes.

Jenny heard a rustle and turned to see Frankie standing in the doorway listening.

"Give me and your sister a moment alone, please."

Frankie moved off reluctantly. It did not sound as if she had gone far.

"I know because, well, he and I . . ." Jenny swallowed. She could tell her cheeks and throat were bright red. Her ears were burning. This was embarrassing and painful, she reminded herself, but it was nothing compared to what Lilly would feel if that message stayed up another day. "He and I are together," she said. "Kind of."

Lilly flinched. All the bravado leaked from her face and she looked stunned and very, very young. Her eyes filled with tears, but it was a moment before she said anything. "Have you had sex with him?"

Jenny took a breath. She knew that any normal, good mother would say *None of your business* if her child asked her that question. This was not a normal situation, however, and anyway, she was not so sure that she was a good mother. What she did know was that it was important that Lilly not nurture any false hopes.

"Not yet," she whispered.

Lilly's expression changed to horror. "But you're going to."

"Maybe," said Jenny. "Probably."

"Oh, my God. Oh, my *God*!" A sob burst out of Lilly and she flung off her blankets to reveal a man's tank top undershirt and a polka-dotted thong. She leaped out of bed and proceeded to hurl clothes around her closet as if she were a thief ransacking the place in search of jewels.

"Look, Lilly, I'll help you paint . . ."

"Don't even talk to me!" She held a flannel shirt to her chest and looked at Jenny with wild loathing. "I *hate* you!" She pushed past Jenny to the door.

Frankie was perched in the soft chair just outside Lilly's room. She glanced at Jenny with alarm as Lilly ran by, half-dressed, toward the shed. "You're not really together with him, are you? With Trinculo? You just said that, right?"

"It's been a long time, Franks, since there was someone I really liked . . ."

"Why would you do that, Mom? Why would you steal him from Lilly?"

"I didn't *steal* him, Frankie." Jenny took a step toward Frankie, her arms extended.

The look on Frankie's face stopped Jenny cold. It was an expression that allowed for no mercy. She remembered seeing it in her English teacher after she turned in yet another essay written on the bus after a night of partying.

Still, Jenny was unprepared for the contempt in Frankie's voice.

"Are you really that desperate?"

Jenny lunged forward and slapped her, hard, across the face. She did it fast, without thinking, like reaching out to grab a child's T-shirt to keep her from running into traffic.

Both Jenny and Frankie stared at each other in shock. A life lived with children was like a hike over changing terrain. Jenny knew that. Yet, in the flash of light that followed that thunderbolt of a blow, she understood something else, too. Some ground, when crossed, left you in a place you did not recognize. And once there, you could not go back.

Frankie pressed her hand against her cheek. Then she turned and darted out the front door after Lilly. Jenny heard the truck start up a few minutes later. She did not run out to tell Lilly to drive carefully, as she usually did, or admonish her to remember that this was their only vehicle. She did not call after the girls and ask if they wanted her help.

She stood in the hallway and shivered. The breeze jostled the wind chime on the front porch and, knocking against itself, it made a discordant music. Jenny remained still and listened for a long time before moving. She was alone.

Jenny spent the afternoon at the cabin without her truck and without her girls. She knew that if she called, Mary Ann would come over. She did not call. Nor did she call Trinculo, whom she suspected would hop in the Mini and barrel down her gravel drive at the smallest invitation. In spite of the sadness she felt, the image made her smile.

Jenny cleaned the kitchen and then she carried her cell phone into the sunporch. She set it on the small table beside her loom in case the girls called or sent a text. She began to weave the header on the fabric she had recently threaded, bringing all of the threads in order. She had dyed the yarn a rich burgundy, woven together with a soft green in a modified herringbone. Into the center she had woven a caracol, the pre-Columbian snail she had copied from a book on Mexican blankets. A small bowl of water sat on the table next to the phone and she dipped her fingers into it and carefully worked the threads with her hands. They expanded slightly. She dipped her fingers again.

She hadn't felt this way in quite a long while, she realized: wrung out and jangly and relieved and nervous. It was the feeling you woke with the morning after a long, wild party where you were not quite sure what you might have said or done. It was hard not to let her mind wander back to before she had hit

Frankie, before she had told Lilly about herself and Trinculo, all the way back to the blanket in the woods on Waldron. Trinculo's fingertips against her skin had been remarkably smooth. This was a man who spent his days on a stage, or a set, reading scripts, discussing characters, drinking wine. Most of the men she had been with, even Phinneas, who supplemented his pottery with odd jobs, had the cracked calloused hands of roofers and contractors and fishermen. They had kissed for the longest time. Faint voices traveled to them from around the fire. Waves pushed against the beach. A breeze moved the pine. His tongue had slid over her lips. She had opened her mouth.

Jenny counted threads out for the fringe and then divided each group in two. Frankie, in her infuriating, adolescent way, had asked if she was desperate. She *was* desperate, to tell the truth, a lot of the time. Desperate for fingers on her skin, a mouth pressed against hers, a long nap in some gentle man's arms after sex. She had been happy to find that weaving often soothed those longings, in a way that some of the other things she'd dabbled in, such as poetry and pottery, never had. It was the repetition, perhaps, and the slow accumulation of fabric under her hands. Sometimes she got up in the middle of the night to sit at her loom. It wasn't working today, though, for some reason. She threaded the needle full of wool through the fringe and her mind kept slipping back to that night. To Trinculo.

Jenny started when she heard the truck on the gravel drive. She had lost track of how long she had been at her loom. She stretched her back and went to stand by the door. She braced herself for Lilly's fury. Whatever Lilly brought, Jenny told herself she would be ready for it.

The door swung open and the girls sauntered in holding large Mint Mocha Chip Frappuccinos from the Starbucks at Roche Harbor. Splotches of green and white paint covered their shorts, tank tops, and hands. Frankie had a stripe of paint in her hair.

"Hi, Mom." Frankie ducked her head shyly, as if she were the one who had hit Jenny and she was waiting to be forgiven.

"Hi, honey." Jenny would be taller than Frankie for a year or two longer, but that was all. She bent to kiss the top of her head. Her hair smelled like smoke, sunlight, and salt. Jenny guessed they had taken a detour to the beach.

"Hey." Lilly acknowledged Jenny with a quick nod.

"Hey, back."

Jenny watched as Lilly removed her iPod from her pocket and stuck the buds in her ears. She flopped into the soft chair and swung her legs over the armrest. She nodded her head to the music and slurped her drink through the straw, just as she had so many times before. She took her phone from her other pocket and began texting someone, probably Miranda, without casting another glance in Jenny's direction. Jenny had expected fury, wailing, accusations, but here was Lilly offering none of the above. All she exhibited when she looked at Jenny was a peculiar flatness. It was disconcerting, to say the least.

Jenny followed Frankie into her bedroom and found her sitting at her desk, sorting her colored pencils. She sat on the bed.

"So what did you guys do?"

"We painted the rock." Frankie swiveled on her chair. "Lilly wanted to write something mean about you, but I convinced her not to. So instead we wrote *The Storm Is Coming* and then the date of the first San Juan show." She grinned. "It was my idea."

Jenny nodded. "Very clever." She smoothed the edge of Frankie's bedspread with the palm of her hand. "What did Lilly want to write?"

Frankie scowled. "Are you sure you want me to tell you?"

"No." Jenny smiled encouragingly at Frankie. "But tell me anyway."

Frankie twisted her fingers together. "She wanted to write *Jennifer Marie Alexander is a* . . . mmm . . . *is a slut.*" She looked up. "I don't think you are one, Mom. Really, I don't."

Jenny came to stand beside her. She rested her hand lightly on her daughter's hair. "I shouldn't have hit you, sweet pea. I'm so sorry."

"It's okay, Mom. I deserved it."

"No. You didn't."

Jenny bent her knees to look Frankie full in the face. Her blue eyes were still luminous and fringed with heavy lashes, but they were newly shadowed underneath from lack of sleep. A smattering of early summer freckles covered her nose. As any mother did, Jenny looked at her children at least fifty times a day. She looked to see if they were doing what they were supposed to (homework, or drying the dishes, or picking their socks up off the kitchen floor) and she looked to see if their clothes had holes in them or covered their body parts adequately and she looked at them, frequently, with a kind of buzzing awe that these *creatures*, these long-legged, opinionated, beautiful creatures had sprung from her own ordinary body.

Knowing her girls so completely, and loving them so much, it was almost impossible for her to look at them clearly. It rarely happened. Perhaps it was her own fatigue, borne of worry, or perhaps it was because of the sense that their lives were on the verge of changing abruptly and in significant ways, but this afternoon the light hit Frankie just right. Jenny was suddenly, just for a moment, able to see Frankie as she appeared in the world now, at thirteen, unencumbered by shimmering images of her as a nursing infant, a toddler in rain boots, a preschooler crawling into Jenny's bed in the middle of the night. She was able to see her daughter through the eyes of a stranger, a person who did not love Frankie, and she shivered. She was beautiful, yes, but no goddess. She was a mortal, trusting child.

"You *never* deserve to be hit," said Jenny emphatically. "Not by me. Not by anybody."

"Okay." Frankie looked down at her lap. "I don't want to talk about it anymore, if that's all right."

"Okay." She nodded toward the empty Frappuccino cup. "Are you still going to want some dinner?"

Frankie nodded. "I'm starving."

Jenny pantomimed the same question to Lilly.

"What are you trying to say?" Lilly removed one of the ear buds and raised her eyebrows.

"Are you going to be hungry for some spaghetti?"

"Don't worry about me. I'm fine." She fit the tiny white knob back into her ear and rolled the volume up.

Jenny could hear voices rising like spirits through the forest of Lilly's hair. "Do you want a million dollars?" she asked then, "and a Jaguar convertible? How about a plane ticket to France?"

Lilly shrugged her shoulders but did not remove the earphones. "Whatever. I said I'm good."

Jenny continued to look at her intently and, though Lilly was quite aware of her mother's gaze, she did not raise her eyes. In her right earlobe she had the two silver earrings, one above the other, that Jenny had given her for her fifteenth birthday. In her left, just an onyx stud. The line of her jaw, sparsely dusted with translucent peach fuzz, had grown sharper than it had been just a year ago, though the ladybug-size mole by her mouth was the same. It was like she was seeing a mirage, thought Jenny, or one of those optical illusions where the old woman turns into a young girl and then an old woman and back again. If she squinted, she could see her daughter grown, without the dreadlocks, sitting at a kitchen table somewhere paying bills.

Jenny bent at the knees until her face was right at the level of Lilly's. Even then, her daughter pretended not to notice her. She was pretty good at it, too. A born actress. Jenny reached out and plucked an earphone from the delicate shell of her daughter's ear.

"What do you want to study, anyway?" she asked. "In college."

Lilly stared. Jenny could almost hear the spell Lilly was wishing she knew how to incant. The one teenage girls through the ages had wished for. The one that made your mother disappear. "Entomology," she said finally, as if she suspected that the quickest way to get her mother to vanish was simply to answer the question.

"Bugs?" Jenny was amazed.

"Well, for organic gardening, you know. Integrated pest management." Lilly dangled the earphones in the air between their faces like a hypnotist's watch. "Do you mind?"

Jenny laid her hand on Lilly's leg. "Remember 'Immigrant Song'?"

When Lilly was about the age Frankie was now, before she had discovered Lil Wayne and Jay-Z, she had been introduced to Led Zeppelin by an older boy. Jenny had been surprised to find that such boys, with their black Stairway to Heaven T-shirts, Viking haircuts, and carpeted Econoline vans still existed in the year 2005 in the Puget Sound. Lilly had been surprised that her mother had heard of Led Zeppelin.

With Lilly looking at her as if she had lost her mind, Jenny sang, "We come from the land of the ice and snow, from the midnight sun where the hot springs blow."

At first it seemed like Lilly might not remember singing "Immigrant Song" with her mother all those years ago, their voices shaking the house.

" 'We sail our ships to new lands'?" Lilly added, unable in the end to resist the lure of the critic. "I mean, *puhleeze.*" She shook her head and fit the earphones neatly into her ears.

Jenny left her and went into the kitchen. She pulled a big silver pot out from the bottom cupboard and filled it with water. Stupid as the lyrics may be, she thought, Lilly had not, in fact, forgotten them. She thought of the time before Frankie was born, when that lanky, pierced, seemingly indifferent stranger was still her only, miraculous child, and set the pot on the stove. She reached for the last box of dried spaghetti and, not realizing it was open, scattered it all over the kitchen floor.

On her hands and knees gathering up dried noodles, it struck her that among the many things that new parenthood and first love shared was the feeling that what you were experiencing was entirely unique. The second time you fell in love you could no longer maintain the illusion that what you felt with your beloved bore no relationship to what the garbage man, or your school principal, felt with his. And after the second baby, you could no longer convince yourself that you could not possibly love a child as much as you did the first. You even started to suspect that perhaps your parents had been as giddy and ecstatic about you when you were a baby. For a lot of people, Jenny included, that could be unnerving.

By the time Lilly was born, Jenny rarely talked to her mother. She tried to imagine her mother lying in bed for hours looking at each part of baby Jenny's body, or kissing the soul of her foot or watching her sleep. If she had done those things, then what could have happened in the time between then and now, when she heard her mother's voice on the answering machine and walked into the other room without picking up the phone? Whatever *had* happened, could she keep it from happening to her and Lilly?

She glanced from the kitchen to Lilly, who was nodding her head, eyes closed, her feet swaying off the ground. She would soon be gone. She brushed the pasta lightly to get the dust off and dumped it in the pot. She looked again at her daughter, comfortably lost in her music and so far away in the world of her own heart, and felt a premonitory ping of loss.

CHAPTER 12

I Might Call Him a Thing Divine

Jenny and Mary Ann reopened the store after the three-day run of the show in Lopez Vineyard. It was midseason now and the island was swarming with tourists. The serviceberry bush behind Jenny's house was heavy with fruit, and every morning she and the girls woke to a cacophony of birds: robins, thrushes, flickers, towhees, waxwings, finches, chickadees, siskins, juncos, quails, crows, and others feasting and calling to their companions. In the three-day break before the first San Juan performance, Mary Ann had said she thought it might be a good idea for them to sell some stuff for a change, considering the fact that they both had to eat and for them, unlike the birds, serviceberries would not suffice.

Jenny answered the call of the front doorbell and spent a few minutes discussing the merits of a set of 1930s china with a woman from Portland who promised to come back later with her husband. She returned to the back of the store to find Mary Ann taking a rest from the inventory. She was perched on the chair with her feet on Jenny's stool reading the *San Juan Islander*.

"Peg's going to love this," she said. "The part about the *stark beauty of design and direction*. Good thing they didn't see her yelling at Chad and Miranda for messing up their makeup backstage."

"I'm glad they finally got together, though. The tension was killing me."

"It was killing all of us." Mary Ann lowered her feet to the ground. "Sit."

Jenny obeyed.

Mary Ann shook the wrinkles out of the paper and smoothed it against her lap. "I love this, too. Listen, as *Ariel adopts balletic poses*. How true is that? And," she raised her eyebrows at Jenny. "The *double-jointed Jester, Trinculo*. Is that accurate, would you say? Is he *double-jointed*?"

Jenny laughed. "None of your business."

Mary Ann looked her in the eyes. "May I ask about his intentions?"

Jenny grew serious. "Geez, I don't know. Go back to New York, I guess." She tried not to smile but couldn't stop. "Though he did mention something about auditioning for next year's show."

"Hmm," said Mary Ann. "That sounds like your kind of arrangement."

"What?" said Jenny. "A boyfriend who's never around?"

"You said it, I didn't."

Jenny chewed her lip. "You're right. I did." She pointed at

the paper. "Have you gotten to the part yet about the sweet-voiced spirits who are both earthy and ethereal?" She waved her hands in the air around her head. Being ethereal.

"Changing the subject, I see." Mary Ann dropped her reading glasses lower down on her nose and scanned the review again. "How is the other spirit doing, anyway?"

"Fine, I guess. Giving both me and Trinculo the cold shoulder. Basking in the adoration of the crowds."

Jenny suspected that she would have to force Lilly into some kind of heart-to-heart before she left for California. She wasn't crazy enough to think that Lilly's studied nonchalance didn't mask a whole mess of hurt, and besides, she had not yet had the opportunity to ask about her visit to Monroe. She comforted herself that they would have plenty of time to talk in the week before Lilly was to leave the island after the actors had gone.

"Oh, I'm not worried about Lilly. Frankie's the one I was asking about. Have you told her yet that her sister's leaving?"

Jenny shook her head. "It just never seems to be the right time. Maybe I'll do it when Phoenix arrives on the island for the show. She's scheduled to come Wednesday night. Frankie's been counting the days."

"Do you think she'd like to work in the store?"

"After school in the fall?"

"Whenever."

"Can you afford to pay her?"

"Sure. Well, not full-time or anything. But a few hours a week."

Jenny tilted herself off the stool and wrapped her arms

around Mary Ann. The skin on the older woman's neck and cheek was a bit damp from the warmth of the store. Hardly anyone had air-conditioning on the island and hot days like this were rare, even in summer. "That is so sweet of you. Really. I think she'd love it."

"And speaking of full-time." Mary Ann patted Jenny gently on the back. "Not much trade in antiques this afternoon, apparently. I think you should go home."

"I told Frankie I'd show her how to make succotash."

"Then go."

"We'll bring you some."

"I'll look forward to it."

Jenny hopped in the truck, tied her hair back with a rubber band she pulled off a bag of peaches from the farmers' market, and turned the key. As she had more often than usual lately, she found herself thinking of her mother. Jenny had fled from Sacramento when she was just a little bit older than Lilly. She had rarely given her parents, her mother with her meat loaf and taco nights and her carefully packed Easter baskets, a second thought. She had run and run and only now, when she was a mother herself, did she understand how often she still needed one. San Juan Island in the Puget Sound was a thousand miles from where she'd been raised. More than twenty years had passed and she was a world away from being able to talk to Helen Phillips, of Sacramento, California, the way she talked to Mary Ann.

The roads were as clogged as they got on the island. Tourists in rental cars inched along, reading signs from their car windows and hunting for parking spaces, and others on mopeds and rented bicycles risked their lives darting past the slow-moving traffic. When she reached Cattle Point Road and an open lane, Jenny hit the gas and the truck filled with lavender-scented wind. God how she hoped that this fight with Lilly wouldn't last long and that they would be able to talk and laugh with each other as they had since Lilly was small. She hoped they would, but if they couldn't, and Lilly in a few years' time was even further away from her than she was now, well, she hoped that she would meet someone like Mary Ann.

The counter was scattered with eggshells and the paprika was out, but the deviled eggs themselves, as well as the deviled-egg-eater, were nowhere in sight. Jenny glanced at the mess and the message light blinking on the answering machine and was tempted to ignore both and go sit at her loom. She had finished the wall-hanging and had begun something new, a scarf to go along with Lilly for when the weather turned cool, and imagined she could get a lot done in the quiet moments before Frankie returned from the pond, or the woods, or wherever she was. Her stomach rumbled and she glanced at her watch. Four-thirty. If they were going to have the succotash that night, as planned, they'd have to start pretty soon. Frankie had wanted to try it out once before Phoenix came, and if it worked well, she would cook it for her by herself.

Jenny stood for long moments in the center of the room, suspended between the gravitational pull of the loom and the kitchen. Finally, she decided that at least she should listen to the message on the machine. The phone sat on a table near an old walnut coat tree that was heavy with coats they wore daily and some they had not worn in years. Jenny pushed the Play button and lifted the sleeve of one of Lilly's old hoodies to her face. She smashed it against her nose and filled her lungs with the scent of patchouli and cloves.

The clicks and humming of the ancient machine were followed by a familiar voice.

"Hello, Jenny? This is Theresa. I won't keep you long because I know you're busy with the play and all, but I did want to call you and let you know that Phoenix won't be able to make it up to the island this week, after all. It turns out she'll be going with one of her cousins to Lake Chelan. I hope it won't be too much of an inconvenience for you. Okay, well, I wanted to get that message to you as soon as possible. Hope you're doing great. Bye."

Jenny, her blood running cold, stared at the speaker from which the disembodied voice had come. Get that message to *you*, Theresa had said. She hadn't even mentioned Frankie. She hadn't even said her name. It was clear that Theresa wanted to get the message to Jenny so that Jenny, at a safe distance, could break her daughter's heart.

Jenny twisted the fabric of Lilly's jacket in her fist. "The *coward*."

It was all she could do not to yank the machine from the wall and hurl it across the room. Instead, she picked up the phone and punched in Theresa's number. Her cell.

"Hello."

"Theresa, this is Jenny."

"Oh, hi. I just left a message on your machine, I . . ."

"Please, Theresa. Please let her come."

If Jenny had intended to yell at her, to say the thing to her directly that she had said to the empty room, the moment she heard the other woman's voice she realized that the main thing, the only thing, was that Phoenix come to the show.

"It's not a question of me *letting* her," said Theresa, defensive. "I gave her the choice, and it's Phoenix who wants to go to Chelan. I can't *make* her go to San Juan."

"Yes, you can, Theresa. You can tell her that her friend is counting on her coming, that it will . . ." Jenny's voice cracked here, and she brought her fist to her mouth, "that it will hurt her terribly if she doesn't come. You can make her."

"That sounds a little extreme, Jenny. It's just one show, after all."

"I'm begging you." Tears were running down Jenny's face now. She wiped at them with her sleeve. "I don't know what to do besides beg."

Theresa sighed. "You're making this so hard."

"Maybe if I talk to Phoenix myself," said Jenny. "Is she there?"

"No." Theresa's voice grew sharp. "She's not. And that's enough. It really is. I'm sorry." The phone went dead.

There was a noise behind Jenny. She turned. Frankie stood just inside the front door holding a piece of driftwood the size of her arm. Her hair was coming out of its braids, spilling around the collar of a jacket that looked like it had been thrown down on the sand and then put on again without a shaking.

She said, "Who was on the phone? Why do you look like that? Is Lilly okay?"

"That was Theresa." Jenny walked forward with one hand outstretched, as if trying to keep a deer from bolting. "Phoenix isn't coming, sweetheart. She can't . . ."

Frankie's face crumpled. It simply collapsed in on itself like a sand castle while Jenny watched. Jenny couldn't finish the sentence, and from the look in Frankie's eyes it was clear she didn't have to. They might never know whether it was Theresa who had proposed the trip to Lake Chelan or whether it was something Phoenix came up with free and clear. Either way, it wasn't that she *couldn't* come, it was that she *wouldn't*.

Frankie gasped and then sobbed. Jenny wrapped herself around her and rocked, trying to contain the storm of the girl's anguish within the bounds of her own ordinary arms. She writhed as if the air itself burned her skin. It seemed unlikely that such rage and grief could come from this small, compact package. It always had. Two, three, four times a day it used to happen like this. When first Lilly and then Frankie were small, any broken toy or squashed finger or bee sting would send them careening onto their mother's lap, shaking and wailing as if the one thing they truly loved, the only thing they could not live without, had vanished from the earth. Just weeks before Jenny had pitched herself against Frankie's sorrow near the downtown playground. After years of mostly blue skies, now here she was again, steeling herself for another storm.

Jenny pressed her lips against Frankie's wet cheek. The very core of her body ached. She contracted her muscles around her fear, fighting the long-forgotten sense that she could split straight down the center into two jagged pieces. Don't shrink from the pain, she could remember the midwife saying when Frankie was born. You won't break. This time she was not so sure. Back then when they were small enough to cradle and her children howled this way, she could not have predicted how their anguish would sound in her ears when they grew to almost her own size. She had not understood that, years later, when they cried as if their hearts were breaking, it would be because it was true.

The kettle whistled and Jenny took it off the stove and grabbed a mug from the cupboard. She carried a cup of chamomile tea into Frankie's room, where she found her lying on her stomach on the bed, staring at the wall. "Tea?"

"No, thanks."

Jenny set down her cup. "I'm getting ready to do a fringe on this scarf. Do you want to help?"

"No, thanks."

"What about tying up some yarn butterflies from the new alpaca? You're so good at that."

"No, thanks."

"Want to talk?"

Frankie shook her head.

"Okay, well, I'll be right out here in case you change your mind."

The phone on the table vibrated and Jenny lunged for it before it rang. She closed her eyes and said a little prayer that the caller was Phoenix, phoning to say that she had changed her mind.

"Jenny?"

Her eyes flew open and she felt a zip of electricity in her spine. The voice was Trinculo's.

"Yes. Hi."

He said, "You three sound surprisingly alike. And it would be just my luck to call and think it was you and ask how the most beautiful woman on the island was doing and to get, say, Lilly." Trinculo waited for a laugh, and when none came he said, "Everything okay?"

"Frankie's best friend backed out of coming to the show. She's crushed."

And here Jenny's own heart was fluttering. It was an organ that was capable of such betrayal. She slipped her hand under the loose linen blouse she was wearing and pressed her palm against her bare chest. It was as if she had caught a frightened bird in her hand.

"I could bring over some dinner, if you wanted," he said. "If you don't feel like cooking this evening, I mean. Maybe a barbecued chicken from the market? Do you think Lilly would let me cross the threshold if I brought a chicken?"

"Lilly would ignore you, most likely, just like she's ignoring me, but she's hiking on Mount Constitution, anyway. It's Frankie. I'm not sure she's up for company."

"I understand if she wants to be alone with her mom."

"I'd need to ask her."

"Of course."

There was a pause, and neither one of them set down the phone immediately. They sat quietly, listening to each other breathe.

Trinculo said, "What if Ariel came, too?"

Jenny glanced out the window. The wind had died and a subtle rose color had begun to seep into the sky. "He's not with Ferdinand tonight?"

"Apparently Ferdinand has begun to pray for guidance about their relationship."

"That doesn't sound like a good sign."

"It's not," said Trinculo. "I'm beginning to think that our Ariel has a weakness for fundamentally unavailable men."

Jenny knew what that was like. She shifted the phone to her other ear and stood up from the stool. "Well, if Ariel were to come, I think that would make the whole enterprise more likely."

"Okay, then."

Jenny listened to him calling out in the background. She could not hear the other man's answer.

"It's a go," said Trinculo, returning to the phone. "I mean, if Frankie says yes."

"Give me a second."

Frankie still lay on her stomach on her bed, staring straight ahead at the wall. She looked up when Jenny entered the room.

Jenny sat down on the edge of the bed. "What would you think if Trinculo came over with dinner for us tonight?"

She wasn't sure why she didn't say right away that Ariel was coming, too. Perhaps she wanted to see Frankie's reaction to Trinculo first.

"No, Mom. Please? After everything that's gone on with him and you and Lilly, I'd really just rather not see anyone tonight, okay?"

"Ariel would be coming with him."

Jenny watched Frankie's expression change. She did not feel any satisfaction at witnessing the conflict of emotions that she saw on her daughter's face but was not surprised either when she said, "Well, okay. If you want them to come. But, Mom . . ."

"What is it, sweet pea?"

"Don't have him stay, okay? When Ariel goes home, have Trinculo go home, too."

Jenny flushed and tried to squash the burst of annoyance she felt. "Geez, Frankie. They're just coming for dinner. Give me a break, okay?" She stood up from the bedside and left the room without waiting for Frankie's response.

Trinculo and Ariel arrived about an hour later with a chicken, a bottle of wine, and a bag of kettle corn. Ariel held this last thing, purchased from the ice cream shop downtown and known by all to be Frankie's favorite, out to her with a feigned expression of distaste.

She lunged for it. "Mom, can I eat some now?"

"Sure. But don't finish it."

"Heaven forbid," said Ariel, going for the corkscrew in the drawer.

Ariel had been a frequent visitor since his arrival with the leotard, and by now he had developed a routine. A glass of wine in hand, he would then head straight to the most comfortable wicker chair on the porch and sit in the sun until dinner. Frankie, of course, would follow him out.

Jenny noticed how her daughter brightened at the sight of Ariel, how her cheeks flushed and her eyes glittered and even her chest seemed to fill with air, tilting her shoulders back. After the news about Phoenix, the contrast between before and after Ariel's arrival was even more pronounced. Moments ago she had appeared to be fighting against gravity; suddenly she was two inches taller and rocking on the balls of her feet. Practical or not, requited or not, thirteen or not, Jenny had to admit that what Frankie was experiencing looked an awful lot like love.

As for Trinculo, it was some trick of memory that her mind, in his absence, could never retain how handsome he truly was. Even if it had been a half hour since she'd seen him last, she was always taken by surprise by his blue eyes and jaw and smile and the artfully tousled hair. Good grief, she said to herself now, even as her heart beat faster at the sight of him, an *actor*. What could she possibly be thinking?

"Here's the bird." He lifted the bagged chicken. "Caught it myself."

Jenny took it from his hands and carried it into the kitchen. "I didn't take you for a hunter."

He followed. "Well, it couldn't run all that fast. Those plastic things holding the ankles together slow them down quite a bit."

"Want a glass of wine?" Jenny poured them each one from the bottle that Ariel had opened.

"Thanks."

Their fingers touched when he accepted the glass. Jenny's desire was so powerful it was like nausea, like seasickness. She hadn't *promised* Frankie that Trinculo wouldn't spend the night, had she? She wished she could think straight.

Trinculo rubbed his palm against the stubble on his cheek and looked pointedly down the hallway. "Do you want to slip into your bedroom? Just for a brief chat?"

"Oh. Yes." Jenny glanced toward the door through which Ariel and Frankie had disappeared. Ariel was on the porch in the chair he liked. Frankie was pointing things out to him in the garden.

"Good," he said. "Because I couldn't eat anything, otherwise."

"Me neither."

The door closed behind them with a gentle click and they

tumbled on the bed together, knocking noses and chins, pressing lips against skin, loosening buckles, zippers, and straps. An image of Frankie flashed into her mind, the moment before she'd slapped her. *Desperate?* she thought. Oh, yes.

They ate outside on the porch. Trinculo and Jenny sat on the step and balanced their plates on their knees. Frankie carried a kitchen chair out the door and set it on the porch next to Ariel's. The last reds of the sunset lit wisps of clouds visible over the ridge. Jenny thought it might have been warm enough that afternoon for Lilly and the other hikers to have taken a swim in Cascade Lake after their climb. Even now, at sunset, it was cool rather than cold. Bullfrogs started croaking from their hiding places in the mud of the nearest neighbor's pond.

"It's like night and day," said Jenny. They were discussing the differences between the Waldron audience and the ones on Shaw. "You saw everyone in jeans and fleece and all, but they were sipping Chardonnay, *expensive* Chardonnay, instead of homebrew, and they drove home in Mercedeses and BMWs. To vacation houses worth millions of dollars."

Frankie said, "Jewel has a house there. Do you know Jewel? The singer?"

"Really?" said Trinculo. "Wow."

Frankie pretended not to have heard him and took a bite from a piece of bread.

"They're used to good theater," said Ariel.

"Oh, they are," mumbled Frankie, mouth full. Her selective hearing was demonstrably complete.

Trinculo drained the wine in his glass. "This *is* good theater."

Ariel met his gaze. "Of course it is."

Jenny said, "They loved it. You should have seen the paper."

"I never read reviews," sniffed Ariel.

Frankie wiped a bit of grease off her cheek with her hand and then wiped her hand on her T-shirt. "One more on Lopez. Then seven on San Juan. And then it's *over*."

Suddenly the little party on the porch was lit up by the brights from a vehicle pulling into the drive.

Jenny shaded her eyes and saw a blue 1979 camper van with a large steal-your-face decal on the side window. She looked at Frankie. "Is that Kevin driving Lilly home?"

Frankie shook her head. "It's Devoney's van now. She bought it from him last month."

"Oh, Lilly, is it?" Ariel stretched his arms over his head with an exaggerated yawn. "Well, it's getting late."

"Too late now," said Trinculo, under his breath, just as the back door slid open with a loud thump and disgorged Lilly in hiking boots, shorts, and a hoodie.

She met the chorus of good-byes from the van with some loud kissing noises and pretended to reel under the few pieces of additional clothing that were tossed at her from inside. Frankie, Jenny, Trinculo, and Ariel sat silently on the porch and watched her. Jenny was quite sure that Lilly was aware of them watching. When the van finally started backing out, she turned and shuffled toward the front steps, dramatically exhausted. She didn't look up until she was practically upon them.

"Oh. Hey everyone. I didn't notice you there."

Ariel crossed his legs and raised his chin with a snort.

Jenny set down her plate and stood up. "Did you have a nice hike?"

"It was a blast." She shifted the things in her arms, which looked like a battered daypack, a beach towel, and a couple of T-shirts or leggings and glanced casually in Ariel's direction. "Ferdinand was there. He is such a crack-up. I couldn't stop laughing all afternoon."

Ariel's spine straightened. He looked past Lilly into the woods as if weighing, for Frankie's sake, what it would be worth to him exactly to separate Lilly's head from her body.

Jenny appreciated his apparent restraint. "There's hot water, Lil, if you want to take a bath." She took a step to the side in order to allow Lilly to pass by them into the house.

Instead, Lilly leaned against the post on the porch.

Trinculo made a motion toward the house. "Do you want a chair?"

She looked at him coldly. "No, thank you."

Jenny wished she had filled up her glass and maybe had one or two more, for good measure. Lilly had not slowed down since the revelation about her mother and Trinculo; quite the opposite. They had seen very little of her; she rarely appeared in a group as small as this. She had been holding court at the after-parties on Shaw and sleeping on the beach on Orcas with an ever-changing crowd of young actors and islanders. She had been zipping around the islands like a first-time tourist, in fact. Doe Bay, Jakle's Lagoon, Lopez Village, Mount Constitution. Like a tourist, thought Jenny, or a girl who knew this summer on the island was to be her last.

"What part of Seattle do you live in, Ariel?" asked Jenny, wishing that Lilly would just go inside.

"My hovel is in the La Salle on Harvard Avenue, Capitol Hill."

Lilly said, "I know Capitol Hill. Ever been to Venom?"

Ariel rolled his eyes. "I know it." He looked at Frankie. "Honey, you are not missing anything," he said. "Believe me. That place is totally ghetto."

Lilly stood up straight. "It is not."

"Oh, but it is." Ariel smiled sweetly at her. "I can see where you wouldn't be able to tell, though, being a girl who's grown up in the woods."

"Jesus, Ariel!" Trinculo sputtered, after nearly choking on a sip of wine.

"Don't you Jesus me," said Ariel softly. "She's not after *your* girlfriend."

Lilly looked like she was about to spit. Jenny could not help but watch in fascination as Lilly's anger washed over her and then ebbed and then turned into something else entirely. Determination, with a hint of pride.

"I'm moving to California in two weeks."

"What?" Frankie had been looking at Ariel. When Lilly spoke she swung herself around.

"To Marin County, California." Lilly did not seem to be aware that Frankie was even there. She was talking to Ariel. "Maybe you've heard of it?"

"Well, that is *so* nice for you," said Ariel. "I couldn't be happier."

"What do you mean you're *moving*?" Frankie stood up and made a motion to go toward Lilly. Halfway there she stopped and looked at Jenny. "She's making that up, right?"

Jenny leaned toward her. "Sue invited her to stay with them and go to College of Marin."

Frankie shrank back. She looked from her mother to Lilly and back again. "You were keeping it a *secret*?"

Jenny said, "It never seemed like the right time to tell you."

"Your mother . . ." began Trinculo.

Jenny, Frankie, and Lilly all turned to him with the same look of warning. *Shut up.* It could not have been more clear if they'd said it aloud.

Ariel pulled himself up and collected the scattered glasses from the porch. He lifted Trinculo's directly from his hand. "It's been a *very* long day," he said. "And I really could not eat another bite."

"You're leaving?" Frankie looked positively stricken.

Ariel paused and then slowly lowered himself back down to the porch. "Soon," he said softly.

Lilly rolled her eyes and let her shoulders rise and fall with an elaborate expression of bored exasperation. "Well, I'll have to catch you all later," she said. "*I'm* going to bed."

Jenny reached out to touch Frankie lightly on the ankle. Frankie moved her leg away. She was suddenly at Ariel's side again. She was his shadow. "What do you mean by that, anyway? Ghetto?"

"Nasty." Ariel sipped his wine. "And cheap." He crossed his legs at the thigh and bounced his foot, on the end of which perched a maroon slipper-like shoe, on the verge of falling off. "You come visit me and I'll take you to see the *real* Capitol Hill."

It was fully dark now and above their heads a moth hurled its small body at the dim uncovered bulb that shed light on the porch.

Frankie rested her chin in her hand. Her eyes kept drifting in the direction that Lilly had gone, but she was clearly interested. "Like what?"

"We'll go see a show at the Egyptian Theater, for one. Stroll down Belmont Street. Sip cappuccinos at the Espresso Vivace Sidewalk Bar." He winked at Jenny. "Decaf."

"When?" Frankie's voice lifted. "When can we do that?"

"I'll take you to Cal Anderson Park for a picnic. There are the most delicious men there on weekends, playing Ultimate Frisbee. A little hairy sometimes, but with nice legs. They jump a lot. Like terriers."

Frankie clapped her hand over her mouth.

A faint alarm went off inside Jenny at the hope and eagerness in Frankie's voice.

Jenny cleared her throat. "Frankie, I . . ."

Frankie shot her mother a look that could have peeled paint off the hull of a boat.

"Fine." Jenny stacked their plates and stood up.

"I'll help," said Trinculo, hopping out of his chair and opening the door.

"Would I stay with you?" continued Frankie. "In your apartment?"

"I can imagine that you would look great dressed up to go dancing," said Ariel. "A little leather. A lot of black." He lifted the hem of her sweater. "Get rid of these old hippie rags, no offense."

The door swung shut behind them and the voices of Ariel and Frankie, the croaking of the bullfrogs, and the distant sound of the occasional car speeding up to enter the curve in the two-lane road at the end of the drive faded away against the hum of the refrigerator and the bright lights of the kitchen. Jenny carried the plates to the sink and turned on the water. Trinculo came up behind her and ran his hands over her rib cage until they met just under her breasts. He rested his chin lightly on the top of her head. She leaned back into him for just a moment and drew comfort from the unaccustomed feeling that her circle of arms was not the strongest in the house. She allowed herself the luxury of feeling small. And then, even though Lilly's room was silent and dark, she wiggled from his embrace and began to rinse the dishes.

The screen door swung open and Frankie, on her way to the bathroom, paused to look at her mother and Trinculo in the kitchen. Her eyes lingered on Jenny for a long while and the expression in them was not anger, as Jenny might have expected or even welcomed, but simple bafflement.

"Why didn't you tell me?"

"You were so sad and I didn't want . . . well, I was afraid that . . ." The words died in Jenny's mouth.

Frankie pulled her sweater tighter around her and disappeared behind the bathroom door.

"We should go," said Trinculo softly.

Jenny nodded. "I'll get you your coat."

· CHAPTER 13 ·

Set Caliban and His Companions Free

The outdoor stage in Roche Harbor was perched at the bottom of a grassy hill. Lights swung from the trees around the stage and the lawn was packed for Props to You's last free performance of the year. Tourists and islanders alike crowded the slope on deck chairs and blankets and even bed and couch pillows dragged from the faux New England time-shares and the big white Hotel de Haro. Many were seeing the production for the very first time.

Some, mostly islanders who had taken the cast members whale watching on their boats, or rented their extra cottages to them or served them meals at the Backdoor Kitchen or Vinny's, were present at the show for the second or even the third time. They sighed when Miranda walked onto the stage in her tattered gown and laughed when Trinculo first appeared, in anticipation of his pratfalls. The stars popped one by one into the sky above their heads and the audience watched the show rapt and melancholic because this was the end.

The last scene belonged to Prospero, and he took the stage alone. The stars glittered above Roche Harbor and, unnoticed by the crowd on the lawn, the water of the bay kissed the hulls of the boats in the dark. People gripped their blankets tighter around their shoulders and mothers shifted sleeping children on their laps. The wistfulness of a good portion of the crowd resonated with the actors who waited backstage listening to Prospero give his final monologue. Peg beamed. Chin in hand, Frankie sat on the barrel from which Trinculo and Stephano had drawn their imaginary wine. Miranda and Lilly distributed clove cigarettes to be smoked directly after the final bow. Tears ran down Caliban's cheeks. Ariel and Ferdinand hovered closely together to one side. Not touching, but closer than they had been in days. Jenny and Trinculo stood to the side and, partially obscured by the curtain, held hands.

> *Now my charms are all o'erthrown,*
> *And what strength I have's mine own,*
> *Which is most faint. Now 'tis true,*
> *I must be here confin'd by you,*
> *Or sent to Naples. Let me not,*
> *Since I have my dukedom got,*
> *And pardon'd the deceiver dwell,*
> *In this bare island by your spell,*
> *But release me from my bands*
> *With the help of your good hands.*

Gentle breath of yours my sails
Must fill, or else my project fails,
Which was to please. Now I want
Spirits to enforce, art to enchant,
And my ending is despair,
Unless I be reliev'd by prayer,
Which pierces so, that assaults
Mercy itself, and frees from all faults.
As you from crimes would pardon'd be,
Let your indulgence set me free.

Those who had seen the play most frequently and read it before then mouthed some of the words along with Prospero, who stood alone on the stage facing the audience for this last speech. But even those audience members, being spectators and not cast, missed some things that the inner circle did not. No one but those in the company had noticed that one of the spirits sang in a voice that was more wavering than usual and that she kept throwing despairing glances at the crowd as if searching for someone who was missing. They might have heard, because gossip on the island was a major pastime, that Lilly had had a crush on Trinculo or perhaps even that the Big Rock had sported a brief and mysterious message, but only those who were on or in back of the stage knew the details of the search for her on Waldron.

Many of those new friends and lovers (rumor had it that Caliban had had some success with the owner of the bead shop) would be around the fire at Dale and Peg's tonight. As was often true for the final party, there might be close to a hundred people trampling the grass, snacking in the kitchen, drinking and smoking by the cars, and singing around the fire.

For days afterward shopkeepers and innkeepers, whale watching captains and real estate agents, schoolteachers and pot farmers, would bump into each other and ask, "Were you there?" For most people the answer would be yes.

"Congratulations! Well done."

"Best year yet."

"You guys were magnificent."

"Thanks. It was a lot of fun. Thanks so much." Jenny returned to the circle around the fire carrying a cup of Peg's now-famous mulled wine that was full enough for her and Trinculo to share.

"I'm going home for a while," said Ferdinand, in response to Stu's question of where he was off to now that the play had ended. "To Ohio."

Ariel slung his arm around Ferdinand. "He's taking me home to meet the parents."

Ferdinand could not keep the look of horror off his face.

"Just kidding," said Ariel, letting his arm fall back to his side.

Stu turned to Ariel. "Well, what *about* you? What's next?"

"New York. I'll be auditioning for the part of Paolo in a new pilot." He smiled wickedly. "He's a Brazilian con man."

Trinculo said, "You can stay with me while you're there, if you want."

"In your bed?"

"On the couch."

Miranda reached her hand into the bag of sunflower seeds that she and Lilly were sharing. "I've got another Shakespeare gig. In Cedar City, Utah. I'll be Desdemona in *Othello*."

Chad looked at her with naked adoration. "You'll be great at that."

Lilly spit a shell into the fire. "I'm going to college."

"Really?"

"What?"

"Where?"

At least three people who had known Lilly since she was a toddler turned to her in surprise.

She raised her eyebrows. "Don't act so shocked, people. It's junior college, not Harvard."

"You could go to Harvard, if you wanted to," said Jenny. "You're smart enough."

Now it was Lilly's turn to look shocked. "Do you think so?"

Jenny nodded.

Lilly's backpack was propped against the wall in her room and nearly full already, though she wasn't scheduled to go for a week. Elliot had offered to drive her to Seattle and from there she would take the bus to San Francisco. Sue would drive her the rest of the way to Marin.

Sally said, "And I, alas, will return to slinging salmon steaks at the Backdoor Kitchen."

Caliban patted his stomach. "It's excellent salmon."

Trinculo leaned in and whispered into Jenny's ear, "I'll come back in a month if I don't get the part in that off-Broadway show. If I do, then I'll come just as soon as it closes."

"That would be great," she said aloud. To herself she added, *we'll see.* But the uncertainty of it did not bother her as much as she might have thought. There were some things about her pre-show life that she missed. The early mornings on her loom, the quiet afternoons in the store with Mary Ann, even the empty winter beaches. During the off-season there were always plenty of parking spaces on the streets downtown.

She craned her neck to peer behind Ariel. "Have you seen Frankie lately?"

"She was here a while ago."

Jenny circled the fire once and then headed for the house. She found Frankie lying on Dale and Peg's bed underneath a quilt, listening to Miranda's iPod. She sat down next to her and moved the edge of the quilt aside so that she could see her face. Frankie glanced over but did not take the ear buds out of her ears.

"Heeellloooo iiiiin theeeere." Jenny mouthed the words in an exaggerated pantomime.

Frankie removed the earphones. "Miranda's got an eighties playlist. Did you ever hear the song 'Venus' by Bananarama? It rocks."

"Hmmm." She stroked Frankie's hair. "What are you doing

in here, anyway? I thought you'd want to be outside with everyone."

Frankie looked past her mother to the wall, which sported a colorful and semiobscene Tantric wall hanging. She glanced away quickly. "They're leaving tomorrow," she said softly. "Well, everyone except for Gonzalo. He's staying till Thursday."

"I know."

"Everyone else."

Everyone, though she did not say it, meant one person primarily. Ariel.

"I know it's hard, hon." Jenny kicked off her shoes and swung her legs onto the bed next to Frankie. "Hey. I forgot to tell you. Eloise Harris, you know, the one who has the clothing store on Shaw? Well, she took ballet all the way through college. She even danced in a city company for a while, when she was young. She said she'd give you some lessons."

Frankie shrugged. "If you want."

"If *you* want. We'll go visit with her next week. When everything calms down."

Frankie did not answer. The bed was soft, and after the cold air and the warm wine it was tempting to crawl under the covers and snuggle up. Jenny scooted closer. Laughter rang from the kitchen and the brief flash of headlights from the field outside shined through the curtains into the room.

"Hey, Mom?"

"What, sweet pea?"

"I'd kind of like to be alone, if that's okay. No offense."

Jenny lifted her daughter's chin to look into her eyes. For

the first time in a long while, she felt like she did not know what was going on behind them. Frankie was sad, that was obvious, but there was more to it than simple sadness.

"Do you . . ." she started to say, but stopped when she saw a look of impatience flutter across Frankie's face. "Okay," she said, and kissed her on the cheek. "None taken. I'll be by the fire if you need me."

When Jenny returned to the fire, the crowd was two verses into John Hardy. Dale was strumming on the guitar and David was wailing away on the harmonica. Peg had even pulled out an old violin and was struggling to add some fiddle.

> *John Hardy stood in that old jail cell,*
> *a tear running down from his eye.*
> *He said, I've been the death of many a poor man,*
> *but my six-shooter's never told a lie, lie, lie.*
> *My six-shooter's never told a lie.*

"Oh, good," said Mary Ann when she saw her. "We're desperate for a soprano."

Jenny tried her best, but she didn't feel like singing. There was an ache inside her, just under her ribs, and though she was layered in a sweatshirt and fleece jacket, jeans and boots, she couldn't seem to get warm. She already missed Lilly in Marin, she missed Frankie in the house, and she, too, was already missing these people around the fire with whom she had spent the last weeks: practicing, eating, laughing, gossiping, playing Frisbee, and, finally, over the course of fourteen magnificent nights, performing.

She glanced at Trinculo's profile and remembered how she had first glimpsed him in the store with Ariel, and later around the fire, with Lilly. Oh, Lilly. Miranda, who had been so very pale when she arrived, was now the gold of a marshmallow that had been swept over the fire. Frankie was not the only one who was bound to feel a little lost tomorrow, when the ferry carried them all away. Jenny imagined that she, too, even worse than in years before, would wander the house in a daze and go through the motions at work in a kind of nostalgic fog. Trinculo leaned in to her, touching her fingertips with his own. She snaked her fingers through his. Yes, she decided, it would be much, much worse than last year. She and Frankie would have to console each other.

"It's my last night," whispered Trinculo.

Jenny feigned surprise. "Really?"

"Oh c'mon. What do you say?" She had not once, since they first got together on Waldron, let him stay over.

Jenny imagined waking to the sound of the birds and finding him still in her bed and she found she wanted that to happen. Very much. She said, "I can't. I've got a full house."

"I know."

He turned his body toward her and tucked his chin under her hair, by her neck. She laughed at the sensation of his burrowing, like a horse after a small golden apple. He raised his mouth to her ear. "Then what about sneaking off with me behind the barn. For old time's sake?"

She whispered back, "I'll go first."

Jenny left the fire circle in the direction of the barn. She knew that no one, certainly not Mary Ann or Dale, David, or Phinneas would be fooled when Trinculo left a few minutes after she did, but at least she would not have to be there to watch him go.

The party lasted until Peg told them all to go home. Although they were scheduled to see the actors off on the late morning ferry, Lilly hugged and kissed everyone with great ostentation before driving out to the lighthouse to hang out with some of her high school friends until the wee hours of the night. Frankie, being asleep, did not have to say good-bye to anyone. Jenny drove the car right up to the door of the house and David deposited Frankie, still wrapped in the quilt, in the backseat. The moon was full and so the dark island roads were illuminated from above and the porch steps, though they had forgotten to leave a lamp on, were bright with reflected light. Jenny led a groggy Frankie through the quiet house and pulled off her shoes before tucking her, fully clothed, into bed.

She glanced at her watch. It was one-thirty in the morning. The morning of the day they were leaving. Certain she would not be able to sleep herself, Jenny padded to the kitchen in her socks and poured herself a glass of wine. She dragged the afghan off the couch and wrapped it around her shoulders. She sat in the wicker chair on the porch, Ariel's chair, and listened to the bullfrogs' calls of lust and longing until the moon retreated and dawn started to lighten the sky.

· CHAPTER 14 ·

With Love in Her Eyes and Flowers
in Her Hair

Lilly's bed had not been slept in by morning, but that was not unusual. Jenny figured she'd make it to the dock to say good-bye to the actors. Or she wouldn't, and that would be all right, too.

Jenny was surprised, however, that Frankie did not want to take the ride into town to see the ferry off. She burrowed under the covers so that her hair was just a tangled nest on the pillow. "My stomach hurts."

Jenny pressed the back of her hand against Frankie's forehead. Her skin was cool. "Is it your period?"

"*Mom*." She turned away from Jenny and mumbled. "I think it might be my appendix."

"Which side?" asked Jenny.

Frankie appeared to hesitate and then raised the blanket and gestured toward her right hip.

"It's not your appendix," said Jenny. She made her tea and

brought her a hot water bottle. She cracked the window to let the fresh air in.

"I'm cold," said Frankie.

Jenny closed the window again. "I told Ariel and the others that we'd come see them off."

"And Trinculo."

"And Trinculo."

"You can go, if you want. Tell them I'm sick."

It was a cool overcast morning and Jenny had put on her winter jeans. She stood and gazed at the blanket-covered lump that was her daughter, considering. She dug both hands down deep into her pockets. With the tips of her fingers on her right hand, she touched cool metal.

"Hey, look what I found." She held the silver dolphin charm out toward the bed.

One eye appeared out from under the blanket. "Lilly gave me that," said a muffled voice.

"Here." Jenny dangled it over the bed.

"Put it on the dresser." Frankie pulled the blanket back over her head.

Jenny felt an unaccountable prick of loss as the charm left her fingers. "I'll be back in one hour."

There was no response from the bed.

It was a cold morning, it was a weekday, and a good fraction of the island's residents were hungover from the party the night before. As a result, there were just a few people assembled on the dock to see the actors off. Mary Ann was snug in a home-made patchwork denim coat with a sheepskin lining. Chad had dragged himself out of bed, knit cap, long underwear, and all, to see off a woman he was sure would have been the love of his life had she only chosen to give up her acting career and stay with him in his cabin. Dale and Peg were there, of course, unbrushed, unwashed, and looking as if they had both aged ten years overnight.

"Morning," said Jenny, and she gave Peg a quick kiss on the cheek. "Great party. You haven't seen Lil, have you?"

"Not since last night," said Dale.

Peg pulled her hair into a wiry bun and secured it with a pencil. "She'll turn up," she said. "If I know Lilly."

The actors stood around Peg in a half circle and several nod-ded their heads in agreement. By now they *all* knew Lilly.

"We'll pick the next play by February," said Peg. "And hold auditions in March."

"I'll be ready," said Trinculo.

"If I don't have a part in a series by then," said Caliban, "I may go back to teaching high school. Maybe I could get a job up here."

Peg laid her hand on his shoulder. "Well, Felix. That would certainly be a loss to the stage. You were wonderful in our show."

Felix. Jenny looked around at the others, standing with their backpacks and suitcases at their feet and thought: Lucy, Corbin, Lawrence. She turned to the man beside her and said softly, "Andre."

Andre, once Trinculo, touched her cheek. "At your service."

"I'll miss you," she said.

"I'll be back," he said, with a predictably good imitation of Schwarzenegger.

"Well, I'll be here."

The captain blasted the horn on the ferry, signaling that it was almost time to go.

Lawrence, formerly Ariel, lifted the handle of his wheeled suitcase and turned his body lightly toward the boat. Jenny stepped forward to wrap her arms around him.

Though there had been plenty of hugging, and more, in the last few weeks, she had never embraced Ariel before, and he looked almost embarrassed as she did so. Embarrassed but pleased, too.

He was a good six inches taller than she was and had to bend to lay his head on her shoulder. "You take care of my girl," he said.

"She would have come. But she wasn't feeling well."

"I get it, Jen. Believe me. You don't need to explain."

"Okay. Be well."

He turned to give a quick parade wave to all of them before he boarded the boat.

Lucy, once Miranda, kissed Jenny on the cheek. "She won't stay mad," said the younger woman, and they both knew she meant Lilly. "I promise."

Jenny hugged her tight. "Thanks, Lucy. I hope you're right."

One by one the others shouldered their packs or picked up the handles of their suitcases and wheeled them toward the boat. Seagulls circled overhead, looking for bits of waffle cone, sandwich crusts, or french fries dropped on the outside dining deck of the Fish Shack.

Andre hung back at Jenny's side. When his companions had all gone, he bent his head to give her a self-conscious kiss on the lips. Even now that Lilly knew about them, they had been hesitant about public displays of affection (the private ones were a different story).

Jenny closed her eyes as his lips touched hers and then, when she opened them, saw that he had already started across the wooden walkway. He was wearing the leather jacket he had worn the night they'd gone to the Colors Ceremony at Roche Harbor. His hair brushed his collar and his jeans came all the way down over his city boots. From where she was standing she could not even see a sliver of his skin, just his broad back growing smaller.

Jenny had been mentally preparing herself for this moment for days. She had been reminding herself that it would be hard on both Frankie and Lilly and that she would need to be attentive to them. What she had not anticipated was how her heart would constrict to the size of a walnut as she watched Andre go. Mary Ann, who was standing next to her, had tucked her arm through Jenny's. Before Andre reached the open mouth of the ferry, Jenny broke away from her friend and ran. She reached him just as the ferry workers were starting to give the all clear for the vehicles to board. They stood near where the bicycles were bungeed to the railing and clung to each other like teenagers.

Jenny was panting from the sprint. "Take me with you."

Andre tilted her chin so he could look into her eyes. "Really? Do you want to come?"

The boat would soon push off from the slip and Jenny, hearing the hope in Andre's voice, came quickly to her senses.

"I wish I could," she said. "But I can't."

Andre gave her the long, sad look of a kicked puppy. "Just what I thought."

She kissed him again. "Come back soon."

Just before stepping onto land, Jenny turned to look and saw him standing there still, his suitcase at his feet.

"Well, well," said Dale, as Jenny joined the islanders on the pier. "I believe that's the first time I've seen Jennifer Alexander chase after anyone."

"Except for Lilly," added Peg.

Jenny shot her a wry glance. "Well, I've certainly done a whole lot of that." She waved to her friends and gave the ferry one last, lingering look before she climbed into her truck and started the engine.

The road was dense with fog and Jenny slowed to let a covey of California quail cross in front of her. Mist clung to the trees alongside the road, and each solitary house she passed, some with hay in round bales dotting a nearby pasture, seemed to exist on its own shrouded island. When she reached the break in the trees and the reflectors that marked their road, she suddenly decided not to turn. Frankie was sleeping. She could go out to San Juan County Park, just for a few moments, and look at the sea. A few children from the campground were playing on the beach in spite of the cold. She perched on the picnic table and watched them climb over the lichen-covered rocks for a while before lifting her eyes to the horizon. The water was as calm as a fishbowl. In the mist beyond, Vancouver Island seemed to waver and then appear as if it had been created that morning for her alone.

Jenny returned to find Frankie sitting on Lilly's bed.

"Feeling better?" She brushed the top of her daughter's head with her palm and then, catching the expression on Frankie's face asked, "Is your sister around?"

"She took her stuff."

"Which stuff?"

Frankie's gaze traveled to the spot in the corner of the room where Lilly's backpack had stood for more than a week. Jenny's followed. The spot was empty. Jenny cast her eyes over the piles of clothes on the floor and the food wrappers on the night table. Lilly's room always looked like she had packed and departed in a hurry. "Did she leave a note?"

Frankie nodded and lifted her favorite article of Lilly's clothing, a beaded peasant blouse, from her lap. "She gave me this."

Jenny took the blouse, and saw the note attached to it. *Tell Mom not to worry cause I have bus fare. You can have this shirt as a going away present.* How Lilly, she thought then. Generous, but within limits. Even as she grieved, the implicit message would not be lost on Frankie, *but keep your paws off the rest of my stuff.*

Jenny was shaking, she realized, as she dialed Lilly's number. Furious. How like her also to leave before the actors did. To stage a mysterious departure of her own. How like her in both its drama and its thoughtlessness. Jenny's message was brief and to the point. *Call me now.*

The next number she dialed was Sue's. Jenny's sister had not heard from Lilly yet that morning, which didn't mean she hadn't heard plenty nonetheless.

"So who is this new guy, Jenny?" she asked. "The one that Lilly liked and that you got instead? Is he going to last, do you think?"

"I didn't *get* him, Sue. We're in a *relationship.*"

"You know what I mean."

"I don't, Sue. Not really," Jenny said, walking farther away from Frankie's door. "It's not important, anyway. What matters is that Lilly is on her way. I need her to call me as soon as you hear from her." She closed her eyes and took a deep breath.

"It's important to Lilly, clearly. And what about Frankie? How is she with all this?"

All what? Jenny wanted to ask. The events of the last twenty-four hours or my whole, entire life? Our lives?

"Frankie is fine," said Jenny, but even as she said so she found her eyes searching anxiously for Frankie's form in the next room. She wished that she were more confident that it was true.

Sue said, "What if Lilly doesn't want to talk to you? Do you want me to phone and tell you that she's arrived?"

"Thank you, yes. That would be nice of you." Why, oh why, she wondered, did she always have to sound like Lilly herself when she talked to her sister?

"Okaaay. Well, talk to you soon."

Jenny stood for a moment longer with the phone in her hand, willing it to ring or for a text to scroll across the screen. She could hear Frankie shuffling around Lilly's room, conducting an inventory of all the things that were missing. She could hear her neighbor mowing a path through the tall yellow grass with a bush hog. It was eleven on an otherwise perfectly ordinary day in August and she was scheduled to work at noon. She thought she ought to make Frankie something to eat before she left for the store. She cradled the phone in her hand like a polished stone. Then she dialed a number she knew by heart but did not call nearly as frequently as she ought to.

"Mom?"

"Jennifer!" Her mother set the phone down. "Arthur! It's Jennifer on the phone." She spoke back into the receiver. "Is something wrong?"

Jenny flinched. "No. Everything's fine." Less than ten words had been spoken and she was already feeling guilty and defensive. "You know, I'm actually dating someone for a change. A very nice man." How strange, she thought, that she still wanted their approval. Even—no, *especially*—now.

"That's wonderful, dear. What does he do?"

"I'm on, Jennifer. Your father's on the phone."

"Hi, Dad."

"What does who do?" asked her father. "Who are we talking about?"

"Jenny's new boyfriend. He is new, isn't he? Or have you been seeing him for a while now?"

Jenny considered the best way to describe Andre to her parents. It struck her that she had allowed so many gaps to develop in their understanding of her life that it would require more explanation than she had energy. Back when she was a girl living at home, they might have failed to grasp what things *meant* to her, her friends, the music that she liked, how she did in school, but at least they knew something about them. They had known the contours of her life if not the center. The very things, she realized, that she knew about Lilly now. For Jenny and her parents the balance had shifted when she moved away. And so it would for her and her daughter. Once Lilly was gone, the only details Jenny would know about her life would be the ones she chose to share.

"He was out here for the summer. He lives in New York."

"Oh, that's too bad." She could hear her mother's enthusiasm draining away.

"It's okay. Really. We plan to visit each other."

Her father cleared his throat. "Can you afford that?"

"Sure. Oh, hey, there was one thing I did want to mention." She had so longed to hear her mother's voice, but now all she wanted to do was get off the phone. "Lilly is on her way down to Sue's on the Greyhound. She might call, you know, if she gets stuck."

Her father said, "The *Grey*hound?"

"She can always call us," said her mother. "And, you know, so can you."

"I *do* know," said Jenny. She was about to hang up.

"So how's my little Fritzie girl?" said her dad. "Is she there? Can we talk to her?"

Jenny carried the phone toward Lilly's room. "Oh, yes. It might cheer her up."

"She needs cheering up?" asked both her parents at once.

Jenny backpedaled fast. "It's always a bit sad when actors that were here for the Shakespeare play leave. That's all. No biggie."

Business was brisk that afternoon and in spite of how distracted she was, Jenny managed to sell a dozen glass figurines to a Canadian couple on their honeymoon. Even as she rang up their purchase, her mind was traveling south on Highway 5, past Shasta and Redding and Weed, following the route of a particular Greyhound bus. She could almost feel the road under the tires. Jenny was a forty-two-year-old mother of two, but somewhere deep inside she was still the girl who had left home to marry a rock and roll musician. When a message from Lilly finally scrolled across her phone, Jenny found she understood both its contours and its melancholy center. *Goin2CA*. Jenny read the message and then, in her mind, she heard the familiar guitar chords that followed. Just as Lilly had known she would. She flipped the phone shut and wiped her eyes. "Going to California," she sang out loud to herself, "with an aching in my heart."

She wandered through the store for the rest of the afternoon without a clear purpose, unable to settle on dusting or inventory or any of the million other things she needed to do. She remembered the burst of adrenaline that sent her charging toward the boat after Andre and realized that that was nothing next to what she was feeling now. She tried to ignore the urgent voice that whispered in her ear, *go, go, go. Go get her back.* Peg was right; she had been chasing after Lilly for years. Was she just supposed to stop now? Could she? What an old liar that Prospero was, she thought as she traded her dust rag for a handful of peppermints. She unwrapped the first and popped it in her mouth. Prospero could have just stepped off-stage at the first scene and let Miranda and Ferdinand be together if he'd wanted to. It could have been a very short play. But he didn't. He made up this big long story about how the obstacles he placed in their path would make them *appreciate* each other more, yada yada yada. She bit down hard and the candy split in half with a satisfying crack. She knew the truth, though. He just didn't want to admit to himself that letting your daughter go, even when the time was right, was too damn hard.

CHAPTER 15

For I Have Lost My Daughter

Two weeks later, Lilly was a full-blown California girl and Frankie was a diligent, if glum, part-time employee at the antique store. Jenny lifted her hand to shield her eyes from the early evening glare. It was hard to believe that the days were slowly growing shorter. In early August the sun still didn't set until after eight p.m.

She said to Mary Ann, "I tried to arrange for her to spend an afternoon with Megan Bermann—you know Erica has a daughter that's in Frankie's grade—and she practically begged me not to call. I offered her ballet lessons and she asked me if she could have the money instead."

Mary Ann looked at Jenny with interest. "I think she's probably earned, what? A hundred or a hundred and fifty dollars by now. What's she saving for?"

"She says she's saving to go visit her sister."

Jenny tucked her arm through Mary Ann's. Their old routine had kicked in now that the play days were behind them:

They would walk downtown for quick glass of wine together before splitting up to go their separate ways. The only difference was that now they visited the wine bar Swirl instead of their old haunt on Second Street and they had a whole new collection of memories to flip through like snapshots when they got there.

"She says?"

"No. I'm sure that's what it is. She wants to go see Lilly." They found a table near the window and sat down. Jenny glanced through the glass and saw David walking across the street from somewhere—China Pearl probably, because he liked their fried rice—toward his car. She waved, but he had his head down and didn't see her. She turned back to Mary Ann. "She asked me to lend her a hundred dollars."

"Did you?"

Jenny shook her head. The smile that played on her lips was a complicated mix of embarrassment, regret, and self-deprecation. "Money's a little tight right now. I sent Lilly some, via Sue. Sue wanted to turn it down, but I told her the decision was Lilly's."

Mary Ann tapped her fingernails on the menu. Neither woman needed to open it anymore; they had its contents memorized. "Let me guess. Lilly kept it."

Jenny's smile was genuine this time. "Bingo."

"I could lend you some."

"No, Mary Ann. Thank you, but no." She toyed with the salt and pepper shakers. "I'm not sure I want her to go down to visit Lilly now, anyway. Those Bay Area kids can be a little wild."

"Lend? What am I talking about? I would *give* it to you."

Jenny reached across the table to place her hand on the back of her friend's. "I know you would."

The waitress paused next to them on her way to deliver an order. She was carrying an armful of plates loaded down with black bean quesadillas, bruschetta, and chicken satay. "A bottle of Chardonnay?"

Mary Ann looked at Jenny for confirmation. "A whole bottle?"

"No. Just a glass. I have to get home to Frankie."

Jenny paused on her front step to pinch some sagging blooms off the pansies and impatiens. It would be nine o'clock in New York and she wondered idly what Trinculo was up to. They had talked a few days before and so she knew he was reading for a part in a play about a man in a feud with his two brothers. It was a serious show, and he thought it would provide a good counterbalance to the comic roles he usually played. She wondered if he'd heard yet. She'd left a message on his voice mail that morning, but so far he hadn't returned her call. He was bound to be busy. Still, she didn't plan to call him again unless he called first.

"Frankie?"

Jenny picked up a sweater that had been knocked off the

coat tree to the floor and hung it back up. She kicked off her shoes and padded into Frankie's room expecting to find her lying on her bed with Miranda's iPod—a parting gift— wrapped around her head. The bed was made and there was no Frankie upon it.

"Honey?"

It wasn't dark yet. There was no need to worry. Even as she told herself those things, Jenny could feel panic rising in the back of her throat like bile. This didn't feel right. Something told her that Frankie was not walking in the woods or on the ridge. That she was not coming home at dusk.

Jenny's hand shook as she punched in the numbers on the phone.

"Hello."

"Mary Ann."

That was all Jenny could say at first. Her friend waited. Jenny could hear her breathing.

"Frankie's not here. She's gone."

"Downtown? I could give her a ride home when I come . . ."

"I don't think so." Jenny swallowed. "I think she might be gone, gone."

"No! What makes you think so? Have you checked her room?"

Jenny dropped the phone. She began frantically opening the drawers of Frankie's dresser and looking for favorite articles of clothing. As she did her pulse started, ever so slightly, to calm. Frankie's Hello Kitty T-shirt was still there, as were the pedal pushers with the patches on the knees that she'd sewn on herself. The silver dolphin charm was on the dresser where Jenny had left it, and without thinking, she stuffed it deep into the pocket of her jeans.

When she found the cap that Frankie wore almost the whole summer, the one that matched Phoenix's, she pressed it to her face and stifled a sob. Surely this was good news? She would not have gone far without her cap? Jenny lowered herself onto the side of Frankie's bed and sat there, thinking she should go back to Mary Ann on the phone. The sun had set now and the light was growing dim. Jenny did not turn on the lamp.

A thought crept up on her, and refusing to examine it too closely, as if it were a dog that would only bite you if you looked it in the eye, Jenny carried the cap into Lilly's room and stood in front of the open door of her closet. Lilly traveled light. Her flowered peasant blouse, the thin long-sleeved cotton shirts she layered under tees, the seventies-style wraparound gypsy pants that she'd found in the secondhand store were all things she'd left behind without appearing to think twice. The closet was dark and the room around Jenny was growing darker. Those things were gone.

She returned to the phone. "She took a bunch of Lilly's things with her."

"I'll be right over."

The wind knocked a tree limb against the house. The rooms were now cold, but neither woman made a move to light a fire in the woodstove. Jenny peered out the window at the swaying trees. It was dark. Frankie had camped out on the beach, she had been to Mount Vernon and to her cousins, she had visited her grandparents in Sacramento, but she had never, ever been by herself all night long.

"Call Sue," said Mary Ann, holding out the phone.

"She won't be there yet." Jenny looked at the clock on the wall. "If she took the ferry to Anacortes, she'd already be on the bus. If she took it to Seattle, she might still be on the boat."

"Let's call the police, then," said Mary Ann. "They'll search the boat. Alert the bus drivers."

"It would scare her to death to be picked up by the police. This is Frankie we're talking about." Jenny stood up. "I'm going to go after her."

"Jenny, sit down. For God's sake, think about it. You won't be able to catch up with her. And neither will you be here if she changes her mind and comes back."

"Oh my God." Jenny dropped her forehead to the table.

"Call Sue. She said she wanted to see Lilly. You should tell your sister to expect her."

"I know. I know," said Jenny, taking the phone from Mary Ann's hand. "Only . . ."

"What? Only what?"

"She took Lilly's things."

"You mean she took them to her?"

Jenny shook her head. "I don't think so. I think she took them to *wear*. And it sounds crazy, but you know how sisters are and, well, I don't think she would have taken them to wear around *Lilly*."

"But where else would she go?"

"I don't know."

The two women sat in silence and looked at each other over the table. Jenny reached for the phone and punched in Sue's number.

"Hello?"

"Sue. It's me."

"She's doing great, Jen. They went windsurfing today over by the ferry terminal. Apparently Lilly has a real talent for it."

"Frankie's gone."

"Gone?"

"I think she . . . she may be on her way to see Lilly. At your place."

"By *herself*?"

"Please go get Lilly. I don't care whether she wants to talk to me or not. Tell her it's an emergency. Tell her her sister is missing."

"One second."

Jenny could hear a TV on in the background. She pictured Lilly sprawled out on Sue's leather couch watching some reality show set in Orange County or New Jersey. Some thumps and scrapes later, the phone was in her hand.

"Frankie ran away? What did you do to her? Where did she go?"

"She didn't call you?"

"No. Was she supposed to?"

Lilly's voice sounded just the same, in spite of the wind-surfing, the recent past, and the distance. Jenny felt a rush of warmth run through her. She took a deep breath and was able, just barely, to hold back a choking sob. Mary Ann reached over the table and wiped the tears off her cheek with a faded dishcloth.

"Did she ever ask about how you got to Sue's?"

"Sure. I told her all about the bus and everything. Greyhound is kind of repulsive, but I met a really nice guy on the route. One of the drivers. But that was weeks ago."

There was shuffling on Lilly's end. Jenny glanced at the clock. It was now ten p.m. Where had the time gone?

"If she took the bus from Seattle," continued Lilly, "she'd probably be to about Tacoma by now. Do you want the number of that driver? His name is Bob and I have his cell."

Jenny carried the phone to the table and fished in the drawer for a pen and a scrap of paper. "Okay. Give it to me."

"206-323-4476. And Mom? Call me when you find her, okay?"

"Will do, sweetie. Bye."

Jenny hit the End button with her thumb and punched in the driver's number without laying down the phone.

"*This is Bob*," said a recorded voice. "*You know what to do and when to do it. Peace and love.*"

Jenny hung up and began to pace. "Lilly gave me the number for some driver on Greyhound. He didn't answer." She gave Mary Ann a look laden with meaning. "She had his cell number."

Mary Ann raised her eyebrows in response. "Call back and leave a message."

"You're right." Jenny told the machine that she was Lilly's mother and that Lilly's sister Frankie was missing. She said that they suspected she might be on the overnight bus to San Francisco. She asked Bob to please, please, please call her back as soon as he got the message.

Jenny had just finished packing when the phone rang. Not knowing how long she would be gone and not knowing how to plan for forever, she had thrown two changes of clothing into a backpack. She made sure to pack her toothbrush and a hairbrush because she figured a woman searching for a child would have better luck if she didn't look like a crazy homeless person. She knew when the phone rang that it was Bob and she knew that he would tell her that Frankie had not been on that bus. Still, she took the phone when Mary Ann held it out to her and she asked him anyway.

"Man, I'm so sorry I couldn't help out," said Bob. "If she's Lilly's sister, then I bet she's pretty cool."

"She's not cool," said Jenny. "She's thirteen."

"Oh, man. Thirteen. That sucks."

Mary Ann and Jenny sat at the kitchen table until the sun began to come up. Jenny's pack was at her feet and she had a half tank of gas in her truck, but there was no way off the island until the first ferry run. That was the thing about living on San Juan. You always had to wait for the ferry. At five in the morning she called Theresa and got her out of bed.

"Jenny! For heaven's sake. What time is it?"

"I need to talk to Phoenix, Theresa. Can you put her on?"

"She's asleep. It's the crack of dawn."

"This is an emergency. Frankie's missing. Please put her on the phone now."

The phone hit something hard, a table most likely, and there was shuffling in the background. Jenny could hear Theresa's exasperated voice and then a more muffled one from Phoenix.

"Hello?"

"This is Jenny, Frankie's mom." Of course Phoenix knew who she was, but she wanted to say it out loud. "She's run off somewhere and I need to know if you know where. Is there any way that she could be on her way to Mount Vernon? To visit you?"

"Why would she?" Phoenix spoke slowly, sleep still clinging to her voice. "We're going on a camping trip today. To Idaho. I told Frankie about it last time she called, so I don't know why she would come here."

"Do you know where she might have gone? *Think* about it, Phoenix. Think hard."

"Maybe she went to see Ariel? She said he invited her."

"She's trying to get to New York?"

"New York? She said Ariel lived in Seattle."

Jenny reached for her sweatshirt and hung up the phone in one fluid motion. She hoisted her pack onto one shoulder.

Mary Ann's expression held the question: What next?

"Frankie doesn't know that Ariel is in New York, and she's gone to Seattle to see him. I'm going to go get her."

"I'll stay here." She put her hand on Jenny's shoulder. "Do you want me to call the police?"

Jenny paused, picturing Frankie getting off the boat at Pier 69, where *The Clipper* docked, and asking directions to Ariel's apartment. Finding it empty and dark. She imagined her sitting on the floor outside his door, wondering what she should do. Perhaps she would call Jenny then, and ask her to come pick her up. Perhaps not.

"Yes. Call the police."

· CHAPTER 16 ·

The City

The first ferry left San Juan Island at six in the morning and was scheduled to arrive in Anacortes just after seven. Jenny put her truck in line and leaned against it while she waited, smoking one cigarette after another. The clerk in the gas station, some kid who had arrived on the island the year before, had raised his eyebrows when she asked for a pack of Camels. She had lifted her gaze from her purse and whatever he saw in her eyes made him look away. He slid the cigarettes to her over the counter.

She ground a butt under her boot and flipped open her phone. Reception could be spotty on some parts of the island. It wasn't unusual for her to miss a message every now and then. There was a call from David, she saw, and three missed calls from a number she didn't recognize with a 718 area code. She knew all the Seattle/Bainbridge area codes, and 718 wasn't among them. Before this summer, she hadn't known to recognize 212 as Manhattan, but now her heart lifted every time she saw it. 718? Most likely a wrong number, but she called it anyway, just to make sure. A woman's voice invited her to leave a message for Marcie or Rebecca. She flipped it closed again. Down the hill by the gift shop entrance a pair of seagulls fought over a discarded sandwich.

Frankie was five, maybe six, and they were reading fairy tales at school. The Pied Piper and Rumpelstiltskin, and the one about Henny Penny and the Fox. Her little eyes shining in the dark, she was starting to understand how vulnerable she was. No one bad is coming to our house, Jenny had said, and smoothed the hair on her forehead, and anyway, all the doors and windows are locked. *Go check*, said Frankie, before flipping over on her other side and secretly, as if Jenny couldn't see, sticking her thumb in her mouth.

What if someone hurt her? Jenny tried not to allow it, but her mind kept creeping back to the edge and peering over. She could see Frankie's beautiful long limbs, dusted with sand on Lopez beach, twisted and broken. Jenny's stomach wrenched and the nicotine taste mingled in the back of her throat with the coffee Mary Ann had forced her to drink before leaving. What if someone killed Frankie? She wondered if Lilly would forgive her if she decided to kill herself, too. Lilly was stronger than they were. Ariel had said so. She flipped her phone open again and tried Andre's number. She left her third message.

"Jenny."

She looked up from her phone to see a neighbor standing in the lot in front of her. "Hello, Stan."

"What are you doing up so early this morning?" Stan looked

like a man who had fished his whole life and lurked in dark bars, but really he had been an investment banker. Seventy now and with blue hands from poor circulation, he had retired and bought a place in Snug Harbor and a Carolina skiff.

Jenny swallowed. "I'm going to Seattle to pick up Frankie." Her voice sounded rough in her own ears.

"Well, say hello to her for me."

Jenny nodded and then climbed back behind the wheel of her truck. She would not get out of it again, not even on the ferry, until she had parked it on Boylston in Seattle, a block from Harvard Avenue. She was walking toward La Salle, a four-story brick box with an arched doorway, when her phone rang. She saw the 212 area code and her heart leaped into her throat. It had to be Andre. Finally, he was calling! She would pour her fears out to him and he would tell her that everything was going to be all right. He was a fine actor and he would make her believe it was true. He was a fine jester, too, but she didn't think even he could make her smile.

Instead, it was Ariel. "Jenny! Mary Ann called and said you were trying to get in touch with me. She said you'd left some message about Frankie running away. What's happened? Where did she go?"

"Oh, God, Ariel. I think she went to see *you*. I mean Lawrence. Sorry."

"Fuck, fuck, fuck. I shouldn't have said all that stuff about her coming to visit. She seemed so sad, though, the crazy kid. I thought it would cheer her up."

"I'm standing outside your apartment building."

"You're in *Seattle?*"

"Yes. At your place. Did Frankie know the apartment number?"

"Oh, my God. Oh, dear." Lawrence's voice trailed off. "God, I am such an utter fool."

"Stop it. Just tell me. Which one is it?"

"224. It's locked, though. There's no one in it."

"I'm going to go up and look anyway."

"Knock on the door at 227. The guy that lives there, Rufus, is a poet. He's an appallingly bad poet, and he's usually in there moping around. The walls are as thin as Madonna's panties, and so he hears *everything* that goes on in the apartments around his."

"Okay. Thanks." The door was propped open with a cinderblock. Jenny slipped in and found herself facing a row of rusty mailboxes packed full of advertisements for cheap sex and cheap food. "I have to go," she said. "Did Andre . . ."

"I haven't been able to get a hold of him," said Lawrence quickly, "his place in the city was broken into and he's been staying in Queens. I'll keep trying, though."

"Right. Okay. Thanks." Worry for Andre flitted through her mind and she pushed it away. There was no time for that now.

She reached the second floor and turned down the hall. "Please be there," she whispered.

There was a dim overhead light in the hallway outside of 224 but no girl sitting on the floor with her backpack on her lap. No Frankie. Jenny let out a moan of anguish. She felt like a passenger on a plane in the middle of a big storm. Falling from unimaginable height to unimaginable height.

Slowly, the door across the hall cracked open. A young man with heavy blond curls and a little soul patch under his bottom lip stuck his head out.

"Rufus?"

He opened the door wider. "Who are you?"

She stepped toward him and saw him step back into his apartment with alarm in his eyes. How must she look, she wondered? How wild and how desperate?

"I'm looking for my daughter. Her name is Frankie and she's just thirteen years old. She ran away from San Juan Island yesterday afternoon. Tall and skinny, with long black hair? Have you seen her?" Jenny's mind kept spiraling onward: She makes deviled eggs, she did her eighth grade history report on the Chelan tribe of the Salish Sea, she has a scar on her left knee from a roller-skating accident when she was nine, she . . .

"Yeah. I saw her."

"When . . . where is she . . ." It was all Jenny could do to keep from grabbing the young man and shaking the information loose.

"She was out here last night. Eight, maybe nine o'clock? Here to see Larry, I guess. I told her he wasn't around. He's in L.A. or New York or somewhere like that. She was pretty busted up. Apparently some street kid ripped off all her shit on the way over here."

"And you let her go?" Jenny's voice rose in disbelief.

"Was I supposed to keep her prisoner? Call the cops? I didn't know she was from somewhere else." His lower lip jutted out in a persecuted sulk. "I gave her twenty bucks. Twenty bucks is a lot of dough."

Jenny closed her eyes and forced herself, before opening them again, to unclench the fists at her side. "Did she say where she was going next?"

"Nah. When I went out to get some grub later, she was gone."

Jenny wasted no time getting from Lawrence's apartment building and the hapless Rufus to a place she thought might be able to offer some real help: the Seattle PD. She gave her name and reason for coming to the receptionist and then waited on a bench under fluorescent lights. She took the opportunity to, once again, check her phone. It was dark. She pushed the button to test and see if it still had any juice, and the time lit up. It was already two in the afternoon. She touched the time button again to make sure. Then she flipped open the phone and dialed Andre's number.

It rang three times and then the ringing was followed by click, and . . . quiet. She waited for the message directing her to voice mail and heard instead a wide-open-sounding silence with a background of . . . was that shuffling?

"Hello? Andre?"

More muffled noises. Then a deep voice that was clearly not Andre's. It sounded like a young person trying to seem older. "This is Andre. Who may I ask is calling?"

"Is your, um, father . . . ?" Jenny could not finish the question. It had occurred to Jenny suddenly to wonder if Trinculo might not have children of his own. The idea of him as a parent was intriguing. But could it really be possible that he had a son and had not told her about him? Maybe the person on the phone was a stepson from a much earlier marriage? She felt she knew Andre well after their weeks together on the island, but how could she be sure? They both had things in their past they had not discussed.

"Excuse me?" the voice asked. "*Excuuuuse* me?"

Jenny lifted the phone away from her ear. She could hear laughter on the other end.

"Mrs. Alexander?"

The officer standing in front of her had blond hair that was combed carefully to the side and a lightly freckled, boyish face. When he held his hand out to her to shake she saw that his nails were short and clean. A wedding ring gleamed on his finger.

He led her down the hallway to a desk and motioned to the squat wooden armchair beside it. "Please sit." He sat in the swivel chair and lifted a pad off the desk. "Florence tells me you have a missing child to report."

Jenny swallowed. "She's been gone overnight. She's somewhere in the city, without any money or anyone to . . ." Her voice broke.

The cop lowered his pad and looked at her with compassion. "I know this must be very, very hard. How old is your daughter?"

"She's thirteen."

He nodded.

"The first thing we'll do is enter her name and description into King County and national databases. We can put out an AMBER alert, and they'll show her picture on the news and to officers around the county. Do you have a photograph of your daughter with you, Mrs. Alexander?"

"Oh, God no, I . . ." Jenny's mind whirled. She could call Mary Ann and ask her to get one from the shoebox under her bed. She thought there was a recent school photograph in that pile. The drugstore had a fax machine. No wait, David had some photographs on his computer. He could e-mail one of them. "Let me call a friend. What e-mail should he send it to?"

The police officer reached for one of the business cards in his desk and handed it to her. She glanced at it. The name said Skip Arnold. *Skip?* Her baby's life depended upon a guy named Skip? She dialed David's number. He answered on the second ring.

"Jenny! Have you found her?"

"No. David, I need you to send a picture. The one you took of Frankie on Jasper's boat last spring." Jenny read the address off the card. Frankie had caught a thorne shark that day, she remembered. And the boat had been followed by a pair of Dall's porpoises halfway back to the harbor.

The cop nodded again. "Good. In the meantime, you can tell me about her. Distinguishing characteristics? Does your daughter have any visible piercings or tattoos?"

Jenny shook her head no.

"Does she have a history of being involved in drugs? Prostitution?"

"No," Jenny whispered.

The officer's tone was matter-of-fact. "If she left them behind, you'll want to confiscate your daughter's BlackBerry, cell phone, computer, anything that might give a clue as to whether she was planning to meet up with someone here in the city."

Jenny pulled her knees up to her chest and rested her boots on the edge of the chair. "She doesn't have any of that stuff. And I know who she came here to see. A friend of ours. Only he's out of town and now she's just . . . lost."

How could that be? Jenny asked herself again. Why hadn't she called?

The officer looked at her for a moment, considering. She wondered what his wife was like. Did they have children? Probably not yet, she thought. The ring on his finger looked new.

He said, "Well, one fifth of runaways return within twenty-four hours. The younger ones, in particular, don't usually go far." He dropped his eyes to the pad in his hands. "The thing is, runaways are not usually running *to* something. They're usually running *away*." He met her eyes. "Can you think of anything that your daughter, Frankie, right, that Frankie might have wanted to get away from? A boyfriend, maybe? Something else?"

Jenny shook her head. He would naturally expect Frankie to have been abused and unhappy, she realized. Most of the children he encountered probably were. He did not know

Frankie. He had not seen her nestled under a pile of coats on Peg's couch or reclining on the prow of a fishing boat. He could not imagine how cherished she was.

"You can call me if you think of anything. One last thing, there are no other friends or relatives in the area?"

Monroe, thought Jenny. Monroe, Monroe, Monroe. The word entered her mind and then lingered there like a hiccup.

"No," she said. "There's no one."

"Will you be staying nearby?"

"As soon as I get a room I'll call and let you know where I am."

"There's a La Quinta hotel right around the corner. You might try there." He stood and offered his hand.

She had trouble pulling herself out of the chair. It was as if her legs suddenly would not hold her. The young man bent slightly and with a hand under her elbow, he helped her to rise.

Jenny waited until she was sitting in her truck again in the parking lot to dial Lilly's cell phone. She could see the Space Needle in the not-too-far distance, but the area immediately around the station was full of dilapidated warehouses and empty parking meters.

Lilly answered the phone immediately. "Did you find her?"

"No." Jenny rubbed her face with the palm of her free hand. It was going to be a hot day. She had only been in the city for a few hours, but already she felt greasy. "Listen to me. Did you ever tell Frankie where your father lived?"

"When did you . . . How?"

"It doesn't matter now, Lil. What matters is *did Frankie know*?"

"I might have mentioned it," said Lilly. She added quickly, "Though I seriously doubt she would go there. She didn't remember one thing about him. And besides, I told her what he was like."

What was he like? Jenny wanted to ask. What was he like to *you*? Instead, she said, "Give me the address."

"I don't remember the exact number. But I can describe where it is." Lilly paused.

Jenny wished she could see her daughter's face. She wanted to scan it for information about her meeting with Monroe. About what it had meant to Lilly to finally see her father after all those years.

"Mom? Hold on, Aunt Sue wants to talk to you."

A car door slammed near her and Jenny jumped in her seat. A few spaces away an elderly Asian woman climbed out from behind the wheel of a rusted Buick and began a slow and deliberate march toward the glass double doors at the entrance to the police station.

"Jenny?" Sue's voice was high and panicked-sounding. "I phoned Mom and Dad. They're waiting by the phone in case Frankie calls."

Jenny could picture her parents in the small front room of

their house in Sacramento. Her mother would be perched on the edge of a chair, pale and full of frightened speculation. Her father would wear a hole in the carpet with his pacing. They would not understand why Jenny had not called them first.

She took a deep breath. "Thank you."

Sue cleared her throat. "Look, Jen. Lilly wants to fly up to Seattle this evening. I know she wants to help, but I don't think it's a good idea to . . ."

"Good," she said, "I'll send you the money for the ticket." Where the money would come from she had no idea, but she felt a rush of relief anyway. They would look together, she and Lilly. They would find her.

Sue hesitated. "It's not that. I just think . . ."

"Please put Lilly on the phone again."

"Lilly?" Sue called and then, quickly into the phone she added, "I'm praying for Frankie."

"What?"

Jenny had barely gotten the word out and Lilly was back on the line.

"Mom?"

Jenny heard more shuffling and suspected that Lilly was carrying the phone into another room. Her suspicion was confirmed when she said, "Aunt Sue did not just say what I think she said, did she? That she was praying for Frankie?"

"Let it go, Lil." She took a deep breath. "Now where did you see your father?"

"Here's the thing." Lilly cleared her throat. "I won't tell you where Monroe lives unless you promise, *promise*, not to go see him until I get there."

"Excuse me?"

"I've got a seat on a plane from SFO to SeaTac. It gets there at six p.m. tonight. We can go after that."

Jenny fished a pen out of her bag. "Okay. Give me the directions."

"Okay that I'm coming or okay that you won't go without me?"

Jenny wiped her eyes with the back of her hand. She wondered if Lilly, somewhere deep inside her, carried the memory of how she had once had set a stuffed dog, cheaply made with appliquéd eyes, on a sobbing Jenny's lap. How she had sung a song about a peanut getting squished on the railroad tracks. *Whoops, peanut butter.*

"Okay to both," lied Jenny.

CHAPTER 17

Monroe

Her first ever words to Monroe had been so banal, she still cringed when she tried to recall what they were. Something about the beer in the cooler being colder than the bottles in the fridge.

She remembered exactly what his reply to her had been, though. He had said, "I'm having a panic attack."

Jenny was balancing a paper plate full of salad on her lap. She set it down on the deck in alarm. "What should I do? Do you want me to call someone?"

He shook his head. "Tell me a story."

That was the moment she should have walked away. Jenny turned on her side on the Motel 6 bed and watched through the open door as a bedraggled family unloaded shopping bags and a cooler and beat-up suitcases from their trunk. He needed help, he was *panicking*, for God's sake, and what happened was that he told her what to do. Not *I want you to tell me a story*, or *It would help if you told me a story*, or even *Please tell me a story*.

He looked at her with those blue eyes, Lilly's eyes, and a rigid jaw and said, *Tell me*. And she did. She *liked* the way he told her what to do. He said it in a way that let her know what she was *going* to do and there was, at that crazy unsettled time in her life, some relief in that. So she told him about how one year when she was about ten and Sue was twelve, their parents took them on a car trip to Wyoming and they stopped at some hot springs. Their dog, a border collie named Rascal and the only dog she had ever loved, hopped out of the car, bolted toward the springs, dove in, and *never came up*.

Monroe laughed.

Jenny stared at him. She had told this story before a number of times. Usually it was greeted with expressions of sympathy or gasps of horror. Never laughter. At the time it happened she thought she would die of grief.

"We stood there for a long time," she continued. "At least twenty minutes. Me and my sister were crying and my dad was poking at the water with a stick."

Jenny laughed then, too. She offered it all up to him without a second thought: her imperfect family, her sister's and her own sadness, her younger self. And this being Monroe, he took it. She left with him that night, and less than a year later they were married.

And that was what Jenny remembered. Not his face. Not the name of the friend who had brought her to the party or the names of the people whose party it was. What she carried with her even to this day was the way it felt when he touched her. As if her life, her *real* life, was just then about to start.

Jenny pulled herself up off the bed to hunt for a phone book. She looked in the *A*s but could find no Monroe Alexander. She would just have to look for him, using Lilly's memories as her guide. But first she dialed Mary Ann's number. When there was no answer there, she dialed her own.

"Jenny, any word?" Mary Ann sounded as exhausted as she felt.

"No. Lilly's arriving tonight to help me look."

"Oh, good. I'm really glad to hear that. Dale and Peg were by earlier. Phinneas has called at least ten times. Chad brought the halibut by for Frankie, and then when he found out what happened he didn't leave for an hour. He's ready to come back at a moment's notice. Everybody is, Jen. Anything you need, you just say."

Jenny rubbed her thumb against a burn spot on the rickety bedside table. It had been left by a cigarette, no doubt. She remembered the pack of Camels in her coat pocket but had no taste for them anymore. Just thinking about smoking made her gag. The hotel room door had been open long enough so that the air had lost some of its musty smell, but the extra light did nothing for the atmosphere. Looking at that room, she felt lonelier than she had in a very long time and she couldn't help thinking that what had happened to her that summer had something to do with it. If she hadn't felt Andre's arms around her before, would she be missing them now?

She said, "I need you to sell my loom."

"What?"

"Anna Birnbaum on Shaw once said she'd give me $700

for it. Tell her that if she'll give me $850 I'll include three boat shuttles, two leash sticks, eight bobbins and, let's see, eight extra heddles."

"Jenny, why?"

"This room costs $70 a night. Lilly and I will have to eat, and I have no idea how long we'll have to stay here. I saw a place downtown where you can wire me the money."

"For goodness sake, don't sell your loom. You saved forever for that. I'll send you the money. How much do you need? $850? $900?"

"No, Mary Ann. Thank you, but this is what I want to do."

"It's no trouble, really. I have three times that in . . ."

"No." Jenny pressed the phone tightly against her ear. It was either that or throw it with all her might against the terrible reproduction of a watercolor of Pike Place Market that hung on the wall. "I love you, Mary Ann, but you either call Anna Birnbaum or I don't want you to be in my home when I return."

If she allowed herself to, she could picture the older woman's eyes filling with tears. The way her jaw, already lightly padded, softened when she was wounded. She pushed the image out of her mind. The stalls in the watercolor were purplish blue. The water was gray blue behind. The pavement stones, slick with rain, were tinged aqua. It was all blue, blue, blue. All of it.

"Okay, Jenny," whispered Mary Ann. "I'll call Anna Birnbaum. Good luck."

"I need it."

The building in which Lilly had found Monroe was in North Seattle, near Aurora Avenue. Jenny found a parking spot in front of Family Pawn, and when she noticed a couple of young guys standing in a doorway noticing *her*, she rolled up the truck windows. The truck wasn't worth much, but she needed it to get around. She reached over to lock the passenger door before getting out onto the curb. She didn't usually lock the truck and so had to remind herself to hold the grip down while she shut her own door, too.

She followed the numbers of the avenues to 97th and then took a right, keeping her eyes open for the four-story brick building that Lilly had described. Jenny walked with her hands in her pockets. She tried to picture Lilly traveling this same sidewalk a year or two before. Would she have brought someone with her? Probably not. She would have come alone.

She followed Lilly's directions to the corner of the building where she'd said Monroe lived. The carpet in the hallway was inky with grime and beer and other liquids too vile to contemplate. She could hear a TV set playing loudly behind one of the doors as she passed. On the door that might have been Monroe's she saw a drawing of some kind of African queen: long profile, headdress, soft, full lips. Underneath the drawing was the stenciled name Alicia. Jenny stood and stared at it for a long time before knocking. This was the first floor, far right corner, facing the street, which is what Lilly had described. Could this Alicia be a girlfriend of Monroe's, she wondered?

A wife? It had not occurred to her until now that he might have other children. She wiped her palms on her jeans and knocked.

She was just about to turn away when she heard some shuffling from inside. A young black woman in a bathrobe opened the door just a crack. Her hair was covered by a shower cap.

"Hi." Jenny smiled, but the woman's expression did not change. "I'm looking for Monroe? Monroe Alexander? Does he still live here?"

"Cross the hall," the woman mumbled, and closed the door.

"Thank you." Jenny swallowed and turned around.

Monroe's door was unmarked. She stood in front of it for what seemed like a long time but was really only a few minutes. The door she had first knocked on cracked open again and the woman peeked out.

"He's in there," she said. "You got to knock loud, you know, cause he takes some shit to get to sleep. Those tweakers upstairs are just too damn noisy."

With the other woman watching, Jenny knocked hard, *one two three.*

She started to turn away, her heart thumping hard in her chest, when the door opened. Suddenly, there stood Monroe in front of her, close enough to touch, his hair shorter than she remembered it and tousled from sleep. He still stood slouched forward as if he was trying to protect his heart with his shoulders, but his arms and chest were padded with muscles he had neither cultivated nor needed as a guitarist in a rock band. He was wearing a thin white T-shirt and loose green army pants that were buttoned but not zipped, the belt hanging open as if he had just thrown them on to answer the door. She did not say anything while he looked at her. She watched recognition creep over his features in a trajectory that went from half-asleep, to disbelief, to surprise.

"Jennifer?" He rubbed the hair on the back of his head with his palm, mussing it up further. "What the fuck?"

"Sorry to barge in on you," said Jenny. *Sorry*? She remembered what Ariel had said and cleared her throat. "Frankie is in Seattle somewhere and I'm trying to find her. I thought she might have been here."

"Fra . . . Come in." He stepped aside for her to enter the apartment.

Jenny ducked past him into the room. There was a sagging blue couch and a leather chair. A small coffee table. A television. The kitchen took up about a fourth of the front room. She stood with her arms crossed on her chest.

"Sit down." Monroe dropped onto the couch and pointed at the leather chair.

Jenny lowered herself down into the chair. There were a few magazines on the table, a can of beer, a plate with some crumbs. No cigarettes. No ashtrays.

"Did you quit smoking?"

He nodded. "About two years ago. I had a heart attack, can you believe it? At forty-five? I almost bought the farm."

Jenny couldn't take her eyes away from his face. The arch of his eyebrows. The blue eyes beneath. His jaw, nose, mouth.

How had she misremembered his face so completely? It wasn't Lilly he resembled, but Frankie. He, or rather she, was the mirror image.

"So what's up with the kid then? Did she run away?"

"Not really." Jenny pressed her eyes with the pads of her fingers. "I mean, she's here in the city somewhere, but I don't think she wants to stay away." She glanced up and couldn't help but get lost for a second in the pools of his eyes. They were so, so familiar. She said softly, "I don't understand why she hasn't called."

He stood up. "Do you want a drink of water? A soda?"

When Jenny shook her head no, he came back with a small white cardboard box and set it on the table next to her. "A scone or something? A cookie? I work at the bakery on Twelfth. Shift starts at one in the morning, but I get to take home pastries that are more than a day old."

She was prepared to say no, but as soon as the pastries were set beside her Jenny realized she had not eaten anything since the night before. It was almost three in the afternoon and she was starving. She bit into a scone. "Have you seen her, then?" she asked through a mouthful. "Have you seen Frankie?" She held her hand under her chin to catch the crumbs.

Monroe stood up and walked into the kitchen. "Don't you think I would have told you right away if I had?" His voice held a touch of irritation. "Here." He handed her a plate and sat back down on the couch. "Have you called the cops? There are a lot of street kids in this city and some of them, man, they are bad news."

Jenny wiped her mouth. "I was there this morning."

"Want something to drink?" asked Monroe again. "I've got some Sunny D in the fridge." He gave her a sheepish look. "Wouldn't make you drink the water in this dump. Who knows what the pipes are made of."

"Sunny D would be great. Thanks."

She brushed the crumbs off her fingers and looked around the apartment. The paint was chipping in places and the Formica on the counters looked a bit warped, but it was better than some places she'd seen. The couch was draped with a bright Mexican blanket. There was even a struggling houseplant in the corner. Monroe was clearly making an effort. She called, "Did Lilly ever come to see you?"

His back was turned so she could not see if his face registered any surprise at the question. By the time he appeared next to her chair with a glass, his expression was mild and friendly.

"Yeah. Bout a year and a half ago, actually." He handed her the drink. "Good-looking girl," he said. "Like her mom." The spot he chose on the couch was closer to her chair, and when he leaned forward his face was less than a couple feet away from her own. "Has a mouth on her, though, that one." He rubbed the whiskers on his jaw. "Can't say I blame her. I've been a pretty shitty father." When he glanced up at Jenny, his eyes were shadowed with the same thick lashes that Frankie had. "Wish I could've done better."

"She's a smart girl," said Jenny. "Funny, too."

He nodded. "You're a good mother, I bet."

Jenny focused her eyes on the wall behind his head. *You will not*, she told herself. *You will not cry.*

"You look great, Jen." Monroe rested his hand ever so gently on her thigh. It could have been a gesture designed to comfort her. Or not. "I'm glad you came by in person, though. I'm not sure I would have recognized your voice if you called."

"It's been a long time," whispered Jenny. She dropped her gaze to stare at his hand. It was about the weight of a child's folded-up sweatshirt, but deeply foreign after all the time that had passed. Strange, but not altogether without an element of comfort. "And these last twenty-four hours have been . . . Well, I've cried so much I've made myself hoarse, I guess . . ."

He gave her an appraising look. "You always did cry a lot."

Around Jenny's body, the temperature dropped. Where moments before her senses had been groggy they now started to pelt her with information. She could hear the cars outside on the busy avenue. The carpet smelled of mold. The leather seat was sticky against her back. Her skin prickled with goose bumps and her stomach twisted in rejection of the scone and the syrupy liquid she had drunk. It was as if a spirit had floated through the room, or perhaps even Juno, goddess of marriage, and stroked her on the cheek. Though long *melted into air, into thin air*, she still had enough power in her touch to wake Jenny from her reverie.

Jenny stood up and reached for her bag. Monroe drew his hand, his whole body back, and looked at her with surprise.

She looked down on him as if from a great distance away. "Take care of yourself, Monroe."

He jumped up and followed. "What's your number, then? Where are you staying? How am I supposed to get a hold of you if I find Frankie?"

She took in his rough, whiskered jaw, the lips she had once kissed and allowed to kiss her, the thick black hair and wide-set blue eyes. She looked hard at his face for one last time, and this time she did not see Frankie or Lilly. She saw only Monroe.

"Here," she said, fishing in her pocket and handing him the business card of one Skip Arnold, detective with the Seattle Police Department. "Call this number if you find her."

She left him reading the name on the card and walked out into the bright sunlight.

CHAPTER 18

Lost Children and Animals

Jenny drove back toward downtown and found a parking space out in front of a Victorian house on Queen Anne. She sat on the curb with her feet in the gutter and dialed Officer Arnold's number, which she had memorized before handing the card to Monroe.

"Well, Mrs. Alexander, your daughter was definitely on the ferry that arrived last night from Friday Harbor into Pier 69. *The Clipper*, as you'd suspected. Apparently she bought a round-trip ticket, which, in my view, is excellent news."

Jenny lifted the hem of her T-shirt to wipe her eyes.

"Are you there? Mrs. Alexander?"

"Yes." Her voice was more of a croak. "I'm here."

"Okay. Well, that's the good news. The bad news is that she hasn't tried to use the second half of the ticket yet. We can tell that from the security tapes. So, she's still here in the city somewhere."

"There's a chance . . ." Jenny cleared her throat before continuing, "that my ex-husband might call. I gave him your number. His name is Monroe."

"He lives here in Seattle?"

"Yes."

She did not need to see his face to know that he was putting that information together with what she had said to him earlier about there being no other friends or family members in the city.

"Okay," he said finally. "We'll watch for his call."

A silver-haired man in a Lexus stopped to look at Jenny's old farm truck before heading slowly down the street. Jenny stood up.

"Oh, Mrs. Alexander? One last thing."

Jenny's heart leaped. "Yes?"

"Frankie wouldn't have cut her hair, would she?"

"I don't think so. Why?"

"There were some reports of a new girl at one of the squats in the University District, where a lot of the street kids hang out. She had short hair and a scar over her left eye."

"Frankie doesn't have a scar."

"I'll call you if we turn up anything else."

"Thank you."

The airport was packed with travelers in shorts and flip-flops dragging huge wheeled suitcases behind them. An exhausted-looking woman with a shoulder bag walked toward security leading two small children by the hand. Jenny watched her until she could no longer see her or the kids.

And then suddenly, there was Lilly. One beloved girl in a stream of anonymous travelers, walking fast, the straps of her backpack covering the straps of her tank top, her skirt brushing the ground. She saw Jenny before Jenny could lift her hand or make a move toward her. She wrapped her arms around her mother before Jenny's knees buckled and she could fall.

"We will so totally find her, Mom." Lilly rested her hand on her mother's shoulder. "I promise."

Jenny wanted so badly to believe her. They walked arm and arm to the truck. "We can go drop off your stuff and then I don't know if it's a good idea," Jenny stopped at the light and glanced over at Lilly, "or a really bad one, to walk downtown where a lot of the kids are." She couldn't say the word *street*. Just kids.

"I thought we were going to go see Monroe." Lilly, Jenny noticed, did not say going to see *Dad*, or even *my father*. Just *Monroe*.

"I did that already."

"Mom! You promised."

"It's done, Lil." She glanced over at her daughter. She was not surprised to see in Lilly's face a touch of relief. "He hadn't seen her."

Lilly chewed her lip. "Did he say anything about me?"

Jenny smiled. "He said you had a mouth on you. But of course, we both knew that."

"He said . . ." Lilly's back straightened with outrage. "Well, I won't even tell you the things that he said."

Jenny held the wheel with her left hand and rested her right gently on Lilly's arm. "It's done, baby. Really. Done."

Lilly nodded and looked out the window. "Okay."

"U District?" Jenny turned and followed the signs for I-5 and Seattle.

"Sure."

It was close to eight p.m. now, but the line of traffic heading out of Seattle was still steady. The lights in the city had begun to pop in the dusk and the sky had one last streak of orange in it that was fading fast.

Lilly flipped open the glove box and began to fish through the odds and ends inside: random maps, flashlights, a takeout menu from the Chinese restaurant in Friday Harbor. "Didn't you used to keep candy in here?"

"There was an old Snickers bar." Jenny glanced at her watch. "I ate it about two hours ago."

Lilly forced a small smile. "Figures."

Jenny said, "We'll get you something to eat."

"No hurry." Lilly pulled her knees up on the seat and wrapped her arms around her legs. The toes of her now-bare feet poked out below the hem of the skirt. "I'm not mad at you anymore, you know. About Trinculo."

Jenny's face burned. "I shouldn't have . . ."

"There are *way* better guys in Marin. Bankers. Movie stars."

Jenny gave her a sharp look and this time, Lilly's smile wasn't forced. "Just kidding."

"Lil, you've got to stop that running around with different boys all the time. I'm serious now. It's not good to . . ."

"I will," said Lilly softly. "I mean I *am*." She glanced over at Jenny briefly and then looked out the window. An eighteen-wheeler pulled up alongside them with Cascade Farms written on it in cursive. "I guess I was just kinda bored. At home." She dropped her feet back to the floor of the cab and slipped them into her sandals. "I think it's great, actually. About you and Trinculo."

Jenny avoided looking at her. "I haven't spoken to him since Frankie disappeared." She merged right toward Exit 169 and the University of Washington, glad that she could concentrate on her driving rather than the expression on Lilly's face.

"Did he break your heart? That *asshole*."

"I'm sure there's a good reason why he hasn't called."

Jenny's mind flashed to the mysterious laughter she'd heard on his end when she called from the police station and she experienced a moment of doubt. She pushed it out of her mind with an image of him sitting beside her on a rock after they had climbed Mount Finlayson. The peak of Mount Rainier stood jagged against the sky and a large navy ship inched its way through the sound like a toy boat in the tub. He had told her about being engaged when he was in college in Boulder. It had ended, he'd said, when he had changed his major from business to theater.

"Practical girl." Jenny had stretched out on the rock to look at the sky.

"No doubt," said Trinculo, and he had lifted her shirt to trace her navel with the tip of his finger.

Beside her, Lilly raised her eyebrows. "Oh please, Mom. Spare me." She shook her head in disbelief. "What a total douchebag." She added, "You know, I never knew why you and David split up anyway. It was fun when he used to come over and bring his harmonica."

"Let's not talk about my love life, okay? We have more serious things to think about."

They parked in the U District and walked through Ravenna Park for what seemed like miles, scanning benches and abandoned patches of grass. They peered into the faces of people as they jogged by, stopping to chat with dog owners, students, and a park worker who was emptying garbage cans near some tennis courts that had fallen into disrepair, the nets sagging and uneven. The sun dropped in the sky and the pedestrians and joggers thinned out. Neither Jenny nor Lilly said much when they were alone. They just walked and looked. Jenny's phone rang in her pocket and they both jumped.

The cop had called once before with a question about Frankie and this time his voice was grim. "Some kids at a squat near I-5 said they might have seen your daughter with a kid whose street name is Pyro. Look, Mrs. Alexander. I have to tell you that if she's with this Pyro character, it's not good news, but we will try to pick her up as fast as we can. I suggest you take your other daughter back to the hotel. We will call you the minute we find her."

Jenny closed the phone and stuck it back into her pocket. She picked up her pace.

"What is it, Mom?" whispered Lilly. "What did he say?"

Jenny could see the park entrance now and the bright lights of the clubs and restaurants beyond. "He said that I should buy you dinner and take you back to the hotel." She looked hard at Lilly. "Can you wait?"

Lilly met her eyes. "Of course."

Jenny started the engine and headed toward the neighborhood of warehouses and industrial complexes near 1-5. She watched the road and wondered, why hadn't Frankie called when she found out that Ariel was gone? The kid across the hall had given her twenty dollars, which was plenty of money for a cab ride to the ferry terminal and a phone call. Why hadn't she simply gotten on the ferry and come home?

They came within sight of the Duwamish River for a stretch, their eyes peeled on the streets and doorways, not sure what they were looking for. They passed several abandoned buildings, a few with broken windows and a place that looked like an art studio that had a wire sculpture on a concrete post marking the door. After a while they moved away from the river back toward the highway where the sound of traffic was constant, like the roar of the sea.

"Stop." Lilly had her hand on the door before Jenny could even pull over and cut the engine. "I thought I saw a light."

Jenny followed Lilly toward a low dark building surrounded

on all sides by a battered chain-link fence. As they got closer, she, too, could see a flickering glow coming from inside one of the windows, though it was faint in the now gray evening light.

She lunged forward and grabbed Lilly's arm. "No."

Lilly tried to yank away. Jenny did not let her loose.

"Frankie might be in there," hissed Lilly. "Let go!"

Jenny pointed to a cinder block that sat in the corner, near the fence. A step, most likely, to use in hoisting yourself over. "You sit there and wait for me. I will be right back."

"But, Mom, no . . ."

"Sit!"

Lilly looked into her mother's face. She figured if Lilly could see even half of the resolve she felt, she would not dare to argue. Lilly crossed her arms over her chest and sat. Jenny left her there. Around the back of the building she found a steel door ajar and lightly pushed it open. She walked in and found herself in a storage area, or what might have been one once, cut off from the flickering light they had seen. A sofa was pushed up against the wall. There was a boy lying on it, asleep, his body curled around a sleeping dog.

Jenny paused to look at him. The white skin of his scalp was visible where he had shaved off part of his hair. He was as skinny as Frankie and Phoenix were, but he looked older, maybe sixteen or seventeen. She'd seen kids like this all through the U District that afternoon, in fact the whole city seemed to be filled with lost children and animals. Her heart was pounding. Another two steps in the dark and she would have stumbled and fallen on top of him.

A small fire was burning at the far end of the space and there were several figures sitting around it. Shapes in one corner looked like they might be the sleeping bodies of yet more people. It wasn't yet nine o'clock and it occurred to her that these kids might rise at night and stay up until dawn, like vampires. She swallowed. To get to them she would have to cross the entire room.

She started walking.

"Who is that?" It was a young girl's voice. "Who's there?"

"My name is Jenny." She tried to speak loud enough so that the girl could hear her but not so loud that she would wake the sleepers on the floor.

"Jenny? Jenny who? What are you doing here?"

It was now almost certain that Frankie was not among them, thought Jenny. Her mother's voice was bound to bring her running. About twenty feet from the circle of light, there were three other kids sitting with the girl who had called out. They were all covered in layers of clothes and bandannas, with glinting nose rings and lip studs and several strands of beads. Jenny was struck by how theatrical they appeared, and how tired.

"I'm looking," she said, "for a girl named Frankie."

There was one boy among them, and at the mention of Frankie's name he snapped his head around to glare at the girl who had spoken first. He whispered, "Is that the new girl that Pyro brought? Jinx?"

"That's who I'm looking for. Jinx." Jenny spoke directly to the boy now. She wanted to shout, but with great effort she was able to keep her voice even.

"Stupid fuck!" The first girl kicked him in the leg with her boot and then glanced sharply at one of the sleeping forms. It was a man wrapped in a blanket. His hair was bushy and blond against the backpack he was using as a pillow.

Jenny walked carefully in that direction. The earlobe she could see was stretched around a disk the size of a junior mint and the man had a series of Roman numerals tattooed crudely on his neck. Jenny knew without a shadow of a doubt that the person she was looking at was Pyro. She was about to kick him awake when the girl hissed at her, "She left."

Jenny turned. "Where did she go?"

"She just booked out of here, okay? A couple of hours ago."

Later when she was back at home, Jenny would remember the fear she heard in that girl's voice and feel faint. For now she just ran.

Lilly was pacing by the fence and smoking.

Jenny charged past her toward the truck. "We're going to find her."

They hopped in the cab and Jenny began cruising at about the pace a lost thirteen-year-old girl might go. Corson led to East Marginal Way, and they followed it down to a little park overlooking the Duwamish.

Lilly saw her first. She was sitting on a bench near the water, hunched over so that all her long black hair was hanging forward over her face like a curtain.

Lilly made a sound and Frankie looked up. Her eyes locked on Jenny. "Mom?" Her face was bruised and bloody on one side.

Jenny drew in her breath and stumbled forward. The grass was muddy near the bench and she slid and almost lost her balance before righting herself and gathering Frankie into her arms.

"I'm sorry," said Frankie, and she started to sob. "I'm so sorry."

"Don't, baby. No. No. It's not your fault." Jenny climbed onto the bench with her. She gasped for breath and her muscles shivered uncontrollably. "Shhh. Shhh. It's okay, now. I'm here." Jenny held Frankie carefully around her thin shoulders so as not to brush against the parts that were injured. "We'll take you to the doctor, okay? Then we'll get you home."

Frankie continued to sob and Jenny could hear both anguish and relief in her voice.

Standing over the bench, Lilly wrinkled her nose and pressed her lips together, clearly trying not to cry. "Frankie? What the fuck?"

Frankie gulped and swallowed. She looked up into her sister's face and then dropped her eyes to the clothes she was wearing. They were covered in blood and grime. She said in a tiny voice, "I shouldn't have taken your stuff."

"Don't be an idiot," said Lilly.

She and Jenny helped Frankie to her feet. The path was too narrow for them to walk three abreast, so Jenny and Frankie went first. Lilly followed close behind, with her hand touching her sister's back. Jenny and Lilly had flown down the trail in seconds, but climbing back up seemed to take forever. Jenny's mind raced ahead to where she had seen the sign for a hospital.

She had to take Frankie there, and yet all she wanted to do was pack her children in her truck and start driving north.

"Hey, lady, is this your truck?" A guy in a delivery uniform was parked with his flashers on.

Jenny ignored his impatience and walked only as fast as Frankie could go. She had taken the keys with her, but she saw now that in addition to blocking the driveway they had left both doors wide open. It looked like a scene from the rapture.

The man stood with his hands on his hips and shook his head while Jenny and the girls approached. Frankie shifted to climb into the cab and the man saw her face.

"Jesus!" he said. "What happened? Do you need any help?"

Jenny shook her head.

The emergency room lobby was unnaturally bright. Jenny held Frankie on her lap, with Frankie's head buried under her arm. She glanced at Lilly and in the fluorescent light she could see how these last hours had drained the color from her face. Her older daughter's eyes rose to meet hers, desperate for reassurance.

"She'll be okay," said Jenny. She was determined, whatever had happened, to make it true.

The receptionist had looked at them through glasses she pushed back on her nose, like a librarian, and told them to have a seat and wait. It had been fifteen minutes now since they'd arrived.

Lilly paced. "She's bleeding! When are they going to call her back?"

Jenny hissed at her, "Sit down, Lilly."

She rocked Frankie the best she could with her gangly legs stretching nearly to the ground. A woman in a bathrobe was momentarily distracted from her own misery by Lilly's pacing and stared openly at her. The intercom called for a Dr. Malvo to please come to Intensive Care. An ambulance screamed into the circular driveway and a team of people wheeled someone from the van through the lobby to the back with astonishing speed. Jenny barely glimpsed a tuft of white hair on the gurney as they passed. Suddenly a nurse was standing in front of them saying Francesca? Francesca Alexander?

Frankie lifted her head, Lilly paused, and, though Jenny had written the name on the card, all three of them stared at the nurse in momentary confusion. Then Frankie slid her feet to the floor and climbed out of Jenny's lap.

The nurse led them through the double doors by the reception area and into a long corridor. "Do we need to do a rape kit?" she asked gently. She was wearing scrubs with small dinosaurs patterned all over them.

Jenny's tongue felt like a balled-up sock in her mouth. She had not considered this as a possibility. She pulled Frankie away from her body so she could look in her face.

Frankie shook her head no.

"Well, thank God for that," said Lilly.

The nurse gave Frankie a gown and Jenny helped her change. In addition to the bloody patch on her face, she had purple bruises on her thigh and side that made Jenny suck in her breath when she saw them.

A young doctor came in and washed his hands in the office sink. For the exam, Frankie sat on the table in a gown with her legs dangling over the side. The remnants of her summer tan made her skin look vaguely yellow in the fluorescent light and her bare feet were large and puppyish at the end of her skinny legs.

The doctor placed his hand under her chin and lifted her face toward the light. She started to cry.

Lilly came to stand beside Jenny and Jenny bent her head to Frankie. Jenny held her smaller child's hand and pressed her cheek ever so gently against her damp skin while Lilly stood close by. She breathed in each small gasp or anguished murmur that escaped from Frankie's mouth. She met each of those noises with soothing sounds of her own.

The doctor pressed the pads of his fingers against her jaw. "Does it hurt here?" He turned her head to the side to look in her ears and Frankie winced. "I want you to call if she has lingering pain in the abdomen. I'll give you a prescription for codeine and a few samples of a disinfectant cream." He directed his instructions at Jenny. "You'll need to put it on three times a day for a week," he said, and he left the room.

Jenny smoothed Frankie's hair down on her head carefully to avoid the wounds on her cheek. "Why didn't you take the ferry back when you found out that Ariel wasn't here? They said you bought a round-trip ticket. Didn't you have it?"

Frankie brought her fingers up to her mouth and gnawed at

her nails, something she had not done for years. "This kid stole my backpack. My ticket was in that little zip purse with the beads, you know, in the side pocket?"

"Oh, honey. Why didn't you call me to come get you? I would have in a second, I . . ."

"There were these other kids . . ." Frankie started to cry again, "Who said they knew the one that did it and they said they would help me get it back again. And if I got it back then I wouldn't have to make you spend all this money to come out here to get me and all, but they were tricking me to get the twenty dollars that guy gave me and I know I shouldn't have listened to them." She gasped for breath. "I'm so sorry, Mommy. I'm so so sorry."

Jenny bit her lip. "It isn't important, Frankie. Shhh. I'm here now. Lilly and I are here with you now."

The nurse returned carrying a pair of scrubs and a sweat-shirt that said Seattle Children's Hospital. She set these on the exam table next to Frankie. Lilly's clothes, the ones Frankie had taken, were in a filthy heap on the floor.

"Wait." Lilly unzipped her hoodie, pulled off her tank top, and then, in front of the nurse, stepped out of her skirt. She handed her clothes to Frankie and reached for the scrubs.

CHAPTER 19

Home

Lilly and Frankie curled up under blankets on the hotel bed to watch *Scooby-Doo* on the Cartoon Network while Jenny ran water in the tub. She scrubbed the sides with a bar of hotel soap and a washcloth before closing the drain. She perched on the side of the tub and moved the hot water around with her hand. She started to call for Frankie and then thought better of it.

Instead she walked to the side of the bed and reached for her hand under the covers. "Come take a bath."

Frankie let herself be led into the bathroom, but until the very last minute she kept her eyes on Daphne, Fred, Velma, and Shaggy. When they got into the bathroom Frankie looked at the water and began to shiver uncontrollably. Jenny pulled the hoodie over Frankie's head and helped her step out of Lilly's skirt. The bruises had begun to turn new colors by then, an ugly yellow and green. Jenny helped her lift her leg over the side of tub and kept holding on to her until she had sat down in the water.

"Okay?" Jenny reached for the shampoo she had bought in the drugstore on their way back from the hospital. Motel 6 didn't provide any for free.

"Stay here." Frankie pulled her knees up to her chest and water splashed over the edge. "Please?"

"Sure. Of course."

Jenny perched on the side of the tub and poured water over Frankie's head with the hotel glass until it was wet through. She squirted some shampoo into the palm of her hand and worked it through Frankie's hair from the scalp all the way down the ends. She soaped the washcloth and washed Frankie's ears, her neck, her back, and holding each one in her hands, her arms. Frankie sat perfectly still with her eyes on the wall of the shower. Tears streamed down her cheeks and her little pointed chin looked soft and dimpled. When she emerged from the hot water Frankie's toes looked like fresh-water pearls. Jenny wrapped her in a towel and retrieved a pair of Lilly's tie-dyed long underwear and a long-sleeved shirt from Lilly's backpack.

"How is she?" whispered Lilly.

Jenny shook her head and carried the clothes into the bathroom. A streetlamp in the hotel's parking lot shone directly into their room, so while the girls snuggled under the covers, Jenny anchored the curtains shut with a chair. She turned the television down low and lay on her back and traced the stains on the ceiling with her eyes. First Frankie, then Lilly, fell asleep on the bed, their legs touching and their faces bathed in the flickering cartoon light. Frankie was sucking her thumb.

The girls were still sleeping at noon, and though she hated to do it, Jenny woke them up. She didn't know how long they'd have to spend at the police station, and the last ferry of the day left Anacortes for Friday Harbor at seven-thirty p.m. She was determined that they not spend another night off the island. Officer Arnold was gentle and mercifully brief, and after interviewing Frankie he let the three of them escape to a diner that served breakfast all day. Jenny ordered pancakes and eggs and biscuits with lots of butter and jam. They hit Interstate 5 with the three of them bouncing in the cab together, Jenny behind the wheel, Lilly on the other side, and Frankie, with a pair of Lilly's shorts over Lilly's long underwear, in the middle.

Jenny had slept little, and the late afternoon sun glinted off the oncoming traffic into her eyes. She put on a pair of cheap sunglasses she kept in the truck and adjusted the sun visor.

Lilly looked at her with concern. "Do you want me to drive for a while?"

"No. I'm okay." It was just over eighty miles now to the ferry landing. They had two hours to get there and get in line.

Frankie stretched her face toward the open window. "I think I'm going to throw up."

"Mom, pull over," said Lilly. "She's not kidding."

Jenny flipped on her blinker and headed for the right lane. Frankie began to gag. They took an exit onto an overpass and just as the truck bounced over the rocks on the shoulder, Frankie vomited down the front of her clothes. Lilly opened the door and tumbled out onto the gravel. Frankie followed, another burst of biscuits and eggs and hot chocolate hurtling from her mouth into a pool on the dirt. She kneeled, retching, until nothing but bile and snot came out of her. Jenny rubbed her back and Lilly fished through her backpack for more clothes. All she could find was the tank top and skirt she had worn the night before.

Frankie wiped at her face with her sleeve and gagged again. "I want to die," she said. "I can't stand it. I want to die."

Jenny took some paper napkins that Lilly handed her from the glove compartment and wiped the vomit and the tears from Frankie's face. "Don't say that, sweetheart. Please. Please don't say that."

Jenny and Lilly helped Frankie change in the truck and then tossed the vomit-covered clothes into the back. Jenny uncapped the water bottle and told Frankie to drink. Just a sip. As soon as they started back toward the freeway, Frankie leaned against Lilly and fell fast asleep.

They drove over the Stillaguamish River and then crossed into Skagit County.

"School will be starting soon," said Lilly softly.

Jenny glanced down at Frankie. Her eyes were moving underneath her closed lids. Her skin was still faintly green. "I know."

Lilly looked straight ahead. "I mean for me."

Now that they were close to home Jenny's exhaustion had been chased away by an end-of-the-road spurt of energy. She took advantage of a straight stretch in the highway to overtake a tractor that was moving so slowly even her own vehicle could shoot past.

"I wish you could stay," she said. Her eyes filled with tears and she chewed the inside of her cheek to keep from crying. "I know it's wrong of me and I do want you to go to school." She smiled at a memory of Lilly doing a sudoku puzzle on the ferry. "I want you to be an entomologist, if that's what you want to be. But, God, Lilly. I'm just going to miss you so much." She gripped the wheel so tightly that her knuckles turned white.

"I know, Mom," said Lilly softly. "I love you, too."

An eighteen-wheeler hauling freight for Walmart slowed abruptly, and she put on the brakes and glanced at Lilly. "It's not the same. When you're a mother it's different, it's as if you . . . well . . ." She sighed with the difficulty, with the enormity of it all. "You'll understand someday."

Lilly shifted Frankie's head to a less bony part of her shoulder. "I *hate* it when you say that."

"Yeah?"

Jenny turned onto the two-lane road that headed through Anacortes to the ferry landing. From the line of headlights facing the opposite direction she figured the boat had already mostly unloaded. She looked at her watch. Jenny had called Mary Ann from the diner and told her they would try for this boat, but if they made it, it would be just barely. "Well, tough."

Lilly poked at her sandal with her bare toe. "You are."

"What?"

"Tough," said Lilly.

Jenny remembered Lawrence, then Ariel, sitting at her kitchen table stirring his tea with a chopstick and said, "I do what I have to do."

The shops selling shells and fishing gear were all familiar now, the drugstores and the banks, the grocery where she and Theresa used to go when the kids were young and load up on cheap food and diapers to take back on the ferry.

"We're just going to make it." Jenny barreled down the hill toward the kiosk where they sold the tickets. "Friday Harbor," she said, and turned for her bag.

Lilly had the money in her hand.

"Slow down," said the uniformed woman as she handed over the ticket. "They see you. They'll wait."

Jenny took the ticket and steered the truck toward the end of the line of cars. She repeated the cashier's words in her mind as they approached. *Slow down.* How much easier that was to say in Anacortes than in Seattle. Soon they would be home and the streets would smell like fish and pine needles rather than urine and garbage. The sidewalks would be full of faces they knew.

Just then Frankie stretched and, rubbing her eyes, sat up and looked around. She saw where they were, the lot, the boat, the water, and for the first time in a long while, perhaps, thought Jenny, since the play had ended, she smiled.

CHAPTER 20

Be Fierce

The weather was changing. The back of the hot spell had been broken and a cold wind from the sea was stirring up fog on the coast. Most of the tourists returning from a day trip to Anacortes or on their way to check into their bed-and-breakfast on San Juan came out on deck for a short time to look at the view and then went shivering back inside. Jenny and her daughters stood in the wind and spray and gulped in the sea air.

Arm in arm on the deck and draped in whatever clean clothing they could find, they made a curious picture against the gray sky and tree-covered ridges. The wind whipped their long hair around their faces. They stood silently and watched the diving birds. As the temperature dropped each fall, the gulls, ducks, auklets, and grebes became desperate to get their fill of the Pacific herring moving through the Sound in huge schools. The auks had short, strong wings, and they dove down into a bait ball, filling their beaks with silver fish and driving the others to the surface for the gulls. Their calls filled the air.

Smoke was rising from the chimneys of the houses tucked away in the trees on the islands they passed. Pleasure craft and fishing boats rocked in their moorings. The stands of trees were shadowed in the mist. Out on the deck with the water crashing against the hull and the waves reaching out to touch the private coves on the smaller islands, the city seemed remote indeed. It was not a dream exactly, but something far, far away.

When the boat passed Lopez Island and entered the narrow channel to San Juan, the engine slowed and the rough wind grew gentler.

"We should go and get in the truck," said Jenny. She gave both girls' arms a slight tug.

Frankie pulled away. "Not yet."

Jenny sighed. She leaned against the railing and watched Friday Harbor come into focus. The rows of boats. The walkway along the water dotted with restaurants and shops. The commercial life of the town lay hidden behind the hill rising behind the terminal, where cars were waiting to board the ferry: Mary Ann's antique store, the wine bar, the grocery, the gas station, the bookstore. Their home.

Lilly narrowed her eyes and leaned over the railing to get a better look. "Is that Phinneas?"

Jenny followed her gaze. "On the dock?"

"Nu-uh. There." Lilly pointed at a tall thin figure in a long flapping coat.

"You're right." Jenny stared ahead as the boat slowly drew closer. "He's not alone, either. Chad's with him. And Sally."

Lilly pulled her hair back and tied it with a bandanna. "Dale and Peg are there, too. Hey, I think that's even Stu Barnes."

They got closer and Jenny could see still more people whom she recognized: Winifred Calloway and the Burtons from Waldron. David. She did not see Mary Ann and knew, without a moment's doubt, that it was because she was in the cabin waiting for them.

Frankie turned and pressed her face against Jenny's chest. "They're all going to be so mad at me."

Jenny grabbed Frankie's shoulders and held her away from her body so that she could see her face. "What are you talking about? Why?"

"For causing so much trouble." Frankie would not meet her mother's eyes.

"Don't be ridiculous," said Lilly. "They love drama. Especially Dale and Peg."

"They love you," said Jenny. "They'll be relieved that you're home safe." She pulled Frankie back into her arms, both to comfort her and because she could not say the word *safe* while looking at the scabs and bruising on her daughter's face.

"I don't want to talk to anyone, okay?" Frankie's hand moved to her damaged face. "I don't want them to see me."

Jenny touched her lips to the top of Frankie's head. "But they want . . ."

"Please?"

"Okay." Jenny rubbed her back. "I'll tell them. Let's go inside."

They walked single file through the warm air of the interior to the windowless stairs that led below deck. Other passengers were already behind the wheels of their cars and waiting for the boat to dock. Frankie curled up into a ball on the seat between Jenny and Lilly and put the hoodie over her head like a tent. Light flooded the passageway around the cars and the uniformed crew member, a woman with her brown hair in a ponytail, waived first the bicyclists, then the motorists, off the boat. David saw Jenny's truck first and jogged toward it, with the others following. Jenny pulled out of the line of cars and stepped out to meet him, with the engine running and the two girls inside.

He pulled her to him in a bear hug. "You've got Lilly, too," he said, waving at her.

Jenny said, "Only for a while."

The others crowded around her, reaching out and rubbing her hair and her back until she began to feel like the Buddha that had once stood in the Westcott Bay Sculpture Park, worn smooth from so many hands. Except that it was she who had been blessed by them, she thought, and not the other way around.

"Thank God, Jen."

"We were so worried."

"How is she?"

Jenny shoved her hands in her pockets. "Exhausted."

Phinneas started toward the truck. "I bet she is."

Jenny reached out and grabbed his arm. "Wait."

"What?" Phinneas turned. His hair under the knit cap was growing long and his pointed beard stretched almost to the round collar of his sweater. His eyes were bright with alarm.

"She doesn't want to see anyone right now. She just wants me to take her home."

The last of the cars leaving the ferry climbed the hill past the knot of people and the idling truck. Jenny stood in the center of the circle, just steps from her children, and watched anger and worry and sadness spread like cracks through their faces.

Peg looked toward the truck. "Of course," she said. "She can have all the time she wants."

David kicked at the curb like a small boy, his face awash with confusion and pain. "Is there something . . ."

"Let us at least make sure that you get home okay," interrupted Phinneas.

Chad added, "I dropped off some halibut and Mary Ann has it in the oven."

"We won't even follow you down the driveway to the house," said Jim Burton.

Dale said, "We'll keep going on Cattle Point."

"It will be like an escort," added Sally.

Peg nodded. "You can call us if you need us."

Jenny looked at each of their faces in turn. "Thank you."

Jenny opened the door and climbed up beside her girls. Frankie shifted under the hoodie, but she did not so much as peek out. Jenny watched as her friends found their cars and then she pulled slowly out into First Avenue. One by one they pulled out behind her, following at a respectful distance.

Lilly turned in her seat to look at the parade of vehicles: a late eighties Honda with mud on the wheel wells, a dented truck, a VW camper van, a Jeep, and a Subaru Outback. She said, "What are they doing? They aren't all coming home with us, are they?"

Jenny slowed for their road and put her blinker on. The cars passed them, one by one, on the right.

Lilly waved out the window and they flashed their lights in return.

The truck rumbled to a stop at the driftwood log.

Frankie lifted her head. "Are we home?"

"Yes, hon. We're home." She took in Frankie's red-rimmed eyes and tousled hair. Her cheeks were rosy from her time spent under the hoodie. "Mary Ann is here."

Frankie said, "That's okay. I don't mind Mary Ann seeing me."

Mary Ann appeared in the doorway. She did not wait for them to unload their things but walked briskly across the path and grass and took Frankie in her arms. She held her tightly. Frankie's eyes were squeezed shut.

"Lilly," said Mary Ann. "Go in the house and set the table."

Lilly obeyed without even her customary rolling of the eyes.

Jenny and Mary Ann stared at each over the top of Frankie's head. Jenny did not realize how close she was to complete collapse until she looked into the older woman's eyes. She swayed on her feet. All the lamps were lit in the front room and Lilly was laying forks onto napkins. The kitchen smelled like rice and butter. There was a bowl of salad on the counter and Mary Ann had put a pitcher with daisies on the table. Jenny craned her neck and saw several slices of grilled fish steaming on the broiler pan.

"Look, Franks. Halibut. Your favorite."

"I'm not hungry." Frankie broke away from Mary Ann and headed straight for her room.

Jenny started to go after her, but Mary Ann stopped her with a gentle touch to the arm. "Let her rest. You look like you need to eat something."

"Hey," said Lilly, looking beyond Jenny to the porch. "Where's Mom's loom?"

Jenny and Mary Ann both glanced at the empty spot where the loom had stood. The small end table was there with a bowl of water still sitting on it, and a few scraps of yarn littered the floor. Jenny glanced back at Mary Ann and started to say something.

Mary Ann pulled at a thread on her napkin. "It's at my house. I know you told me not to be here, but, well, I'm sorry. I couldn't do it."

"Do what?" asked Lilly. She sat down and began loading her plate with salad.

"It's okay," said Jenny. She gave Mary Ann a quick peck on the cheek. "Frankie's home now."

They both knew without saying so that there were circumstances that might have stretched even this friendship to the breaking point.

Mary Ann handed Lilly a pot of rice to put on the table. "I'll ask David to bring it back over tomorrow."

Jenny let herself be led to the table and seated before a plate of fish, salad, and rice. Mary Ann sat across from her.

Lilly ripped a piece off the loaf of bread and stuffed a hunk of it in her mouth. "I'm so starving you'd think it was me that lost my cookies on the ride."

Jenny reached for the food that Mary Ann had so lovingly prepared. She willed herself to eat it.

"Trinculo called," said Mary Ann.

Jenny stopped chewing. "Andre? When?"

"His name is *Andre*?" Lilly rested her elbows on the table and looked at each of the two women in turn. "I can't believe I didn't know that was his name after all this time. Even after we . . ." Her voice trailed off.

Jenny looked at her sharply.

Lilly blushed and averted her eyes. "We didn't do all that much, actually."

Mary Ann spread butter on a piece of bread and tucked it next to the rice on Jenny's plate. "Earlier this afternoon. He said that his phone had been stolen from his apartment and that he had been trying to call you from his friends' house in Queens."

Queens. She remembered the woman's voice on the answering machine and flushed. Now that she had a chance to put this together with what Lawrence had said about the break-in at Andre's, she did not need to check a directory to know that 718 would be the area code for Queens.

Lilly pointed at the untouched piece of fish on her mother's plate. "Are you going to eat that?"

Jenny pushed her chair back from the table without answering. She fished in the pocket of her jeans for the phone she had kept there, except for a brief window in the hotel when it was charging, since Frankie had gone missing. Frankie's silver dolphin charm emerged from the depths of her pocket along with the phone. Jenny considered dropping it into the dish by the door where she kept her keys and then changed her mind. Whatever luck it might have brought them, and they had been lucky indeed, she wanted just a little more.

She slipped through the door to the porch, scrolling through the missed calls until she found one with the 718 area code. It was the first of four missed calls. She pressed the button, her heart hammering while she waited for an answer. The phone rang once and then twice. With it still pressed against her ear, she crossed the dark garden to the fence that was supposed to keep out the animals. She closed a hole in the chicken wire large enough for a rabbit to slip through.

"Hello?" It was a different woman's voice this time.

"Hi. This is . . . my name is Jenny Alex . . ."

"Oh, Jenny! Marcie and I have heard all about you. Andre's not here, though. He left this afternoon."

"He did?" Jenny's heart lifted and fell and then lifted again, as if it were a balloon in the hand of a running child. Marcie and Marcie's companion, this woman on the phone, had heard about her? Andre was gone?

"Sure. He's on his way."

Jenny straightened. "On his way where?" She turned to look at the bright windows of her small house. She could see Mary Ann moving in the kitchen. Washing dishes.

"Well, out to Washington State. At least that's what I thought." The woman held the phone away from her mouth. "Dre went back out to Washington, didn't he?" she called to someone in the room.

Jenny heard a muffled response and then the first woman's voice speaking back into the phone. "Yeah. That's where he went. His plane was going to leave about six o'clock."

"Thank you." Alone in the moonlight, Jenny pulled a sunflower toward her as if it were a person and kissed it square in the middle of its yellow face.

When Jenny came back through the door she found Mary Ann holding her plate out to her again. Lilly had eaten the fish, but her rice and salad remained untouched.

The older woman urged, "You should eat something. It will help you sleep."

Jenny took the plate, although eating was the furthest thing from her mind. "Andre's on his way out here."

Mary Ann said, "Don't sound so surprised."

Jenny smiled. "I can't help it. He'll probably arrive some-time tomorrow morning."

Lilly walked by carrying a glass of orange juice. "Precisely when all the hard work has been done."

Mary Ann and Jenny both watched her disappear into her room.

"That gives you plenty of time to get some rest," said Mary Ann.

Jenny shook her head. "I won't sleep."

"Yes," said Mary Ann. "You will. Because . . ." She went into the kitchen and returned with an open bottle of wine and a water glass. "You are going to drink." She poured the glass half full and set it before Jenny on the table with such force that the yellow liquid sloshed.

Jenny took a sip, then a gulp. "What if Frankie gets up in the night?"

"I'll be here," said Mary Ann.

Jenny took another large pull on her wine and then, sud-denly dizzy, she took a small bite of rice. Mary Ann watched her take a few more bites and then drink the rest of the wine like a nurse watching a patient take her medicine. Then Jenny stumbled into bed.

The morning sun was bright on her face when Jenny awoke and she was sweating under a heavy quilt. She padded into the kitchen in her socks to find Mary Ann sitting in the arm-chair by the door with her eyes closed. When she was awake the brightness of her friend's eyes and her easy smile distracted Jenny from the lines spreading over her face. Mary Ann's hair was more gray than blond now, Jenny could see, and the grooves alongside her mouth and etched into her forehead were thick and deep. She tiptoed to Frankie's room and inched the door open. The shock of black hair visible on the pillow and the curled lump underneath the blanket reassured her that her younger child was still asleep. She glanced at the clock on the mantle and saw that it was already eleven-fifteen. From the hallway she could see that Lilly's door was ajar. Both her bed and her room were empty.

There was coffee on the counter, though the pot was cool. Jenny poured the coffee into a saucepan and turned on the burner. She pulled the milk from the refrigerator and noticed that there was a bowl with milk and a few soggy cornflakes sitting in the sink.

"How do you feel?"

Jenny turned to find Mary Ann's eyes open. The older woman's head was still back against the top of the chair and her legs were stretched out over the footrest.

Jenny stirred the coffee with a wooden spoon. "Where's Lilly?"

"In town."

"I don't know why I even bothered to ask." She reached for a mug and tipped the saucepan to pour the coffee into it. "Frankie's been sleeping for over fourteen hours."

"She was up for a while."

Jenny carried her coffee to the table and turned her chair to face Mary Ann. "When?"

"At about midnight. We sat and talked. I made her some warm milk with honey in it. Then she went back to sleep."

"What did she say?" Jenny sipped her coffee.

"I heard most of the story, I think. How she handed her backpack to some boy and he ran off with it. She talked about this group of kids, Tinker Bell and Rash. A boy named Lightning. She says this Pyro character was diagnosed with some kind of illness, occasional explosive syndrome or something like that, and thrown out of his house when he was fourteen."

Jenny snorted. "Syndrome or not, he was a violent, aggressive jerk."

Mary Ann added softly, "He wanted to have sex with her and hit and kicked her when she said no."

"Jesus." Jenny thought of the bruises on Frankie's hip and felt her stomach turn. She remembered how she had stood over a sleeping Pyro and it was all she could do not to wail out loud for having missed her chance to do him harm. "Why didn't she tell me?"

Mary Ann sighed. "You're her mother. She wants to protect you."

"I wanted to protect her, too." Jenny pushed the heels of her palms against her eyes. "And I ended up doing a fine job with that, didn't I?"

"She got away, Jen. Little Frankie fought back and got away."

Jenny chewed her lip. "She made excuses for him," she said. She met Mary Ann's eyes and wondered if the older woman could see her panic. "The police officer kept telling her that whatever happened wasn't her fault, but I could tell that she didn't believe a word of it."

"Maybe you have to believe it, too," said Mary Ann gently.

Jenny straightened. "How could I possibly think it was her fault? She's a child."

"That's not what I mean."

Jenny stared at her hands. How well she could remember standing on Mary Ann's doorstep all those years ago with her children and her life and little else and finding herself fully taken in by that gaze. Those green eyes in the face of her friend had been her salvation once. She forced herself to look up. "What do you mean?"

Mary Ann's face softened. "What I mean is that maybe *you* have to believe it. Maybe in order for Frankie to forgive herself you have to show her how to do it. You have to believe, you know, that *it's not your fault.*"

Jenny buried her face in her hands. She was not, it had to be said, Juno. Whatever powers she possessed were of the distinctly human kind. "I don't know," she said in a very small voice. "I don't know if I can do that." She did not need Mary Ann to tell her that for Frankie's sake, and for her own, she had to try.

They sat without speaking. The silence was interrupted by the sound of a flock of waxwings just outside the window getting drunk on serviceberries, and a rhythmic, knocking sound that Jenny did not immediately recognize.

She asked, "What's that noise?"

Mary Ann glanced at the window. "David is outside chopping wood for your woodpile."

Jenny said, "But I know how to chop wood."

Mary Ann sighed. "Let him do it, will you?"

Jenny slipped her feet into a pair of Lilly's shoes that were by the door and carried her mug outside. David had paused to wipe the sweat off his forehead with the bandanna from his pocket. He wore jeans and heavy boots and a T-shirt that must have been given to him by Phinneas. It said *Potters for Peace.*

"Can I get you a glass of water?" asked Jenny.

David jumped a little at hearing her voice. "Sure. Thanks." He lifted the ax again and brought it down hard on the wood that he had stood upright on the stump. It split straight down the middle.

Jenny went into the house and returned with the glass. David emptied it and handed it back. His skin was ruddy from sun and wind and in his whiskers of a few days were a few silver ones glinting among the reddish blond. She could remember how those rough points felt against her skin when he burrowed his face under her hair and pressed his lips against her neck. She wondered if she could have really broken his heart, as she'd heard him complain more than once. She was sorry if she had.

He leaned the blade against the stump. "Do you love that guy?"

Jenny touched his arm. "Yeah, actually. I think I do." The hesitation was all for David's sake, and she could see in his eyes that he knew it.

"I'll be here, you know," he said. "If you ever change your mind."

The woodpile was already three quarters full. David balanced another log on the stump for chopping.

She said, "Thank you."

"No problem," he said, and brought the ax down.

Back in the house, Mary Ann had risen from her chair and was cracking eggs into a bowl. She looked up when Jenny approached. "Cheese omelet?"

"Sure." She glanced back in the direction she'd come. "How long has he been out there?"

"Bout an hour." She poured the eggs into the pan. "You'll have to tell him later," she said, "when you want him to stop. That is unless you want to be responsible for the deforestation of San Juan Island."

Jenny laughed. It was an odd sound, she thought, coming from her mouth. "I will, I promise." She glanced toward the window, through which David's form was intermittently visible when he went to retrieve pieces of wood that had gone flying. "But not quite yet."

At the sound of a truck rumbling up the drive, both Jenny and Mary Ann walked to the front door and looked out. The truck was Elliot's. It came to a halt and Elliot, Lilly, and another high school friend of Lilly's, a girl named May, tumbled out. It looked like there was another kid in the bed of the truck, but the cab obscured too much of him for Jenny to make out who it was. She was soon enough distracted by Lilly, who pushed through the front door carrying a box in her arms.

"Hey Mom! Mary Ann! Where's Frankie? I have something for her. It's a big box and it's from Ariel."

"Ariel sent me a present?"

Frankie stood in the doorway to her room in jeans and bare feet. The pants, which had fit her well when she left, hung around her hips to expose a strip of smooth, pale skin between the waistband and the bottom of her T-shirt.

Jenny glanced at the box and could see neither the address nor postage. She wondered how Lilly could be so sure that it came from Ariel.

May stepped forward to give Jenny a hug. "My mom says that you should call her if you have time to make ten place mats before Thanksgiving."

Jenny nodded. "I can do that."

Lilly placed the box in Frankie's hands. Frankie looked at it in wonder before setting it on the table to open it. Jenny got the scissors and returned to find Frankie ripping it open with her hands.

Frankie opened the flaps and Jenny gasped.

Staring up at them was the face of a wolf. The snout was covered with gray and black fur, with a wet-looking nose at the tip. The eyes were pitch black. There was an opening underneath one row of jagged teeth and after the opening, another row below. The opening was for the eyes and nose, Jenny guessed, for when Frankie lifted the thing from its box she could see that it was a mask. She looked at Mary Ann in alarm.

"I love it," breathed Frankie, and she placed it on her head.

A curtain of thin gray fabric fell to her shoulders below the frightening jaw. Because the opening was in the mouth, it tilted the snout slightly toward the ceiling and made it look as if the wolf were both baring its teeth and about to howl at the moon.

"Check this out." Lilly reached into the box and pulled out the rest of the costume: a gray shirt and leggings with loops of gray and black yarn attached to them like matted fur with black and mother-of-pearl sequins sewn on at odd intervals. She shook it and a note fluttered to the floor.

"Cool," said Elliot.

"Awesome," added May.

Jenny bent to pick up the note. "It says, *Dear Iris. This is from an Off-Broadway production of* Peter and the Wolf. *I hope you like it. Be fierce. Love Ariel.*"

Frankie gathered the rest of the costume in her arms and disappeared into her room to change. Jenny looked at her slender back and thin pale arms and remembered what Mary Ann had said about her fighting back.

Lilly turned to Jenny with a mysterious smile on her face and for a moment Jenny wondered if the present might actually have come from Lilly.

"Frankie got a delivery from Ariel," said Lilly, as if reading her mother's mind. "But you got something, too. It's outside."

"What?" Jenny's heart charged ahead of her. Could it be?

"The delivery man."

Jenny rushed toward the door. "Do you mean to say you left him out there all this time? Lilly, you're impossible!"

Lilly called, "Too light winning makes the prize light."

Jenny burst out into the bright sun of midday, trying and failing to keep the grin off her face. Imagine Lilly quoting Prospero. Even Lilly had by now, it seemed, read the play.

Andre had climbed out of the bed of the truck and was now leaning against it. He was wearing black jeans, a Ramones T-shirt, and dark sunglasses, which he took off the moment he saw Jenny.

Jenny was in his arms in seconds. He kissed her forehead and her ear and then, after bumping his nose against her jaw, her lips.

"How was I supposed to know that was you calling? Why didn't you leave a message?"

He lifted her chin to look at her eyes. "I couldn't stop thinking that if it hadn't been for the whole thing with you and me, and me bringing Ariel over and all that, then Frankie might not have . . ."

"Stop it." She kissed him again. "Stop it, you stupid man. You stupid, beautiful man." She slipped her hand under the Ramones T-shirt and ran it up over his chest. For two days she had eaten only the scone at Monroe's and half a plate of eggs at the diner before leaving Seattle. And two bites of rice the night before. His skin was damp on the back of his neck. She slid her hand across it and shivered. She hadn't been hungry. Until now.

It wasn't until she heard David's ax fall on the wood that she realized that he was still there. She flushed and took a step back.

Turning away from Andre, she called out to him, "David, do you want some eggs?"

He did not look up but stared grimly at his work.

Thump. "No." *Split.* "Thank." *Thump.* "You."

Jenny cooked eggs for everyone but David, who did not come back in the house to say good-bye before heading down the road to home. She would call him later, she resolved, to make amends.

Lilly lifted a chunk of scrambled eggs with two fingers and tipped her head before dropping it into her mouth. She looked like a trainer at SeaWorld feeding a porpoise. Before Jenny could scold her, Lilly turned to Andre and asked, "So how long are you planning to hang around?"

"I have to go back on Monday." He tilted his chair so that the two front legs were in the air and stared back at her. "I guess I could ask you the same thing."

Lilly frowned. She seemed nonplussed by the fact that her question had not rattled him. "Well, I'm leaving as soon as I possibly can."

"Lilly!" Jenny's head whipped around to face the door to Frankie's room.

Frankie stood in her doorway in full wolf regalia. They gray fabric of the suit was flimsy enough, but the layers of yarn gave her weight and bulk. She said, "It's okay. I know Lilly is not going to stay here forever."

Jenny patted the seat next to Elliot. "Come eat." She wondered if Frankie would be able to fit a forkful of omelet through the mouth hole. Well, she guessed they would all find out.

Lilly moved her fork around on her empty plate, thinking. When she looked up the expression on her face was dead serious and her attention was focused squarely on Andre. "If you break my mother's heart, I'll kick your butt."

"For heaven's sake." Jenny barely kept herself from dropping the spatula.

"Whoa," said Elliot. May sat next to him looking thrilled.

Andre nodded toward the arm that held Lilly's fork. It was brown and more cut than usual from a summer of lifting twenty-five-pound bags of potting soil and holding a sail against the winds off San Francisco Bay. He said, "I think you could do it, too."

"Damn straight," said Lilly. She looked enormously pleased.

· CHAPTER 21 ·

Love's Labour

Jenny stood up from her loom just in time to see Dale saun-
tering into the room with a paper sack filled with popcorn
and a copy of *Love's Labour's Lost* peeking out of his leather
shoulder bag. David stood behind him, wiping his hands on
his jeans.

Fall had arrived. Mushrooms had begun sprouting up
through decomposing logs and in piles of fir needles and amid
the ferns on Jakle's Lagoon trail. Cone lovers, flat tops, and
redbelts worked in their dark corners to reclaim the under-
growth for food and fuel. The rental cottages were empty and
the nights were growing long, so that when Dale arrived each
evening to read aloud, dark had long since settled around the
cabin.

"I'll get bowls," said Frankie.

Jenny began clearing the dinner dishes from the table where
she had left them. "No Peg?"

"She said to go on without her. She's got a headache."

David quipped, "No Shakespeare tonight, dear, I've got a headache."

Dale raised his eyebrows. "Is that a wisecrack? From Mr. Travers? Could he be getting a little frisky these days?"

Jenny pulled out a chair. "Leave him alone and sit down."

The scent of popcorn mingled with the smell of leftover rice. Jenny poured wine into her glass and got one each for Dale and David.

Dale settled into the chair with the play resting on his substantial belly and began to read. He happily took all the parts and was good with the voices, particularly that of Don Adriano de Armado, the heavily accented Spanish swordsman. To Berowne, noble companion to the king who has banished all the women, he gave a debonair affect, and to Costard, the clown, a lisp.

"*Costard.* O Lord, sir, they would know whether the three Worthies shall come in or no.

Berowne. What, are there but three?

Costard. No, sir, but it is vara fine, for every one pursents three.

Berowne. And three times thrice is nine.

Costard. Not so, sir, under correction, sir, I hope it is not so. You cannot beg us, sir, I can assure you, sir, we know what we know. I hope, sir, three times thrice, sir—

Berowne. Is not nine.

Costard. Under correction, sir, we know whereuntil it doth amount.

Berowne. By Jove, I always took three threes for nine.

Costard. Oh Lord, sir, it were a pity you should get your living by reck'ning, sir."

Frankie laughed. She had a bowl of popcorn on her lap and her bare feet were on an empty chair. "He's funny, Costard. That would be a good role for Trinculo. I mean Andre."

Dale's eyes met Jenny's across the table and he smiled. "It might indeed."

"Moth is a nice part," said David, looking from Dale to Jenny and back again.

"Well, who knows," said Dale dryly, "With your sudden gift for comedy you might be a good fit."

"Keep reading," said Frankie. "Please."

"What my lady doth command," said Dale, pulling at his beard with his fingers and bending his head to the book.

"But only for a little while longer," said Jenny, glancing at the kitchen clock. "It's a school night and Frankie needs to go to bed."

Dale tilted his head toward David and gave Jenny a hang-dog look. "Just like the king in our story, you would deprive us of the company of women?"

Frankie sat up straight and put her feet on the floor. Unlike Lilly, her feelings were all played out clearly on the canvas of her face. They could see her thinking, *Women? Does that mean me?*

Dale leaned forward and touched her cheek. "For where is any author in the world teaches such beauty as a woman's eye?"

Frankie blushed.

David started a kindling fire in the woodstove. Dale read until Costard appeared as Pompey in the play within the play and then he tucked his book in his bag and kissed Jenny goodnight. David made a move to linger, suddenly needing to haul more logs for the fire, but Jenny pushed him out into the night soon after.

Jenny watched Frankie getting ready for bed through the open door of the bathroom. Frankie brushed her hair slowly, her eyes roaming her own reflection in the glass. Jenny suspected that she was searching for whatever it was that Dale had seen. To Jenny, as indeed to any adult, it was obvious that Frankie was perfectly poised on the edge of womanhood. Jenny pulled herself out of her chair. However many chances she might have had that she hadn't acted upon, this felt like the one chance she had left with Frankie. A window was closing. It might already be too late.

She padded to the bathroom and leaned against the doorjamb. "Your father used to hit me, you know. When you and Lilly were small."

Frankie turned and searched her mother's face with troubled eyes.

"A lot?" she asked.

"Enough."

"Were you scared?"

Jenny steadied her breath. Mothering her two girls had always had a tightrope quality, but this felt like a wire strung between skyscrapers. With each arm reaching out in a different direction, she was stretched as far as she could go, one hundred stories above the street.

She said, "I didn't have any money and I had two little girls to take care of." She tried to reconcile her memories with the long lean shape of her daughter's body. "You were just a tiny baby."

Frankie frowned. "If you didn't have me, you might have run away earlier."

Jenny shook her head. Reading for the first time how Prospero had described being cast away with his child, she had shuddered. She had known all too well what it was like to *cry to the sea that roar'd to us*. But however lost she had been, she had not been alone. Like Prospero, who in telling the tale to Miranda had declared, *Thou wast that did preserve me*, she had carried her own deliverance in her arms. She wiped her eyes. How could a sixteenth-century writer have known so much? How was it possible that he could have seen inside a woman's heart?

"If I didn't have you, I might not have run away at all," she said. "You and your sister gave me the courage to leave when I did." She looked straight into Frankie's eyes. "Wanting to keep you safe is what saved me. That is the one thing that I'm sure of."

A log burned through in the woodstove and collapsed into itself with a muffled thud.

Frankie turned back to her reflection in the mirror. Her bruises had faded and her skin was once again as pale as fine sand against her dark brows. She murmured, *"When love speaks, the voice of all the gods makes heaven drowsy with the harmony."*

Jenny tried to place the line. Was it Prospero, she asked herself? Ariel? She watched the brush travel through her daughter's shining hair and it struck her suddenly that it wasn't *The Tempest* at all, but *Love's Labour's Lost* that she was quoting. Frankie had moved on.